G. W. Dasent

A Selection from the Norse Tales for the Use of Children

G. W. Dasent

A Selection from the Norse Tales for the Use of Children

ISBN/EAN: 9783337344559

Printed in Europe, USA, Canada, Australia, Japan

Cover: Foto ©Andreas Hilbeck / pixelio.de

More available books at **www.hansebooks.com**

A SELECTION

FROM

THE NORSE TALES

FOR THE USE OF CHILDREN.

BY

G. W. DASENT, D.C.L.

EDINBURGH:

EDMONSTON AND DOUGLAS.

1862.

NOTICE.

———◆———

IT was said by one of old time that a child's heart is a holy place, and Scripture in awful words has uttered woe on him who wounds the feelings "of one of these little ones." So this selection has been made to meet the scruples of those good people who thought some of *The Norse Tales* too outspoken for their children. Whether these worthy folk were not mistaken; whether here, too, "evil to him who evil thinks" might not have been a fitting answer; it is now needless to ask. The book is printed. "Hacon Grizzlebeard," "Why the Sea is salt," "The Master Smith," "The Mastermaid," "The Master Thief," and other naughty stories, are blotted out, and no doubt the rest feel glad to be rid of such bad company, and proud to be raised to the rank of "Moral Tales." The beautiful illustrations and bright binding will make them vain too. They had best be ware. Pride and Vanity hand in hand can hardly fail to trip. But if any little readers before whose eyes either of the earlier editions may have come, should chance to miss some of their old friends, and ask why they have been left out of this volume, it is hoped that their mothers will be better able to answer the question than the writer of these lines can ever be, for he still sees no harm at all in them.

BROAD SANCTUARY, *Dec.* 6, 1861.

CONTENTS.

—————ooo—————

LIST OF ILLUSTRATIONS.

———o———

TALES FROM THE NORSE.

TRUE AND UNTRUE.

ONCE on a time there were two brothers; one was called True, and the other Untrue. True was always upright and good towards all, but Untrue was bad and full of lies, so that no one could believe what he said. Their mother was a widow, and had n't much to live on; so when her sons had grown up, she was forced to send them away that they might earn their bread in the world. Each got a little scrip with some food in it, and then they went their way.

Now, when they had walked till evening, they sat down on a windfall in the wood, and took out their scrips, for they were hungry after walking the whole day, and thought a morsel of food would be sweet enough.

"If you're of my mind," said Untrue, "I think

B

we had better eat out of your scrip, so long as
there is anything in it, and after that we can take
to mine."

Yes! True was well pleased with this, so they
fell to eating, but Untrue got all the best bits,
and stuffed himself with them, while True got
only the burnt crusts and scraps.

Next morning they broke their fast off True's
food, and they dined off it too, and then there was
nothing left in his scrip. So when they had
walked till late at night, and were ready to eat
again, True wanted to eat out of his brother's
scrip, but Untrue said "No," the food was his,
and he had only enough for himself.

"Nay! but you know you ate out of my scrip
so long as there was anything in it," said True.

"All very fine, I daresay," answered Untrue;
" but if you are such a fool as to let others eat up
your food before your face, you must make the
best of it; for now all you have to do is to sit
here and starve."

"Very well!" said True, " you're Untrue by
name and untrue by nature; so you have been,
and so you will be all your life long."

Now when Untrue heard this, he flew into a

rage, and rushed at his brother, and plucked out both his eyes. " Now, try if you can see whether folk are untrue or not, you blind buzzard !" and so saying, he ran away and left him.

Poor True! there he went, walking along and feeling his way through the thick wood. Blind and alone, he scarce knew which way to turn, when all at once he caught hold of the trunk of a great bushy lime-tree ; so he thought he would climb up into it, and sit there till the night was over for fear of the wild beasts.

" When the birds begin to sing," he said to himself, " then I shall know it is day, and I can try to grope my way farther on." So he climbed up into the lime-tree. After he had sat there a little time, he heard how some one came and began to make a stir and clatter under the tree, and soon after others came ; and when they began to greet one another, he found out it was Bruin the bear, and Greylegs the wolf, and Slyboots the fox, and Longears the hare, who had come to keep St. John's eve under the tree. So they began to eat and drink, and be merry ; and when they had done eating they fell to gossipping together. At last the Fox said—

" Shan't we, each of us, tell a little story while we sit here ?"

Well ! the others had nothing against that. It would be good fun, they said, and the Bear began ; for you may fancy he was king of the company.

" The king of England," said Bruin, " has such bad eyesight, that he can scarce see a yard before him ; but if he only came to this lime-tree in the morning, while the dew is still on the leaves, and took and rubbed his eyes with the dew, he would get back his sight as good as ever."

" Very true !" said Greylegs. " The king of England has a deaf and dumb daughter too ; but if he only knew what I know, he would soon cure her. Last year she went to the communion. She let a crumb of the bread fall out of her mouth, and a great toad came and swallowed it down ; but if they only dug up the chancel floor they would find the toad sitting right under the altar rails, with the bread still sticking in his throat. If they were to cut the toad open and take and give the bread to the princess, she would be like other folk again as to her speech and hearing."

"That is all very well," said the Fox; "but if the king of England knew what I know, he would not be so badly off for water in his palace; for under the great stone, in his palace-yard, is a spring of the clearest water one could wish for, if he only knew to dig for it there."

"Ah!" said the Hare in a small voice; "the king of England has the finest orchard in the whole land, but it does not bear so much as a crab, for there lies a heavy gold chain in three turns round the orchard. If he got that dug up, there would not be a garden like it for bearing in all his kingdom."

"Very true, I dare say," said the Fox; "but now it's getting very late, and we may as well go home."

So they all went away together.

After they were gone, True fell asleep as he sat up in the tree; but when the birds began to sing at dawn, he woke up, and took the dew from the leaves, and rubbed his eyes with it, and so got his sight back as good as it was before Untrue plucked his eyes out.

Then he went straight to the king of England's palace, and begged for work, and got it on the spot. So one day the king came out into the palace-yard, and when he had walked about a bit, he wanted to drink out of his pump; for you must know the day was hot, and the king very thirsty; but when they poured him out a glass, it was so muddy, and nasty, and foul, that the king got quite vexed.

"I don't think there's ever a man in my whole kingdom who has such bad water in his yard as I, and yet I bring it in pipes from far, over hill and dale," cried out the king.

"Like enough, your Majesty;" said True, "but if you would let me have some men to help me to dig up this great stone which lies here in the middle of your yard, you would soon see good water, and plenty of it."

Well! the king was willing enough; and they had scarcely got the stone well out, and dug under it a while, before a jet of water sprang out high up into the air, as clear and full as if it came out of a conduit, and clearer water was not to be found in all England.

A little while after the king was out in his palace-yard again, and there came a great hawk flying after his chicken, and all the king's men

began to clap their hands and bawl out, "There
he flies! There he flies!" The king caught up
his gun and tried to shoot the hawk, but he
could'nt see so far, so he fell into great grief.

"Would to Heaven," he said, "there was any
one who could tell me a cure for my eyes; for I
think I shall soon go quite blind!"

"I can tell you one soon enough," said True;
and then he told the king what he had done to
cure his own eyes, and the king set off that very
afternoon to the lime-tree, as you may fancy, and
his eyes were quite cured as soon as he rubbed
them with the dew which was on the leaves in the
morning. From that time forth there was no one
whom the king held so dear as True, and he had
to be with him wherever he went, both at home
and abroad.

So one day as they were walking together in
the orchard, the king said, "I can't tell how it is
that I can't! there isn't a man in England who
spends so much on his orchard as I, and yet I
can't get one of the trees to bear so much as a
crab."

"Well! well!" said True; "if I may have
what lies three times twisted round your orchard

and men to dig it up, your orchard will bear well
enough."

Yes! the king was quite willing, so True got
men and began to dig, and at last he dug up the
whole gold chain. Now True was a rich man,
far richer indeed than the king himself, but still
the king was well pleased, for his orchard bore so
that the boughs of the trees hung down to the
ground, and such sweet apples and pears nobody
had ever tasted.

Another day too the king and True were
walking about, and talking together, when the
princess passed them, and the king was quite
downcast when he saw her.

"Isn't it a pity, now, that so lovely a princess
as mine should want speech and hearing," he said
to True.

"Ay, but there is a cure for that," said True.

When the king heard that, he was so glad
that he promised him the princess to wife, and
half his kingdom into the bargain, if he could get
her right again. So True took a few men, and
went into the church, and dug up the toad which
sat under the altar-rails. Then he cut open the
toad, and took out the bread and gave it to the

king's daughter; and from that hour she got back her speech, and could talk like other people.

Now True was to have the princess, and they got ready for the bridal feast, and such a feast had never been seen before; it was the talk of the whole land. Just as they were in the midst of dancing the bridal-dance, in came a beggar lad, and begged for a morsel of food, and he was so ragged and wretched that every one crossed themselves when they looked at him; but True knew him at once, and saw that it was Untrue, his brother.

"Do you know me again?" said True.

"Oh! where should such a one as I ever have seen so great a lord," said Untrue.

"Still you *have* seen me before," said True. "It was I whose eyes you plucked out a year ago this very day. Untrue by name, and untrue by nature. So I said before, and so I say now; but you are still my brother, and so you shall have some food. After that, you may go to the lime-tree where I sat last year; if you hear anything that can do you good, you will be lucky."

So Untrue did not wait to be told twice. "If True has got so much good by sitting in the lime-

tree, that in one year he has come to be king over
half England, what good may not I get," he
thought. So he set off and climbed up into the
lime-tree. He had not sat there long, before all
the beasts came as before, and ate and drank, and
kept St. John's eve under the tree. When they
had left off eating, the Fox wished that they
should begin to tell stories, and Untrue got ready
to listen with all his might, till his ears were
almost fit to fall off. But Bruin the bear was
surly, and growled and said—

"Some one has been chattering about what
we said last year, and so now we will hold our
tongues about what we know;" and with that the
beasts bid one another "Good night," and parted,
and Untrue was just as wise as he was before,
and the reason was, that his name was Untrue,
and his nature untrue too.

THE OLD DAME AND HER HEN.

ONCE on a time there was an old widow who lived far away from the rest of the world, up under a hillside, with her three daughters. She was so poor that she had no stock but one single hen, which she prized as the apple of her eye; in short, it was always cackling at her heels, and she was always running to look after it. Well! one day, all at once, the hen was missing. The old wife went out, and round and round the cottage, looking and calling for her hen, but it was gone, and there was no getting it back.

So the woman said to her eldest daughter, "You must just go out and see if you can find our hen, for have it back we must, even if we have to fetch it out of the hill."

Well! the daughter was ready enough to go, so she set off and walked up and down, and looked and called, but no hen could she find. But all at once, just as she was about to give up the hunt, she heard some one calling out in a cleft in the rock—

"Your hen trips inside the hill!
Your hen trips inside the hill!"

So she went into the cleft to see what it was, but she had scarce set her foot inside the cleft, before she fell through a trap-door, deep, deep down, into a vault under ground. When she got to the bottom she went through many rooms, each finer than the other; but in the innermost room of all, a great ugly man of the hill-folk came up to her and asked, "Will you be my sweetheart?"

"No! I will not," she said. She wouldn't have him at any price! not she; all she wanted was to get above ground again as fast as ever she could, and to look after her hen which was lost. Then the Man o' the Hill got so angry that he took her up and wrung her head off, and threw both head and trunk down into the cellar.

While this was going on, her mother sat at home waiting and waiting, but no daughter came. So after she had waited a bit longer, and neither heard nor saw anything of her daughter, she said to her midmost daughter, that she must go out and see after her sister, and she added—

"You can just give our hen a call at the same time."

Well! the second sister had to set off, and the very same thing befell her; she went about looking and calling, and all at once she too heard a voice away in the cleft of the rock saying—

"Your hen trips inside the hill!
Your hen trips inside the hill!"

She thought this strange, and went to see what it could be; and so she too fell through the trap-door, deep, deep down, into the vault. There she went from room to room, and in the innermost one the Man o' the Hill came to her and asked if she would be his sweetheart? No! that she wouldn't; all she wanted was to get above ground again, and hunt for her hen which was lost. So the Man o' the Hill got angry, and took her up and wrung her head off, and threw both head and trunk down into the cellar.

Now, when the old dame had sat and waited seven lengths and seven breadths for her second daughter, and could neither see nor hear anything of her, she said to the youngest,—

"Now, you really must set off and see after your sisters. 'T was silly to lose the hen, but 't will be sillier still if we lose both your sisters; and you can give the hen a call at the same time,"—for the old dame's heart was still set on her hen.

Yes! the youngest was ready enough to go; so she walked up and down, hunting for her sisters and calling the hen, but she could neither see nor hear anything of them. So at last she too came up to the cleft in the rock, and heard how something said—

> " Your hen trips inside the hill!
> Your hen trips inside the hill!"

She thought this strange, so she too went to see what it was, and fell through the trap-door too, deep, deep down, into a vault. When she reached the bottom she went from one room to another, each grander than the other; but she wasn't at all afraid, and took good ti   to look about her. So as she was peeping into this and that, she cast her eye on the trap-door into the cellar, and looked down it, and what should she see there but her sisters, who lay dead. She had scarce time to slam to the trap-door before the Man o' the Hill came to her and asked—

"Will you be my sweetheart?"

"With all my heart," answered the girl, for she saw very well how it had gone with her sisters.

So, when the Man o' the Hill heard that, he got her the finest clothes in the world; she had only to ask for them, or for anything else she had a mind to, and she got what she wanted, so glad was the Man o' the Hill that any one would be his sweetheart.

But when she had been there a little while, she was one day even more doleful and downcast than was her wont. So the Man o' the Hill asked her what was the matter, and why she was in such dumps.

"Ah!" said the girl, "it's because I can't get home to my mother. She's hard pinched, I know, for meat and drink, and has no one with her."

"Well!" said the Man o' the Hill, "I can't let you go to see her; but just stuff some meat and drink into a sack, and I'll carry it to her."

Yes! she would do so, she said, with many thanks; but at the bottom of the sack she stuffed a lot of gold and silver, and afterwards she laid a little food on the top of the gold and silver. Then she told the ogre the sack was ready, but he must be sure not to look into it. So he gave his word he wouldn't, and set off. Now, as the Man o' the Hill walked off, she peeped out after him through a chink in the trap door; but when he had gone a bit on the way, he said,—

"This sack is so heavy, I'll just see what there is inside it."

And so he was about to untie the mouth of the sack, but the girl called out to him,—

"I see what you're at!
I see what you're at!"

"The deuce you do!" said the Man o' the Hill; "then you must have plaguy sharp eyes in your head, that's all!"

So he threw the sack over his shoulder, and dared not try to look into it again. When he reached the widow's cottage, he threw the sack in through the cottage door, and said,—

"Here you have meat and drink from your daughter; she doesn't want for anything."

So, when the girl had been in the hill a good bit longer, one day a billy-goat fell down the trapdoor.

"Who sent for you, I should like to know? you long-bearded beast!" said the Man o' the Hill, who was in an awful rage, and with that he whipped up the goat, and wrung his head off, and threw him down into the cellar.

"Oh!" said the girl, "why did you do that? I might have had the goat to play with down here."

"Well!" said the Man o' the Hill, "you needn't be so down in the mouth about it, I should think, for I can soon put life into the billy-goat again."

So saying, he took a flask which hung up against the wall, put the billy-goat's head on his body again, and smeared it with some ointment out of the flask, and he was as well and as lively as ever again.

"Ho! ho!" said the girl to herself; "that flask is worth something—that it is."

So when she had been some time longer in the hill, she watched for a day when the Man o' the Hill was away, took her eldest sister, and putting her head on her shoulders, smeared her with some of the ointment out of the flask, just as she had seen the Man o' the Hill do with the billy-goat, and in a trice her sister came to life again. Then the girl stuffed her into a sack, laid a little food over her, and as soon as the Man o' the Hill came home, she said to him,—

"Dear friend! Now do go home to my mother

C

with a morsel of food again; poor thing! she's both hungry and thirsty, I'll be bound; and besides that, she's all alone in the world. But you must mind and not look into the sack."

Well! he said he would carry the sack; and he said, too, that he would not look into it; but when he had gone a little way, he thought the sack got awfully heavy; and when he had gone a bit farther he said to himself,—

"Come what will, I must see what's inside this sack, for however sharp her eyes may be, she can't see me all this way off."

But just as he was about to untie the sack, the girl who sat inside the sack called out,—

" I see what you're at!
I see what you're at!"

"The deuce you do!" said the ogre; "then you must have plaguy sharp eyes;" for he thought all the while it was the girl inside the hill who was speaking. So he didn't dare so much as to peep into the sack again, but carried it straight to her mother as fast as he could, and when he got to the cottage door he threw it in through the door, and bawled out —

"Here you have meat and drink from your daughter; she wants for nothing."

Now, when the girl had been in the hill a while longer, she did the very same thing with her other sister. She put her head on her shoulders, smeared her with ointment out of the flask, brought her to life, and stuffed her into the sack; but this time she crammed in also as much gold and silver as the sack would hold, and over all laid a very little food.

"Dear friend," she said to the Man o' the Hill, "you really must run home to my mother with a little food again; and mind you don't look into the sack."

Yes! the Man o' the Hill was ready enough to do as she wished, and he gave his word too that he wouldn't look into the sack; but when he had gone a bit of the way he began to think the sack got awfully heavy, and when he had gone a bit further, he could scarce stagger along under it, so he set it down, and was just about to untie the string and look into it, when the girl inside the sack bawled out,—

"I see what you're at!
I see what you're at!"

"The deuce you do!" said the Man o' the Hill, "then you must have plaguy sharp eyes of your own."

Well, he dared not try to look into the sack, but made all the haste he could, and carried the sack straight to the girl's mother. When he got to the cottage door he threw the sack in through the door, and roared out,—

"Here you have food from your daughter; she wants for nothing."

So when the girl had been there a good while longer, the Man o' the Hill made up his mind to go out for the day; then the girl shammed to be sick and sorry, and pouted and fretted.

"It's no use your coming home before twelve o'clock at night," she said, "for I shan't be able to have supper ready before—I'm so sick and poorly."

But when the Man o' the Hill was well out of the house, she stuffed some of her clothes with straw, and stuck up this lass of straw in the corner by the chimney, with a besom in her hand, so that it looked just as if she herself were standing there. After that she stole off home, and got a sharp-shooter to stay in the cottage with her mother.

So when the clock struck twelve, or just about it, home came the Man o' the Hill, and the first thing he said to the straw-girl was, "Give me something to eat."

But she answered him never a word.

"Give me something to eat I say!" called out the Man o' the Hill, "for I am almost starved."

No! she hadn't a word to throw at him.

"Give me something to eat!" roared out the ogre the third time. "I think you'd better open your ears and hear what I say, or else I'll wake you up, that I will!"

No! the girl stood just as still as ever; so he flew into a rage, and gave her such a slap in the face, that the straw flew all about the room; but when he saw that, he knew he had been tricked, and began to hunt everywhere; and at last, when he came to the cellar, and found both the girl's sisters missing, he soon saw how the cat jumped, and ran off to the cottage, saying, "I'll soon pay her off!"

But when he reached the cottage, the sharp-shooter fired off his piece, and then the Man o' the Hill dared not go into the house, for he thought it was thunder. So he set off home again as fast as he could lay legs to the ground, but what do you think, just as he got to the trap-door, the sun rose and the Man o' the Hill burst.

Oh! if one only knew where the trap-door was, I'll be bound there's a whole heap of gold and silver down there still!

EAST O' THE SUN AND WEST O' THE MOON.

ONCE on a time there was a poor husbandman who had so many children that he hadn't much of either food or clothing to give them. Pretty children they all were, but the prettiest was the youngest daughter, who was so lovely there was no end to her loveliness.

So one day, 'twas on a Thursday evening late at the fall of the year, the weather was so wild and rough outside, and it was so cruelly dark, and rain fell and wind blew, till the walls of the cottage shook again. There they all sat round the fire busy with this thing and that. But just then, all at once something gave three taps on the window-pane. Then the father went out to see what was the matter; and, when he got out of doors, what should he see but a great big White Bear.

" Good evening to you !" said the White Bear.

"The same to you," said the man.

"Will you give me your youngest daughter? If you will, I'll make you as rich as you are now poor," said the Bear.

Well, the man would not be at all sorry to be so rich; but still he thought he must have a bit of a talk with his daughter first; so he went in and told them how there was a great White Bear waiting outside, who had given his word to make them so rich if he could only have the youngest daughter.

The lassie said "No!" outright. Nothing could get her to say anything else; so the man went out and settled it with the White Bear, that he should come again the next Thursday evening and get an answer. Meantime he talked his daughter over, and kept on telling her of all the riches they would get, and how well off she would be herself; and so at last she thought better of it, and washed and mended her rags, made herself as smart as she could, and was ready to start. I can't say her packing gave her much trouble.

Next Thursday evening came the White Bear to fetch her, and she got upon his back with her bundle, and off they went. So, when they had gone a bit of the way, the White Bear said,—

"Are you afraid?"

"No! she wasn't."

"Well! mind and hold tight by my shaggy coat, and then there's nothing to fear," said the Bear.

So she rode a long, long way, till they came to a great steep hill. There, on the face of it, the White Bear gave a knock, and a door opened, and they came into a castle, where there were many rooms all lit up; rooms gleaming with silver and gold; and there too was a table ready laid, and it was all as grand as grand could be. Then the White Bear gave her a silver bell; and when she wanted anything, she was only to ring it, and she would get it at once.

Well, after she had eaten and drunk, and evening wore on, she got sleepy after her journey, and thought she would like to go to bed, so she rang the bell; and she had scarce taken hold of it before she came into a chamber, where there was a bed made, as fair and white as any one would wish to sleep in, with silken pillows and curtains and gold fringe. All that was in the

room was gold or silver; but when she had gone
to bed, and put out the light, a man came and
laid himself alongside her. That was the White
Bear, who threw off his beast shape at night; but
she never saw him, for he always came after she
had put out the light, and before the day dawned
he was up and off again. So things went on
happily for a while, but at last she began to get
silent and sorrowful; for there she went about
all day alone, and she longed to go home to see
her father and mother, and brothers and sisters.
So one day, when the White Bear asked what it
was that she lacked, she said it was so dull and
lonely there, and how she longed to go home to
see her father and mother, and brothers and
sisters, and that was why she was so sad and
sorrowful, because she couldn't get to them.

"Well, well!" said the Bear, "perhaps there's
a cure for all this; but you must promise me
one thing, not to talk alone with your mother,
but only when the rest are by to hear; for she'll
take you by the hand and try to lead you into
a room alone to talk; but you must mind and
not do that, else you'll bring bad luck on both
of us."

So one Sunday the White Bear came and said, now they could set off to see her father and mother. Well, off they started, she sitting on his back; and they went far and long. At last they came to a grand house, and there her brothers and sisters were running about out of doors at play, and everything was so pretty, 'twas a joy to see.

"This is where your father and mother live now," said the White Bear; "but don't forget what I told you, else you'll make us both unlucky."

"No! bless her, she'd not forget;" and when she had reached the house, the White Bear turned right about and left her.

Then when she went in to see her father and mother, there was such joy, there was no end to it. None of them thought they could thank her enough for all she had done for them. Now, they had everything they wished, as good as good could be, and they all wanted to know how she got on where she lived.

Well, she said, it was very good to live where she did; she had all she wished. What she said beside I don't know; but I don't think any of them had the right end of the stick, or that they

got much out of her.   But so in the afternoon,
after they had done dinner, all happened as the
White Bear had said.   Her mother wanted to talk
with her alone in her bedroom ; but she minded
what the White Bear had said, and wouldn't go
up stairs.

"Oh ! what we have to talk about, will keep,"
she said, and put her mother off. But some how
or other, her mother got round her at last, and she
had to tell her the whole story.   So she said, how
every night, when she had gone to bed, a man
came and lay down beside her as soon as she had
put out the light, and how she never saw him,
because he was always up and away before the
morning dawned ; and how she went about woeful and sorrowing, for she thought she should
so like to see him, and how all day long she
walked about there alone, and how dull, and dreary,
and lonesome it was.

"My !" said her mother; "it may well be a
Troll you slept with ! But now I 'll teach you a
lesson how to set eyes on him. I 'll give you a
bit of candle, which you can carry home in your
bosom ; just light that while he is asleep, but take
care not to drop the tallow on him."

Yes! she took the candle and hid it in her bosom, and as night drew on, the White Bear came and fetched her away.

But when they had gone a bit of the way, the White Bear asked if all hadn't happened as he had said?

"Well she couldn't say it hadn't."

"Now, mind," said he, "if you have listened to your mother's advice, you have brought bad luck on us both, and then, all that has passed between us will be as nothing."

"No," she said, "she hadn't listened to her mother's advice."

So when she reached home, and had gone to bed, it was the old story over again. There came a man and lay down beside her; but at dead of night, when she heard he slept, she got up and struck a light, lit the candle, and let the light shine on him, and so she saw that he was the loveliest Prince one ever set eyes on, and she fell so deep in love with him on the spot, that she thought she couldn't live if she didn't give him a kiss there and then. And so she did, but as she kissed him, she dropped three hot drops of tallow on his shirt, and he woke up.

"What have you done?" he cried; "now you have made us both unlucky, for had you held out only this one year, I had been freed. For I have a step-mother who has bewitched me, so that I am a White Bear by day, and a Man by night. But now all ties are snapt between us; now I must set off from you to her. She lives in a Castle which stands EAST O' THE SUN AND WEST O' THE MOON, and there, too, is a Princess, with a nose three ells long, and she's the wife I must have now."

She wept and took it ill, but there was no help for it; go he must.

Then she asked if she mightn't go with him?

No, she mightn't.

"Tell me the way then," she said; "and I'll search you out; *that* surely I may get leave to do."

"Yes, she might do that," he said; "but there was no way to that place. It lay EAST O' THE SUN AND WEST O' THE MOON, and thither she'd never find her way."

So next morning, when she woke up, both Prince and castle were gone, and then she lay on a little green patch, in the midst of the gloomy thick wood, and by her side lay the same bundle of rags she had brought with her from her old home.

So when she had rubbed the sleep out of her eyes, and wept till she was tired, she set out on her way, and walked many, many days, till she came to a lofty crag. Under it sat an old hag, and played with a gold apple which she tossed about. Her the lassie asked if she knew the way to the Prince, who lived with his step-mother in the Castle, that lay EAST O' THE SUN AND WEST O' THE MOON, and who was to marry the Princess, with a nose three ells long.

"How did you come to know about him?" asked the old hag; "but maybe you are the lassie who ought to have had him?"

Yes, she was.

"So, so; it's you, is it?" said the old hag. "Well, all I know about him is, that he lives in the castle that lies EAST O' THE SUN AND WEST O' THE MOON, and thither you'll come, late or never; but still you may have the loan of my horse, and on him you can ride to my next neighbour. Maybe she'll be able to tell you; and when you get there, just give the horse a switch under the left ear, and beg him to be off home; and, stay, this gold apple you may take with you."

So she got upon the horse, and rode a long long time, till she came to another crag, under which sat another old hag, with a gold carding-comb. Her the lassie asked if she knew the way to the castle that lay EAST O' THE SUN AND WEST O' THE MOON, and she answered, like the first old hag, that she knew nothing about it, except it was east o' the sun and west o' the moon.

"And thither you'll come, late or never, but you shall have the loan of my horse to my next neighbour; maybe she'll tell you all about it; and when you get there, just switch the horse under the left ear, and beg him to be off home."

And this old hag gave her the golden carding-comb; it might be she'd find the use for it, she said. So the lassie got up on the horse, and rode a far far way, and a weary time; and so at last she came to another great crag, under which sat another old hag, spinning with a golden spinning-wheel. Her, too, she asked if she knew the way to the Prince, and where the castle was that lay EAST O' THE SUN AND WEST O' THE MOON. So it was the same thing over again.

"Maybe it's you who ought to have had the Prince?" said the old hag.

Yes, it was.

But she, too, didn't know the way a bit better than the other two, "East o' the sun and west o' the moon it was," she knew—that was all.

"And thither you'll come, late or never; but I'll lend you my horse, and then I think you'd best ride to the East Wind and ask him; maybe he knows those parts, and can blow you thither. But when you get to him, you need only give the horse a switch under the left ear, and he'll trot home of himself.

And so, too, she gave her the gold spinning-wheel. "Maybe you'll find a use for it," said the old hag.

Then on she rode many many days, a weary time, before she got to the East Wind's house, but at last she did reach it, and then she asked the East Wind if he could tell her the way to the Prince who dwelt east o' the sun and west o' the moon. Yes, the East Wind had often heard tell of it, the Prince, and the castle, but he couldn't tell the way, for he had never blown so far.

"But, if you will, I'll go with you to my brother the West Wind, maybe he knows, for he's much stronger. So, if you will just get on my back, I'll carry you thither."

Yes, she got on his back, and I should just think they went briskly along.

So when they got there, they went into the West Wind's house, and the East Wind said the lassie he had brought was the one who ought to have had the Prince who lived in the castle EAST O' THE SUN AND WEST O' THE MOON; and so she had set out to seek him, and how he had come with her, and would be glad to know if the West Wind knew how to get to the castle.

"Nay," said the West Wind, "so far I've never blown; but if you will, I'll go with you to our brother the South Wind, for he's much stronger than either of us, and he has flapped his wings far and wide. Maybe he'll tell you. You can get on my back, and I'll carry you to him."

Yes! she got on his back, and so they travelled to the South Wind, and weren't so very long on the way, I should think.

When they got there, the West Wind asked him if he could tell her the way to the castle that

lay EAST O' THE SUN AND WEST O' THE MOON,
for it was she who ought to have had the Prince
who lived there.

"You don't say so. That's she, is it?" said
the South Wind.

"Well, I have blustered about in most places
in my time, but so far have I never blown; but if
you will, I'll take you to my brother the North
Wind; he is the oldest and strongest of the
whole lot of us, and if he don't know where it is,
you'll never find any one in the world to tell you.
You can get on my back, and I'll carry you
thither."

Yes! she got on his back, and away he went
from his house at a fine rate. And this time, too,
she wasn't long on her way.

So when they got to the North Wind's house,
he was so wild and cross, cold puffs came from
him a long way off.

"BLAST YOU BOTH, WHAT DO YOU WANT?"
he roared out to them ever so far off, so that it
struck them with an icy shiver.

"Well," said the south Wind, "you needn't be
so foul-mouthed, for here I am, your brother the
South Wind, and here is the lassie who ought to

have had the Prince who dwells in the castle that lies EAST O' THE SUN AND WEST O' THE MOON, and now she wants to ask you if you ever were there, and can tell her the way, for she would be so glad to find him again."

"YES, I KNOW WELL ENOUGH WHERE IT IS," said the North Wind; "once in my life I blew an aspen-leaf thither, but I was so tired I couldn't blow a puff for ever so many days after. But if you really wish to go thither, and aren't afraid to come along with me, I'll take you on my back and see if I can blow you thither."

Yes! with all her heart; she must and would get thither if it were possible in any way; and as for fear, however madly he went, she wouldn't be at all afraid.

"Very well then," said the North Wind, "but you must sleep here to-night, for we must have the whole day before us if we're to get thither at all."

Early next morning the North Wind woke her, and puffed himself up, and blew himself out, and made himself so stout and big, 'twas gruesome to look at him; and so off they went, high up through the air, as if they would never stop till they got to the world's end.

Down here below there was such a storm; it threw down long tracts of wood and many houses, and when it swept over the great sea ships foundered by hundreds.

So they tore on and on,—no one can believe how far they went,—and all the while they still went over the sea, and the North Wind got more and more weary, and so out of breath he could scarce bring out a puff, and his wings drooped and drooped, till at last he sunk so low that the crests of the waves dashed over his heels.

"Are you afraid?" said the North Wind.

No! she wasn't.

But they weren't very far from land; and the North Wind had still so much strength left in him that he managed to throw her up on the shore under the windows of the castle which lay EAST O' THE SUN AND WEST O' THE MOON; but then he was so weak and worn out, he had to stay there and rest many days before he could get home again.

Next morning the lassie sat down under the castle window, and began to play with the gold apple; and the first person she saw was the Long-nose who was to have the Prince.

"What do you want for your gold apple, you lassie?" said the Long-nose, and threw up the window.

"It's not for sale for gold or money," said the lassie.

"If it's not for sale for gold or money, what is it that you will sell it for! You may name your own price," said the Princess.

"Well! if I may get to the Prince, who lives here, and be with him to night, you shall have it," said the lassie whom the North Wind had brought.

Yes! she might; that could be done. So the Princess got the gold apple; but when the lassie came up to the Prince's bed-room at night he was fast asleep; she called him and shook him, and between whiles she wept sore; but all she could do she couldn't wake him up. Next morning, as soon as day broke, came the Princess with the long nose, and drove her out again.

So in the daytime she sat down under the castle windows and began to card with her golden carding-comb, and the same thing happened. The Princess asked what she wanted for it; and she said it wasn't for sale for gold or money, but if she might get leave to go up to the Prince and be with him that night, the Princess should have it. But when she went up, she found him fast asleep again, and all she called, and all she shook, and wept, and prayed, she couldn't get life into him; and as soon as the first gray peep of day came, then came the Princess with the long nose, and chased her out again.

So, in the day time, the lassie sat down outside under the castle window, and began to spin with her golden spinning-wheel, and that, too, the Princess with the long nose wanted to have. So she threw up the window and asked what she wanted for it. The lassie said, as she had said twice before, it wasn't for sale for gold or money; but if she might go up to the Prince who was there, and be with him alone that night, she might have it.

Yes! she might do that and welcome. But now you must know there were some christian folk who had been carried off thither, and as they sat in their room, which was next the Prince, they had heard how a woman had been in there, and wept and prayed, and called to him two nights running, and they told that to the Prince.

That evening, when the Princess came with

her sleepy drink, the Prince made as if he drank, but threw it over his shoulder, for he could guess it was a sleepy drink. So, when the lassie came in, she found the Prince wide awake; and then she told him the whole story how she had come thither.

"Ah," said the Prince, "you've just come in the very nick of time, for to-morrow is to be our wedding-day; but now I won't have the Long-nose, and you are the only woman in the world who can set me free. I'll say I want to see what my wife is fit for, and beg her to wash the shirt which has the three spots of tallow on it; she'll say yes, for she doesn't know 'tis you who put them there; but that's a work only for christian folk, and not for such a pack of Trolls, and so I'll say that I won't have any other for my bride than the woman who can wash them out, and ask you to do it."

So there was great joy and love between them all that night. But next day, when the wedding was to be, the Prince said,—

"First of all, I'd like to see what my bride is fit for."

"Yes!" said the step-mother, with all her heart.

"Well," said the Prince, "I've got a fine shirt which I'd like for my wedding shirt, but somehow or other it has got three spots of tallow on it, which I must have washed out; and I have sworn never to take any other bride than the woman who's able to do that. If she can't, she's not worth having."

Well, that was no great thing they said, so they agreed, and she with the long-nose began to wash away as hard as she could, but the more she rubbed and scrubbed, the bigger the spots grew.

"Ah!" said the old hag, her mother, "you can't wash; let me try."

But she hadn't long taken the shirt in hand, before it got far worse than ever, and with all her rubbing, and wringing, and scrubbing, the spots grew bigger and blacker, and the darker and uglier was the shirt.

Then all the other Trolls began to wash, but the longer it lasted, the blacker and uglier the shirt grew, till at last it was as black all over as if it had been up the chimney.

"Ah!" said the Prince, "you're none of you worth a straw; you can't wash. Why there, outside, sits a beggar lassie, I'll be bound she knows

how to wash better than the whole lot of you.
COME IN LASSIE !" he shouted.

Well, in she came.

" Can you wash this shirt clean, lassie, you ?"
said he.

" I don't know," she said, " but I think I
can."

And almost before she had taken it and dipped
it in the water, it was as white as driven snow,
and whiter still.

" Yes ; you are the lassie for me," said the
Prince.

At that the old hag flew into such a rage, she
burst on the spot, and the Princess with the long
nose after her, and the whole pack of Trolls after
her, — at least I've never heard a word about
them since.

As for the Prince and Princess, they set free
all the poor christian folk who had been carried
off and shut up there ; and they took with them
all the silver and gold, and flitted away as far as
they could from the Castle that lay EAST O' THE
SUN AND WEST O' THE MOON.

BOOTS WHO ATE A MATCH WITH THE TROLL.

ONCE on a time there was a farmer, who had three sons; his means were small, and he was old and weak, and his sons would take to nothing. A fine large wood belonged to the farm, and one day the father told his sons to go and hew wood, and try to pay off some of his debts.

Well, after a long talk, he got them to set off, and the eldest was to go first. But when he had got well into the wood, and began to hew at a mossy old fir, what should he see coming up to him but a great sturdy Troll.

"If you hew in this wood of mine," said the Troll, " I'll kill you!"

When the lad heard that, he threw the axe down, and ran off home as fast as he could lay legs to the ground; so he came in quite out of breath, and told them what had happened, but his father called him "hare-heart,"—no Troll would ever have scared him from hewing when he was young, he said."

Next day the second son's turn came, and he fared just the same. He had scarce hewn three strokes at the fir, before the Troll came to him too, and said,—

"If you hew in this wood of mine, I'll kill you!"

The lad dared not so much as look at him, but threw down the axe, took to his heels, and came scampering home just like his brother. So when he got home, his father was angry again, and said no Troll had ever scared him when he was young.

The third day Boots wanted to set off.

"You, indeed!" said the two elder brothers; "you'll do it bravely, no doubt! you, who have scarce ever set your foot out of the door."

Boots said nothing to this, but only begged them to give him a good store of food. His mother had no cheese, so she set the pot on the fire to make him a little, and he put it into a scrip and set off. So when he had hewn a bit, the Troll came to him too, and said,—

"If you hew in this wood of mine, I'll kill you."

But the lad was not slow; he pulled his cheese out of the scrip in a trice, and squeezed it till the whey spurted out.

"Hold your tongue!" he cried to the Troll, "or I'll squeeze you as I squeeze the water out of this white stone."

"Nay, dear friend!" said the Troll, "only spare me, and I'll help you to hew."

Well, on those terms the lad was willing to spare him, and the Troll hewed so bravely, that they felled and cut up many, many fathoms in the day.

But when even drew near the Troll said,—

"Now you'd better come home with me, for my house is nearer than yours."

So the lad was willing enough; and when they reached the Troll's house, the Troll was to make up the fire, while the lad went to fetch water for their porridge, and there stood two iron pails so big and heavy, that he couldn't so much as lift them from the ground.

"Pooh!" said the lad, "it isn't worth while to touch these finger-basins. I'll just go and fetch the spring itself."

"Nay, nay, dear friend!" said the Troll; "I

can't afford to lose my spring; just you make up the fire, and I'll go and fetch the water."

So when he came back with the water, they set to and boiled up a great pot of porridge.

"It's all the same to me," said the lad; "but if you're of my mind, we'll eat a match!"

"With all my heart," said the Troll, for he thought he could surely hold his own in eating. So they sat down; but the lad took his scrip unawares to the Troll, and hung it before him, and so he spooned more into the scrip than he ate himself; and when the scrip was full, he took up his knife and made a slit in the scrip. The Troll looked on all the while, but said never a word. So when they had eaten a good bit longer, the Troll laid down his spoon, saying, "Nay! but I can't eat a morsel more."

"But you shall eat," said the youth; "I'm only half done; why don't you do as I did, and cut a hole in your paunch? You'll be able to eat then as much as you please."

"But doesn't it hurt one cruelly?" asked the Troll.

"Oh," said the youth, "nothing to speak of."

So the Troll did as the lad said, and then you

must know very well that he lost his life; but the
lad took all the silver and gold that he found in
the hill-side, and went home with, it and you may
fancy it went a great way to pay off the debt.

BOOTS, WHO MADE THE PRINCESS SAY, "THAT'S A STORY."

ONCE on a time there was a king who had a daughter, and she was such a dreadful story-teller that the like of her was not to be found far or near. So the king gave out, that if any one could tell such a string of lies as would get her to say, "That's a story," he should have her to wife, and half the kingdom besides. Well, many came, as you may fancy, to try their luck, for every one would have been very glad to have the Princess, to say nothing of the kingdom; but they all cut a sorry figure, for the Princess was so given to story telling, that all their lies went in at one ear and out of the other. Among the rest came three brothers to try their luck, and the two elder went first, but they fared no better than those who had gone before them. Last of all the third, Boots, set off and found the Princess in the farm-yard.

"Good morning," he said, "and thank you for nothing."

"Good morning," said she, "and the same to you."

Then she went on—

"You haven't such a fine farm-yard as ours, I'll be bound; for when two shepherds stand, one at each end of it, and blow their ram's horns, the one can't hear the other."

"Haven't we though!" answered Boots; "ours is far bigger; for when a cow begins to go with calf at one end of it, she doesn't get to the other end before the time to drop her calf is come."

"I daresay!" said the Princess. "Well, but you haven't such a big ox, after all, as ours yonder; for when two men sit, one on each horn, they can't touch each other with a twenty-foot rule."

"Stuff!" said Boots; "is that all? why, we have an ox who is so big, that when two men sit, one on each horn, and each blows his great mountain-trumpet, they can't hear one another."

"I dare say!" said the Princess; "but you haven't so much milk as we, I'll be bound; for we milk our kine into great pails, and carry them in-doors, and empty them into great tubs, and so we make great, great cheeses."

E

"Oh! you do, do you?" said Boots. "Well, we milk ours into great tubs, and then we put them in carts and drive them in-doors, and then we turn them out into great brewing vats, and so we make cheeses as big as a great house. We had, too, a dun mare to tread the cheese well together when it was making; but once she tumbled down into the cheese, and we lost her; and after we had eaten at this cheese seven years, we came upon a great dun mare, alive and kicking. Well, once after that I was going to drive this mare to the mill, and her backbone snapped in two; but I wasn't put out, not I, for I took a spruce sapling, and put it into her for a back-bone, and she had no other back-bone all the while we had her. But the sapling grew up into such a tall tree, that I climbed right up to heaven by it, and when I got there, I saw the Virgin Mary sitting and spinning the foam of the sea into pig's-bristle ropes; but just then the spruce-fir broke short off, and I couldn't get down again; so the Virgin Mary let me down by one of the ropes, and down I slipped straight into a fox's hole, and who should sit there but my mother and your father cobbling shoes; and just as I stepped in, my mother gave your father such a box on the ear, that it made his whiskers curl."

"That's a story!" said the Princess; "my father never did any such thing in all his born days!"

So Boots got the Princess to wife, and half the kingdom besides.

THE TWELVE WILD DUCKS.

ONCE on a time there was a Queen who was out driving, when there had been a new fall of snow in the winter; but when she had gone a little way, she began to bleed at the nose, and had to get out of her sledge. And so, as she stood there, leaning against the fence, and saw the red blood on the white snow, she fell a thinking how she had twelve sons and no daughter, and she said to herself,

"If I only had a daughter as white as snow and as red as blood, I shouldn't care what became of all my sons."

But the words were scarce out of her mouth before an old witch of the Trolls came up to her.

"A daughter you shall have," she said, "and she shall be as white as snow, and as red as blood; and your sons shall be mine, but you may keep them till the babe is christened."

So when the time came the Queen had a

daughter, and she was as white as snow, and as red as blood, just as the Troll had promised, and so they called her "Snow-white and Rosy-red." Well, there was great joy at the King's court, and the Queen was as glad as glad could be; but when what she had promised to the old witch came into her mind, she sent for a silversmith, and bade him make twelve silver spoons, one for each prince, and after that she bade him make one more, and that she gave to Snow-white and Rosy-red. But as soon as ever the Princess was christened, the Princes were turned into twelve wild ducks, and flew away. They never saw them again,—away they went, and away they stayed.

So the Princess grew up, and she was both tall and fair, but she was often so strange and sorrowful, and no one could understand what it was that failed her. But one evening the Queen was also sorrowful, for she had many strange thoughts when she thought of her sons. She said to Snow-white and Rosy-red,

"Why are you so sorrowful, my daughter? Is there anything you want? if so, only say the word, and you shall have it."

" Oh, it seems so dull and lonely here," said Snow-white and Rosy-red; "every one else has brothers and sisters, but I am all alone; I have none; and that's why I'm so sorrowful."

" But you *had* brothers, my daughter," said the Queen; "I had twelve sons who were your brothers, but I gave them all away to get you;" and so she told her the whole story.

So when the Princess heard that, she had no rest; for, in spite of all the Queen could say or do, and all she wept and prayed, the lassie would set off to seek her brothers, for she thought it was all her fault; and at last she got leave to go away from the palace. On and on she walked into the wide world, so far, you would never have thought a young lady could have strength to walk so far.

So, once, when she was walking through a great, great wood, one day she felt tired, and sat down on a mossy tuft and fell asleep. Then she dreamt that she went deeper and deeper into the wood, till she came to a little wooden hut, and there she found her brothers; just then she woke, and straight before her she saw a worn path in the green moss, and this path went deeper into the

wood; so she followed it, and after a long time
she came to just such a little wooden house as
that she had seen in her dream.

Now, when she went into the room there was
no one at home, but there stood twelve beds, and
twelve chairs, and twelve spoons—a dozen of
everything, in short. So when she saw that, she
was so glad, she hadn't been so glad for many a
long year, for she could guess at once that her
brothers lived here, and that they owned the
beds, and chairs, and spoons. So she began to
make up the fire, and sweep the room, and make
the beds, and cook the dinner, and to make the
house as tidy as she could; and when she had done
all the cooking and work, she ate her own dinner,
and crept under her youngest brother's bed, and lay
down there, but she forgot her spoon upon the table.

So she had scarcely laid herself down before
she heard something flapping and whirring in the
air, and so all the twelve wild ducks came sweep-
ing in; but as soon as ever they crossed the
threshold they became Princes.

"Oh, how nice and warm it is in here," they
said. "Heaven bless him who made up the fire,
and cooked such a good dinner for us."

And so each took up his silver spoon, and was going to eat. But when each had taken his own, there was one still left lying on the table, and it was so like the rest that they couldn't tell it from them.

"This is our sister's spoon," they said; "and if her spoon be here, she can't be very far off herself."

"If this be our sister's spoon, and she be here," said the eldest, "she shall be killed, for she is to blame for all the ill we suffer."

And this she lay under the bed and listened to.

"No," said the youngest; "'twere a shame to kill her for that. She has nothing to do with our suffering ill; for if any one's to blame, it's our own mother."

So they set to work hunting for her both high and low, and at last they looked under all the beds, and so when they came to the youngest Prince's bed, they found her, and dragged her out. Then the eldest Prince wished again to have her killed, but she begged and prayed so prettily for herself.

"Oh! gracious goodness! don't kill me, for I've gone about seeking you these three years, and if I could only set you free, I'd willingly lose my life."

"Well!" said they, "if you will set us free, you may keep your life; for you can if you choose."

"Yes; only tell me," said the Princess; "how it can be done, and I'll do it, whatever it be."

"You must pick thistle-down," said the Princes, "and you must card it, and spin it, and weave it; and after you have done that, you must cut out and make twelve coats, and twelve shirts, and twelve neckerchiefs, one for each of us, and while you do that, you must neither talk, nor laugh, nor weep. If you can do that, we are free."

"But where shall I ever get thistle-down enough for so many neckerchiefs, and shirts, and coats?" asked Snow-white and Rosy-red.

"We'll soon shew you," said the Princes; and so they took her with them to a great wide moor, where there stood such a crop of thistles, all nodding and nodding in the breeze, and the down all floating and glistening like gossamers through the air in the sunbeams. The Princess had never seen such a quantity of thistle-down in her life, and she began to pluck and gather it as fast and as well as she could; and when she got home at

night she set to work carding and spinning yarn
from the down. So she went on a long long time,
picking, and carding, and spinning, and all the
while keeping the Princes' house, cooking and
making their beds. At evening home they came,
flapping and whirring like wild ducks, and all
night they were Princes, but in the morning off
they flew again, and were wild ducks the whole
day.

But now it happened once, when she was out
on the moor to pick thistle-down,—and if I don't
mistake, it was the very last time she was to go
thither,—it happened that the young King who
ruled that land was out hunting, and came riding
across the moor and saw her. So he stopped
there and wondered who the lovely lady could be
that walked along the moor picking thistle-down,
and he asked her her name, and when he could
get no answer, he was still more astonished; and
at last he liked her so much, that nothing would
do but he must take her home to his castle and
marry her. So he ordered his servants to take
her and put her upon his horse. Snow-white and
Rosy-red, she wrung her hands, and made signs
to them, and pointed to the bags in which her

work was, and when the King saw she wished to
have them with her, he told his men to take up
the bags behind them. When they had done
that the Princess came to herself little by little,
for the King was both a wise man and a handsome
man too, and he was as soft and kind to her as a
doctor. But when they got home to the palace,
and the old Queen, who was his stepmother, set
eyes on Snow-white and Rosy-red, she got so
cross and jealous of her because she was so lovely,
that she said to the king,—

"Can't you see now, that this thing whom
you have picked up, and whom you are going to
marry, is a witch. Why? she can't either talk, or
laugh, or weep!"

But the King didn't care a pin for what she
said, but held on with the wedding, and married
Snow-white and Rosy-red, and they lived in great
joy and glory; but she didn't forget to go on
sewing at her shirts.

So when the year was almost out Snow-
white and Rosy-red brought a Prince into the
world; and then the old Queen was more spiteful
and jealous than ever, and at dead of night, she
stole in to Snow-white and Rosy-red, while she

slept, and took away her babe, and threw it into a pit full of snakes. After that she cut Snow-white and Rosy-red in her finger, and smeared the blood over her mouth, and went straight to the King.

"Now come and see," she said, "what sort of a thing you have taken for your Queen; here she has eaten up her own babe."

Then the King was so downcast, he almost burst into tears, and said—

"Yes, it must be true, sure I see it with my own eyes; but she'll not do it again, I'm sure, and so this time I'll spare her life."

So before the next year was out she had another son, and the same thing happened. The King's step-mother got more and more jealous and spiteful. She stole in to the young Queen at night while she slept, took away the babe, and threw it into a pit full of snakes, cut the young Queen's finger, and smeared the blood over her mouth, and then went and told the King she had eaten up her own child. Then the King was so sorrowful, you can't think how sorry he was, and he said,—

"Yes, it must be true, since I see it with my own eyes; but she'll not do it again, I'm sure, and so this time too I'll spare her life."

Well! before the next year was out, Snow-
white and Rosy-red brought a daughter into the
world, and her, too, the old Queen took and threw
into the pit full of snakes, while the young Queen
slept. Then she cut her finger, smeared the blood
over her mouth, and went again to the King and
said,—

"Now you may come and see if it isn't as I
say; she's a wicked, wicked witch, for here she has
gone and eaten up her third babe too."

Then the King was so sad, there was no end
to it, for now he couldn't spare her any longer,
but had to order her to be burnt alive on a pile of
wood. But just when the pile was all a-blaze,
and they were going to put her on it, she made
signs to them to take twelve boards and lay them
round the pile, and on these she laid the neckerchiefs, and the shirts, and the coats for her brothers,
but the youngest brother's shirt wanted its left arm,
for she hadn't had time to finish it. And as soon as
ever she had done that, they heard such a flapping
and whirring in the air, and down came twelve
wild ducks flying over the forest, and each of them
snapped up his clothes in his bill and flew off
with them.

"See now!" said the old Queen to the King, "wasn't I right when I told you she was a witch; but make haste and burn her before the pile burns low."

"Oh!" said the King, "we've wood enough and to spare, and so I'll wait a bit, for I have a mind to see what the end of all this will be."

As he spoke, up came the twelve princes riding along, as handsome well-grown lads as you'd wish to see; but the youngest prince had a wild duck's wing instead of his left arm.

"What's all this about?" asked the Princes.

"My Queen is to be burnt," said the King, "because she's a witch, and because she has eaten up her own babes."

"She hasn't eaten them at all," said the Princes. "Speak now, sister; you have set us free and saved us, now save yourself."

Then Snow-white and Rosy-red spoke, and told the whole story; how every time she was brought to bed, the old Queen, the King's step-mother, had stolen into her at night, had taken her babes away, and cut her little finger, and smeared the blood over her mouth; and then the Princes took the King, and shewed him the snake-pit where three babes lay playing with adders and toads, and lovelier children you never saw.

So the King had them taken out at once, and went to his stepmother, and asked her what punishment she thought that woman deserved who could find it in her heart to betray a guiltless Queen and three such blessed little babes.

"She deserves to be fast bound between twelve unbroken steeds, so that each may take his share of her," said the old Queen.

"You have spoken your own doom," said the King, "and you shall suffer it at once."

So the wicked old Queen was fast bound between twelve unbroken steeds, and each got his share of her. But the King took Snow-white and Rosy-red, and their three children, and the twelve Princes; and so they all went home to their father and mother, and told all that had befallen them, and there was joy and gladness over the whole kingdom, because the Princess was saved and set free, and because she had set free her twelve brothers.

THE GIANT WHO HAD NO HEART IN HIS BODY.

ONCE on a time there was a king who had seven sons, and he loved them so much that he could never bear to be without them all at once, but one must always be with him. Now, when they were grown up, six were to set off to woo, but as for the youngest, his father kept him at home, and the others were to bring back a princess for him to the palace. So the king gave the six the finest clothes you ever set eyes on, so fine that the light gleamed from them a long way off, and each had his horse, which cost many, many hundred dollars, and so they set off. Now, when they had been to many palaces, and seen many princesses, at last they came to a king who had six daughters; such lovely king's daughters they had never seen, and so they fell to wooing them, each one, and when they had got them for sweethearts, they set off home again, but they quite forgot that they were to bring back with them a sweetheart for Boots, their brother, who stayed at home, for they were over head and ears in love with their own sweethearts.

But when they had gone a good bit on their way, they passed close by a steep hill-side, like a wall, where the giant's house was, and there the giant came out, and set his eyes upon them, and turned them all into stone, princes and princesses and all. Now, the king waited and waited for his six sons, but the more he waited, the longer they stayed away; so he fell into great trouble, and said he should never know what it was to be glad again.

"And if I had not you left," he said to Boots, " I would live no longer, so full of sorrow am I for the loss of your brothers."

"Well, but now I've been thinking to ask your leave to set out and find them again; that's what I'm thinking of," said Boots.

"Nay, nay!" said his father; "that leave you shall never get, for then you would stay away too."

But Boots had set his heart upon it; go he would; and he begged and prayed so long that

F

the king was forced to let him go. Now, you
must know the king had no other horse to give
Boots but an old broken-down jade, for his six
other sons and their train had carried off all his
horses; but Boots did not care a pin for that, he
sprang up on his sorry old steed.

"Farewell, father," said he; "I'll come back,
never fear, and like enough I shall bring my six
brothers back with me;" and with that he rode
off.

So when he had ridden a while he came to a
Raven, which lay in the road and flapped its
wings, and was not able to get out of the way,
it was so starved.

"Oh, dear friend," said the Raven, "give me
a little food, and I'll help you again at your
utmost need."

"I haven't much food," said the Prince, "and
I don't see how you'll ever be able to help me
much; but still I can spare you a little. I see
you want it."

So he gave the Raven some of the food he had
brought with him.

Now, when he had gone a bit further, he came
to a brook, and in the brook lay a great Salmon,

which had got upon a dry place and dashed itself about, and could not get into the water again.

"Oh, dear friend," said the Salmon to the Prince, "shove me out into the water again, and I'll help you again at your utmost need."

"Well!" said the Prince, "the help you'll give me will not be great, I daresay, but it's a pity you should lie there and choke;" and with that he shot the fish out into the stream again.

After that he went a long, long way, and there met him a Wolf, which was so famished that it lay and crawled along the road on its belly.

"Dear friend, do let me have your horse," said the Wolf; "I'm so hungry the wind whistles through my ribs; I've had nothing to eat these two years."

"No," said Boots, "this will never do; first I came to a Raven, and I was forced to give him my food; next I came to a Salmon, and him I had to help into the water again; and now you will have my horse. It can't be done, that it can't, for then I should have nothing to ride on."

"Nay, dear friend, but you can help me," said Greylegs the wolf; "you can ride upon my back, and I'll help you again in your utmost need."

"Well! the help I shall get from you will not be great, I'll be bound," said the Prince; "but you may take my horse, since you are in such need."

So when the wolf had eaten the horse, Boots took the bit and put it into the Wolf's jaw, and laid the saddle on his back; and now the Wolf was so strong, after what he had got inside, that he set off with the Prince like nothing. So fast he had never ridden before.

"When we have gone a bit farther," said Greylegs; "I'll shew you the Giant's house."

So after a while they came to it.

"See here is the Giant's house," said the Wolf; "and see, here are your six brothers, whom the Giant has turned into stone; and see here are their six brides, and away yonder is the door, and in at that door you must go."

"Nay, but I daren't go in," said the Prince; "he'll take my life."

"No! no!" said the Wolf; "when you get in you'll find a Princess, and she'll tell you what to do to make an end of the Giant. Only mind and do as she bids you."

Well! Boots went in, but, truth to say, he was very much afraid. When he came in the Giant was away, but in one of the rooms sat the Princess, just as the wolf had said, and so lovely a princess Boots had never yet set eyes on.

"Oh! heaven help you! whence have you come?" said the Princess, as she saw him; "it will surely be your death. No one can make an end of the Giant who lives here, for he has no heart in his body."

"Well! well!" said Boots; "but now that I am here, I may as well try what I can do with him; and I will see if I can't free my brothers, who are standing turned to stone out of doors; and you, too, I will try to save, that I will."

"Well, if you must, you must," said the Princess; "and so let us see if we can't hit on a plan. Just creep under the bed yonder, and mind and listen to what he and I talk about. But, pray, do lie as still as a mouse."

So he crept under the bed, and he had scarce got well underneath it, before the Giant came.

"Ha!" roared the Giant, "what a smell of Christian blood there is in the house!"

"Yes, I know there is," said the Princess, "for there came a magpie flying with a man's bone, and let it fall down the chimney. I made all the haste

I could to get it out, but all one can do, the smell does n't go off so soon."

So the Giant said no more about it, and when night came, they went to bed. After they had lain a while, the Princess said,—

"There is one thing I'd be so glad to ask you about, if I only dared."

"What thing is that?" asked the Giant.

"Only where it is you keep your heart, since you do n't carry it about you," said the Princess.

"Ah! that's a thing you've no business to ask about; but if you must know, it lies under the door-sill," said the Giant.

"Ho! ho!" said Boots to himself under the bed, "then we'll soon see if we can't find it."

Next morning the Giant got up cruelly early, and strode off to the wood; but he was hardly out of the house before Boots and the Princess set to work to look under the door-sill for his heart; but the more they dug, and the more they hunted, the more they could n't find it.

"He has baulked us this time," said the Princess, "but we'll try him once more."

So she picked all the prettiest flowers she could find, and strewed them over the door-sill which they had laid in its right place again; and when the time came for the Giant to come home again, Boots crept under the bed. Just as he was well under, back came the Giant.

Snuff—snuff, went the Giant's nose. "My eyes and limbs, what a smell of Christian blood there is in here," said he.

"I know there is," said the Princess, "for there came a magpie flying with a man's bone in his bill, and let it fall down the chimney. I made as much haste as I could to get it out, but I daresay it's that you smell."

So the Giant held his peace, and said no more about it. A little while after, he asked who it was that had strewed flowers about the door-sill.

"Oh, I, of course," said the Princess.

"And, pray, what's the meaning of all this," said the Giant.

"Ah!" said the Princess, "I'm so fond of you that I couldn't help strewing them, when I knew that your heart lay under there."

"You don't say so," said the Giant; "but after all it doesn't lie there at all."

So when they went to bed again in the evening, the Princess asked the Giant again where his heart was, for she said she would so like to know.

"Well," said the Giant, "if you must know, it lies away yonder in the cupboard against the wall."

"So, so!" thought Boots and the Princess; "then we'll soon try to find it."

Next morning the Giant was away early, and strode off to the wood, and so soon as he was gone Boots and the Princess were in the cupboard hunting for his heart, but the more they sought for it the less they found it.

"Well," said the Princess, "we'll just try him once more."

So she decked out the cupboard with flowers and garlands, and when the time came for the Giant to come home, Boots crept under the bed again.

Then back came the Giant.

Snuff—snuff! "My eyes and limbs, what a smell of Christian blood there is in here!"

"I know there is," said the Princess; "for a little while since there came a magpie flying with a man's bone in his bill, and let it fall down the chimney. I made all the haste I could to get it out of the house again; but after all my pains, I dare say it's that you smell."

When the Giant heard that he said no more about it; but a little while after, he saw how the cupboard was all decked about with flowers and garlands; so he asked who it was that had done that? Who could it be but the Princess.

"And, pray, what's the meaning of all this tomfoolery?" asked the Giant.

"Oh, I'm so fond of you, I couldn't help doing it when I knew that your heart lay there," said the Princess.

"How can you be so silly as to believe any such thing?" said the Giant.

"Oh yes; how can I help believing it, when you say it," said the Princess.

"You're a goose," said the Giant; "where my heart is, you will never come."

"Well," said the Princess; "but for all that, 'twould be such a pleasure to know where it really lies."

Then the poor Giant could hold out no longer, but was forced to say,—

"Far, far away in a lake lies an island; on that island stands a church; in that church is a well; in that well swims a duck; in that duck there is an egg, and in that egg there lies my heart,—you darling!"

In the morning early, while it was still gray dawn, the Giant strode off to the wood.

"Yes! now I must set off too," said Boots; "if I only knew how to find the way. He took a long, long farewell of the Princess, and when he got out of the Giant's door, there stood the Wolf waiting for him. So Boots told him all that had happened inside the house, and said now he wished to ride to the well in the church, if he only knew the way. So the Wolf bade him jump on his back, he'd soon find the way; and away they went till the wind whistled after them, over hedge and field, over hill and dale. After they had travelled many, many days, they came at last to the lake. Then the Prince did not know how to get over it, but the Wolf bade him only not be afraid, but stick on, and so he jumped into the lake with the Prince on his back, and swam over to the island. So they came to the church; but the church keys hung high, high up on the top of the tower, and at first the Prince did not know how to get them down.

"You must call on the Raven," said the Wolf.

So the Prince called on the Raven, and immediately the Raven came, and flew up and fetched the keys, and so the Prince got into the church. But when he came to the well, there lay the duck, and swam about backwards and forwards, just as the Giant had said. So the Prince stood and coaxed it and coaxed it, till it came to him, and he grasped it in his hand; but just as he lifted it up from the water the duck dropped the egg into the well, and then Boots was beside himself to know how to get it out again.

"Well, now you must call on the Salmon, to be sure," said the Wolf; and the king's son called on the Salmon, and the Salmon came and fetched up the egg from the bottom of the well.

Then the Wolf told him to squeeze the egg, and as soon as ever he squeezed it the Giant screamed out.

"Squeeze it again," said the Wolf; and when the Prince did so, the Giant screamed still more piteously, and begged and prayed so prettily to be spared, saying he would do all that the Prince wished if he would only not squeeze his heart in two.

" Tell him, if he will restore to life again your six brothers and their brides, whom he has turned to stone, you will spare his life," said the Wolf. Yes, the Giant was ready to do that, and he turned the six brothers into king's sons again, and their brides into king's daughters.

" Now, squeeze the egg in two," said the Wolf. So Boots squeezed the egg to pieces, and the Giant burst at once.

Now, when he had made an end of the Giant, Boots rode back again on the Wolf to the Giant's house, and there stood all his six brothers alive and merry, with their brides. Then Boots went into the hill-side after his bride, and so they all set off home again to their father's house. And you may fancy how glad the old king was when he saw all his seven sons come back, each with his bride;—" But the loveliest bride of all was the bride of Boots after all," said the king, "and he shall sit uppermost at the table, with her by his side."

So he sent out, and called a great wedding-feast, and the mirth was both loud and long, and if they have not done feasting, why they are still at it.

THE FOX AS HERDSMAN.

ONCE on a time there was a woman who went out to hire a herdsman, and she met a bear.

"Whither away, Goody?" said Bruin.

"Oh, I'm going out to hire a herdsman," answered the woman.

"Why not have me for a herdsman?" said Bruin.

"Well, why not?" said the woman. "If you only knew how to call the flock; just let me hear?"

"OW, OW!" growled the bear.

"No, no! I wont have you," said the woman, as soon as she heard him say that, and off she went on her way.

So, when she had gone a bit further, she met a wolf.

"Whither away, Goody?" asked the Wolf.

"Oh!" said she, "I'm going out to hire a herdsman."

"Why not have me for a herdsman?" said the Wolf.

"Well, why not? if you can only call the flock; let me hear?" said she.

"Uh, uh!" said the Wolf.

"No, no!" said the woman; "you will never do for me."

Well, after she had gone a while longer, she met a fox.

"Whither away, Goody?" asked the Fox.

"Oh, I'm just going out to hire a herdsman," said the woman.

"Why not have me for your herdsman?" asked the Fox.

"Well, why not?" said she; "if you only knew how to call the flock; let me hear?"

"Dil-dal-holom," sung out the Fox, in such a fine clear voice.

"Yes; I'll have you for my herdsman," said the woman; and so she set the Fox to herd her flock.

The first day the Fox was herdsman he ate up all the woman's goats; the next day he made an end of all her sheep; and the third day he ate up all her kine. So, when he came home at even, the woman asked what he had done with all her flocks?

"Oh!" said the Fox, "their skulls are in the stream, and their bodies in the holt."

Now, the Goody stood and churned when the fox said this, but she thought she might as well step out and see after her flock; and while she was away the Fox crept into the churn and ate up the cream. So when the Goody came back and saw that, she fell into such a rage, that she snatched up the little morsel of the cream that was left, and threw it at the fox as he ran off, so that he got a dab of it on the end of his tail, and that's the reason why the fox has a white tip to his brush.

THE CAT ON THE DOVREFELL.

ONCE on a time there was a man up in Finn-
mark who had caught a great white bear,
which he was going to take to the king of Den-
mark Now, it so fell out, that he came to the
Dovrefell just about Christmas Eve, and there he
turned into a cottage where a man lived, whose
name was Halvor, and asked the man if he could
get house-room there, for his bear and himself.

"Heaven never help me, if what I say isn't
true!" said the man; "but we can't give any one
house-room just now, for every Christmas Eve
such a pack of Trolls come down upon us, that
we are forced to flit, and haven't so much as a
house over our own heads, to say nothing of
lending one to any one else."

"Oh!" said the man, "if that's all, you can
very well lend me your house; my bear can lie
under the stove yonder, and I can sleep in the
side-room."

Well, he begged so hard, that at last he got

THE CAT ON THE DOVREFELL.

leave to stay there; so the people of the house flitted out, and before they went, everything was got ready for the Trolls; the tables were laid, and there was rice porridge, and fish boiled in lye, and sausages, and all else that was good, just as for any other grand feast.

So, when everything was ready, down came the Trolls. Some were great and some were small; some had long tails and some had no tails at all; some, too, had long, long noses; and they ate and drank, and tasted every thing. Just, then, one of the little Trolls caught sight of the white bear, who lay under the stove; so he took a piece of sausage and stuck it on a fork, and went and poked it up against the bear's nose, screaming out—

"Pussy, will you have some sausage?"

Then the white bear rose up and growled, and hunted the whole pack of them out of doors, both great and small.

Next year Halvor was out in the wood, on the afternoon of Christmas Eve, cutting wood before the holidays, for he thought the Trolls would come again; and just as he was hard at work, he heard a voice in the wood calling out,—

" Halvor, Halvor !"

" Well," said Halvor, "here I am."

" Have you got your big cat with you still ?"

" Yes, that I have," said Halvor ; " she's lying at home under the stove, and what's more, she has now got seven kittens, far bigger and fiercer than she is herself."

" Oh, then, we'll never come to see you again," bawled out the Troll away in the wood, and he kept his word ; for since that time the Trolls have never eaten their Christmas brose with Halvor on the Dovrefell.

ONCE on a time there was a man who had a meadow which lay high up on the hill-side, and in the meadow was a barn, which he had built to keep his hay in. Now, I must tell you, there hadn't been much in the barn for the last year or two, for every St. John's night, when the grass stood greenest and deepest, the meadow was eaten down to the very ground the next morning, just as if a whole drove of sheep had been there feeding on it over night. This happened once, and it happened twice; so at last the man grew weary of losing his crop of hay, and said to his sons—for he had three of them, and the youngest was nicknamed Boots, of course—that now one of them must just go and sleep in the barn in the outlying field when St. John's night came, for it was too good a joke that his grass should be eaten, root and blade, this year, as it had been the last two years. So whichever of them went must keep a sharp look-out; that was what their father said.

Well, the eldest son was ready to go and watch the meadow; trust him for looking after the grass! It shouldn't be his fault if man or beast, or the fiend himself got a blade of grass. So, when evening came, he set off to the barn, and lay down to sleep; but a little on in the night came such a clatter, and such an earthquake that walls and roof shook, and groaned, and creaked; then up jumped the lad, and took to his heels as fast as ever he could; nor dared he once look round till he reached home; and as for the hay, why it was eaten up this year just as it had been twice before.

The next St. John's night, the man said again it would never do to lose all the grass in the out-lying field year after year in this way, so one of his sons must just trudge off to watch it, and watch it well too. Well, the next oldest son was ready to try his luck, so he set off, and lay down to sleep in the barn as his brother had done before him; but as the night wore on, there came on a rumbling and quaking of the earth, worse even than on the last St. John's night, and when the lad heard it, he got frightened, and took to his heels as though he were running a race.

Next year the turn came to Boots; but when he made ready to go, the other two began to laugh and to make game of him, saying,—

"You're just the man to watch the hay, that you are; you, who have done nothing all your life but sit in the ashes and toast yourself by the fire."

But Boots did not care a pin for their chattering, and stumped away as evening drew on up the hill-side to the outlying field. There he went inside the barn and lay down; but in about an hour's time the barn began to groan and creak, so that it was dreadful to hear.

"Well," said Boots to himself, "if it isn't worse than this, I can stand it well enough."

A little while after came another creak and an earthquake, so that the litter in the barn flew about the lad's ears.

"Oh!" said Boots to himself, "if it isn't worse than this, I daresay I can stand it out."

But just then came a third rumbling, and a third earthquake, so that the lad thought walls and roof were coming down on his head; but it passed off, and all was still as death about him.

"It'll come again, I'll be bound," thought Boots; but no, it didn't come again; still it was, and still it stayed; but after he had lain a little while, he heard a noise as if a horse were standing just outside the barn-door, and cropping the grass. He stole to the door, and peeped through a chink, and there stood a horse feeding away. So big, and fat, and grand a horse, Boots had never set eyes on; by his side on the grass lay a saddle and bridle, and a full set of armour for a knight, all of brass, so bright that the light gleamed from it.

"Ho, ho!" thought the lad; "it's you, is it, that eats up our hay? I'll soon put a spoke in your wheel, just see if I don't."

So he lost no time, but took the steel out of his tinder-box, and threw it over the horse; then it had no power to stir from the spot, and became so tame that the lad could do what he liked with it. So he got on its back, and rode off with it to a place which no one knew of, and there he put up the horse. When he got home, his brothers laughed and asked how he had fared?

You didn't lie long in the barn, even if you had the heart to go so far as the field."

"Well," said Boots, "all I can say is, I lay in the barn till the sun rose, and neither saw nor heard anything; I can't think what there was in the barn to make you both so afraid."

"A pretty story," said his brothers; "but we'll soon see how you have watched the meadow;" so they set off; but when they reached it, there stood the grass as deep and thick as it had been over night.

Well, the next St. John's eve it was the same story over again; neither of the elder brothers dared to go out to the outlying field to watch the crop; but Boots, he had the heart to go, and everything happened just as it had happened the year before. First a clatter and an earthquake, then a greater clatter and another earthquake, and so on a third time; only this year the earthquakes were far worse than the year before. Then all at once everything was as still as death, and the lad heard how something was cropping the grass outside the barn-door, so he stole to the door, and peeped through a chink; and what do you think he saw? why, another horse standing right up

against the wall, and chewing and champing with
might and main. It was far finer and fatter than
that which came the year before, and it had a
saddle on its back, and a bridle on its neck, and
a full suit of mail for a knight lay by its side, all
of silver, and as grand as you would wish to see.

"Ho, ho!" said Boots to himself; "it's you
that gobbles up our hay, is it? I'll soon put a
spoke in your wheel; and with that he took the
steel out of his tinder-box, and threw it over the
horse's crest, which stood as still as a lamb. Well,
the lad rode this horse too to the hiding-place
where he kept the other one, and after that he
went home.

"I suppose you'll tell us," said one of his
brothers, "there's a fine crop this year too, up in
the hayfield."

"Well, so there is," said Boots; and off ran
the others to see, and there stood the grass thick
and deep, as it was the year before, but they
didn't give Boots softer words for all that.

Now when the third St. John's eve came, the
two elder still hadn't the heart to lie out in the
barn and watch the grass, for they had got so
scared at heart the night they lay there before,

that they couldn't get over the fright; but Boots,
he dared to go; and, to make a long story short,
the very same thing happened this time as had
happened twice before. Three earthquakes came,
one after the other, each worse than the one which
went before, and when the last came, the lad
danced about with the shock from one barn wall
to the other; and after that, all at once, it was
still as death. Now, when he had lain a little
while, he heard something tugging away at the
grass outside the barn, so he stole again to the
door-chink, and peeped out, and there stood a
horse close outside—far, far bigger and fatter than
the two he had taken before.

"Ho, ho!" said the lad to himself, "it's you,
is it, that comes here eating up our hay? I'll
soon stop that—I'll soon put a spoke in your
wheel." So he caught up his steel and threw it
over the horse's neck, and in a trice it stood as if
it were nailed to the ground, and Boots could do
as he pleased with it. Then he rode off with it
to the hiding, where he kept the other two, and
then went home. When he got home, his two
brothers made game of him as they had done
before, saying, they could see he had watched the

grass well, for he looked for all the world as if he were walking in his sleep, and many other spiteful things they said; but Boots gave no heed to them, only asking them to go and see for themselves; and when they went, there stood the grass as fine and deep this time as it had been twice before.

Now, you must know that the king of the country where Boots lived had a daughter, whom he would only give to the man who could ride up over the hill of glass, for there was a high, high hill, all of glass, as smooth and slippery as ice, close by the king's palace. Upon the tip top of the hill the king's daughter was to sit, with three golden apples in her lap, and the man who could ride up and carry off the three golden apples, was to have half the kingdom, and the Princess to wife. This the king had stuck up on all the church-doors in his realm, and had given it out in many other kingdoms besides. Now, this Princess was so lovely, that all who set eyes on her, fell over head and ears in love with her, whether they would or no. So I need n't tell you how all the princes and knights who heard of her were eager to win her to wife, and half the kingdom beside; and how they came riding from all parts of the world

on high prancing horses, and clad in the grandest
clothes, for there wasn't one of them who hadn't
made up his mind that he, and he alone, was to
win the Princess.

So when the day of trial came, which the king
had fixed, there was such a crowd of princes and
knights under the glass hill, that it made one's
head whirl to look at them ; and every one in the
country who could even crawl along was off to
the hill, for they all were eager to see the man
who was to win the Princess. So the two elder
brothers set off with the rest; but as for Boots,
they said outright he shouldn't go with them, for
if they were seen with such a dirty changeling, all
begrimed with smut from cleaning their shoes and
sifting cinders in the dust-hole, they said folk
would make game of them.

"Very well," said Boots; "it's all one to me.
I can go alone, and stand or fall by myself."

Now, when the two brothers came to the hill
of glass, the knights and princes were all hard at
it, riding their horses till they were all in a foam ;
but it was no good, by my troth ; for as soon as
ever the horses set foot on the hill, down they
slipped, and there wasn't one who could get a yard

or two up; and no wonder, for the hill was as
smooth as a sheet of glass, and as steep as a
house-wall.   But all were eager to have the
Princess and half the kingdom.   So they rode and
slipped, and slipped and rode, and still it was the
same story over again.   At last all their horses
were so weary that they could scarce lift a leg, and
in such a sweat that the lather dripped from them,
and so the knights had to give up trying any
more.   So the king was just thinking that he
would proclaim a new trial for the next day, to
see if they would have better luck, when all at
once a knight came riding up on so brave a steed,
that no one had ever seen the like of it in his
born days, and the knight had mail of brass, and
the horse a brass bit in his mouth, so bright that
the sunbeams shone from it.   Then all the others
called out to him he might just as well spare himself the trouble of riding at the hill, for it would
lead to no good; but he gave no heed to them,
and put his horse at the hill, and went up it like
nothing for a good way, about a third of the
height; and when he had got so far, he turned
his horse round, and rode down again.   So lovely
a knight the Princess thought she had never yet

seen; and while he was riding, she sat and thought to herself—

"Would to heaven he might only come up and down the other side."

And when she saw him turning back, she threw down one of the golden apples after him, and it rolled down into his shoe. But when he got to the bottom of the hill he rode off so fast that no one could tell what had become of him. That evening all the knights and princes were to go before the king, that he who had ridden so far up the hill might show the apple which the princess had thrown, but there was no one who had anything to show. One after the other they all came, but not a man of them could show the apple.

At even the brothers of Boots came home too, and had such a long story to tell about the riding up the hill.

"First of all," they said, "there was not one of the whole lot who could get so much as a stride up; but at last came one who had a suit of brass mail, and a brass bridle and saddle, all so bright that the sun shone from them a mile off. He was a chap to ride, just! He rode a third of the way up the hill of glass, and he could easily have ridden the whole way up, if he chose; but he turned round and rode down, thinking, maybe that was enough for once."

"Oh! I should so like to have seen him, that I should," said Boots, who sat by the fireside, and stuck his feet into the cinders, as was his wont.

"Oh!" said his brothers, "you would, would you? You look fit to keep company with such high lords, nasty beast that you are, sitting there amongst the ashes."

Next day the brothers were all for setting off again, and Boots begged them this time, too, to let him go with them and see the riding; but no, they wouldn't have him at any price, he was too ugly and nasty, they said.

"Well, well!" said Boots; "if I go at all, I must go by myself. I'm not afraid."

So when the brothers got to the hill of glass, all the princes and knights began to ride again, and you may fancy they had taken care to shoe their horses sharp; but it was no good,—they rode and slipped, and slipped and rode, just as they had done the day before, and there was not one who could get so far as a yard up the hill.

And when they had worn out their horses, so that
they could not stir a leg, they were all forced to
give it up as a bad job.   So the king thought he
might as well proclaim that the riding should take
place the day after for the last time, just to give
them one chance more; but all at once it came
across his mind that he might as well wait a little
longer, to see if the knight in brass mail would
come this day too.   Well! they saw nothing of
him; but all at once came one riding on a steed,
far, far braver and finer than that on which the
knight in brass had ridden, and he had silver
mail, and a silver saddle and bridle, all so bright
that the sunbeams gleamed and glanced from them
far away.   Then the others shouted out to him
again, saying, he might as well hold hard, and not
try to ride up the hill, for all his trouble would be
thrown away; but the knight paid no heed to
them, and rode straight at the hill, and right up
it, till he had gone two-thirds of the way, and then
he wheeled his horse round and rode down again.
To tell the truth, the Princess liked him still better
than the knight in brass, and she sat and wished
he might only be able to come right up to the
top, and down the other side; but when she saw

him turning back, she threw the second apple after him, and it rolled down and fell into his shoe. But as soon as ever he had come down from the hill of glass, he rode off so fast that no one could see what became of him.

At even, when all were to go in before the king and the Princess, that he who had the golden apple might show it; in they went, one after the other, but there was no one who had any apple to show, and the two brothers, as they had done on the former day, went home and told how things had gone, and how all had ridden at the hill, and none got up.

"But, last of all," they said, "came one in a silver suit, and his horse had a silver saddle and a silver bridle. He was just a chap to ride; and he got two-thirds up the hill, and then turned back. He was a fine fellow, and no mistake; and the Princess threw the second gold apple to him."

"Oh!" said Boots, "I should so like to have seen him too, that I should."

"A pretty story," they said. "Perhaps you think his coat of mail was as bright as the ashes you are always poking about and sifting, you nasty dirty beast."

The third day everything happened as it had happened the two days before. Boots begged to go and see the sight, but the two wouldn't hear of his going with them. When they got to the hill there was no one who could get so much as a yard up it; and now all waited for the knight in silver mail, but they neither saw nor heard of him. At last came one riding on a steed, so brave that no one had ever seen his match; and the knight had a suit of golden mail, and a golden saddle and bridle, so wondrous bright that the sunbeams gleamed from them a mile off. The other knights and princes could not find time to call out to him not to try his luck, for they were amazed to see how grand he was. So he rode right at the hill, and tore up it like nothing, so that the Princess hadn't even time to wish that he might get up the whole way. As soon as ever he reached the top, he took the third golden apple from the Princess's lap, and then turned his horse and rode down again. As soon as he got down, he rode off at full speed, and was out of sight in no time.

Now, when the brothers got home at even, you may fancy what long stories they told, how the riding had gone off that day; and amongst other

II

things, they had a deal to say about the knight in golden mail.

"He just was a chap to ride!" they said; "so grand a knight isn't to be found in the wide world."

"Oh!" said Boots, "I should so like to have seen him; that I should."

"Ah!" said his brothers, "his mail shone a deal brighter than the glowing coals which you are always poking and digging at; nasty dirty beast that you are."

Next day all the knights and princes were to pass before the king and the Princess—it was too late to do so the night before, I suppose—that he who had the gold apple might bring it forth; but one came after another, first the princes, and then the knights, and still no one could show the gold apple.

"Well," said the king, "some one must have it, for it was something that we all saw with our own eyes, how a man came and rode up and bore it off."

So he commanded that every one who was in the kingdom should come up to the palace and see if they could show the apple. Well, they all

came one after another, but no one had the golden
apple, and after a long time the two brothers of
Boots came. They were the last of all, so the
king asked them if there was no one else in the
kingdom who hadn't come.

"Oh, yes," said they; "We have a brother,
but he never carried off the golden apple. He
hasn't stirred out of the dusthole on any of the
three days."

"Never mind that," said the king; "he may
as well come up to the palace like the rest."

So Boots had to go up to the palace.

"How, now," said the king; "have you got the
golden apple? Speak out!"

"Yes, I have," said Boots; "here is the first,
and here is the second, and here is the third too;"
and with that he pulled all three golden apples
out of his pocket, and at the same time threw off
his sooty rags, and stood before them in his
gleaming golden mail.

"Yes!" said the king; "you shall have my
daughter, and half my kingdom, for you well
deserve both her and it."

So they got ready for the wedding, and Boots
got the Princess to wife, and there was great

merry-making at the bridal-feast, you may fancy, for they could all be merry though they couldn't ride up the hill of glass; and all I can say is, if they haven't left off their merry-making yet, why they're still at it.

HOW ONE WENT OUT TO WOO.

ONCE on a time there was a lad who went out to woo him a wife. Amongst other places, he came to a farm-house, where the household were little better than beggars; but when the wooer came in, they wanted to make out that they were well to do, as you may guess. Now the husband had got a new arm to his coat.

"Pray, take a seat," he said to the wooer "but there's a shocking dust in the house."

So he went about rubbing and wiping all the benches and tables with his new arm, but he kept the other all the while behind his back.

The wife she had got one new shoe, and she went stamping and sliding with it up against the stools and chairs, saying, "How untidy it is here! Everything is out of its place!"

Then they called out to their daughter to come down and put things to rights; but the daughter, she had got a new cap; so she put her head in at the door, and kept nodding and nodding, first to this side, and then to that.

"Well! for my part," she said, "I can't be everywhere at once."

Ay! ay! that was a well-to-do houschold the wooer had come to.

———

THE COCK AND HEN.

[In this tale the notes of the Cock and Hen must be imitated.]

Hen—"You promise me shoes year after year, year after year, and yet I get no shoes!"

Cock—"You shall have them, never fear Henny penny!"

Hen—"I lay egg after egg, egg after egg, and yet I go about barefoot!"

Cock—"Well, take your eggs, and be off to the tryst, and buy yourself shoes, and don't go any longer barefoot!"

THE TWO STEP-SISTERS.

ONCE on a time there was a couple, and each of them had a daughter by a former marriage. The woman's daughter was dull and lazy, and could never turn her hand to anything, and the man's daughter was brisk and ready; but somehow or other she could never do anything to her stepmother's liking, and both the woman and her daughter would have been glad to be rid of her.

So it fell one day the two girls were to go out and spin by the side of the well, and the woman's daughter had flax to spin, but the man's daughter got nothing to spin but bristles.

"I don't know how it is," said the woman's daughter, "you're always so quick and sharp, but still I'm not afraid to spin a match with you."

Well, they agreed that she whose thread first snapped, should go down the well. So they span away; but just as they were hard at it, the man's daughter's thread broke, and she had to go down

the well. But when she got to the bottom, she
saw far and wide around her a fair green mead,
and she hadn't hurt herself at all.

So she walked on a bit, till she came to a
hedge which she had to cross.

"Ah! don't tread hard on me, pray don't,
and I'll help you another time, that I will," said
the Hedge.

Then the lassie made herself as light as she
could, and trode so carefully she scarce touched a
twig.

So she went on a bit further, till she came to
a brindled cow, which walked there with a milking-
pail on her horns. 'Twas a large pretty cow, and
her udder was so full and round.

"Ah be so good as to milk me, pray," said
the Cow; "I'm so full of milk. Drink as much
as you please, and throw the rest over my hoofs,
and see if I don't help you some day."

So the man's daughter did as the cow begged.
As soon as she touched the teats, the milk spouted
out into the pail. Then she drank till her thirst
was slaked; and the rest she threw over the cow's
hoofs, and the milking-pail she hung on her horns
again.

So when she had gone a bit further, a big wether met her, which had such thick long wool, it hung down and draggled after him on the ground, and on one of his horns hung a great pair of shears.

"Ah, please clip off my wool," said the Sheep, "for here I go about with all this wool, and catch up everything I meet, and besides it's so warm, I'm almost choked. Take as much of the fleece as you please, and twist the rest round my neck, and see if I don't help you some day."

Yes! she was willing enough, and the sheep lay down of himself on her lap, and kept quite still, and she clipped him so neatly, there wasn't a scratch on his skin. Then she took as much of the wool as she chose, and the rest she twisted round the neck of the sheep.

A little further on, she came to an apple-tree, which was loaded with apples; all its branches were bowed to the ground, and leaning against the stem was a slender pole.

"Ah! do be so good as to pluck my apples off me," said the Tree, "so that my branches may straighten themselves again, for it's bad work to stand so crooked; but when you beat them down, don't strike me too hard. Then eat as many as you please, lay the rest round my root, and see if I don't help you some day or other."

Yes, she plucked all she could reach with her hands, and then she took the pole and knocked down the rest, and afterwards she ate her fill, and the rest she laid neatly round the root.

So she walked on a long, long way, and then she came to a great farm-house, where an old hag of the Trolls lived with her daughter. There she turned in to ask if she could get a place.

"Oh!" said the old hag, "it's no use your trying. We've had ever so many maids, but none of them was worth her salt."

But she begged so prettily that they would just take her on trial, that at last they let her stay. So the old hag gave her a sieve, and bade her go and fetch water in it. She thought it strange to fetch water in a sieve, but still she went, and when she came to the well, the little birds began to sing—

"Daub in clay,
Stuff in straw!
Daub in clay,
Stuff in straw."

Yes, she did so, and found she could carry water

in a sieve well enough; but when she got home with the water, and the old witch saw the sieve, she cried out.

"THIS YOU HAVEN'T SUCKED OUT OF YOUR OWN BREAST."

So the old witch said, now she might go into the byre to pitch out dung and milk kine; but when she got there, she found a pitchfork so long and heavy, she couldn't stir it, much less work with it. She didn't know at all what to do, or what to make of it; but the little birds sung again that she should take the broom-stick and toss out a little with that, and all the rest of the dung would fly after it. So she did that, and as soon as ever she began with the broom-stick, the byre was as clean as if it had been swept and washed.

Now she had to milk the kine, but they were so restless that they kicked and frisked; there was no getting near them to milk them.

But the little birds sung outside,—

> "A little drop, a tiny sup,
> For the little birds to drink it up."

Yes, she did that; she just milked a tiny drop, 'twas as much as she could, for the little birds outside; and then all the cows stood still and let her milk them. They neither kicked nor frisked; they didn't even lift a leg.

So when the old witch saw her coming in with the milk, she cried out,—

"THIS YOU HAVEN'T SUCKED OUT OF YOUR OWN BREAST. BUT NOW JUST TAKE THIS BLACK WOOL AND WASH IT WHITE."

This the lassie was at her wit's end to know how to do, for she had never seen or heard of any one who could wash black wool white. Still she said nothing, but took the wool and went down with it to the well. There the little birds sung again, and told her to take the wool and dip it into the great butt that stood there; and she did so, and out it came as white as snow.

"Well! I never!" said the old witch, when she came in with the wool, "it's no good keeping you. You can do everything, and at last you'll be the plague of my life. We'd best part, so take your wages and be off."

Then the old hag drew out three caskets, one red, one green, and one blue, and of these the lassie was to choose one as wages for her service.

Now she didn't know at all which to choose, but the little birds sung—

"Don't take the red, don't take the green,
But take the blue, where may be seen
Three little crosses all in a row,
We saw the marks, and so we know."

So she took the blue casket, as the birds sang.

"Bad luck to you, then," said the old witch; "see if I don't make you pay for this!"

So when the man's daughter was just setting off, the old witch shot a red-hot bar of iron after her, but she sprang behind the door and hid herself, so that it missed her, for her friends, the little birds, had told her beforehand how to behave. Then she walked on and on as fast as ever she could; but when she got to the apple tree, she heard an awful clatter behind her on the road, and that was the old witch and her daughter coming after her.

So the lassie was so frightened and scared, she didn't know what to do.

"Come hither to me, lassie, do you hear," said the Apple Tree, "I'll help you; get under my branches and hide, for if they catch you, they'll tear you to death, and take the casket from you."

Yes! she did so, and she had hardly hidden herself before up came the old witch and her daughter.

"Have you seen any lassie pass this way, you apple tree," said the old hag.

"Yes, yes," said the Apple Tree; "one ran by here an hour ago; but now she's got so far a-head, you'll never catch her up."

So the old witch turned back and went home again.

Then the lassie walked on a bit, but when she came just about where the sheep was, she heard an awful clatter beginning on the road behind her, and she didn't know what to do, she was so scared and frightened; for she knew well enough it was the old witch who had thought better of it.

"Come hither to me, lassie," said the Wether, "and I'll help you. Hide yourself under my fleece, and then they'll not see you; else they'll take away the casket, and tear you to death."

Just then up came the old witch, tearing along.

"Have you seen any lassie pass here, you sheep?" she cried to the wether.

"Oh, yes," said the Wether, "I saw one an hour ago, but she ran so fast, you'll never catch her."

So the old witch turned round and went home.

But when the lassie had come to where she met the cow, she heard another awful clatter behind her.

"Come hither to me, lassie," said the Cow, "and I'll help you to hide yourself under my udder, else the old hag will come and take away your casket, and tear you to death."

True enough, it wasn't long before she came up.

"Have you seen any lassie pass here, you cow?" said the old hag.

"Yes, I saw one an hour ago," said the Cow, "but she's far away now, for she ran so fast I don't think you'll ever catch her up."

So the old hag turned round, and went back home again.

When the lassie had walked a long, long way farther on, and was not far from the hedge, she heard again that awful clatter on the road behind her, and she got scared and frightened, for she knew well enough it was the old hag and her daughter, who had changed their minds.

"Come hither to me, lassie," said the Hedge, "and I'll help you. Creep under my twigs, so that they can't see you; else they'll take the casket from you, and tear you to death."

Yes! she made all the haste she could to get under the twigs of the hedge.

"Have you seen any lassie pass this way, you hedge?" said the old hag to the hedge.

"No, I haven't seen any lassie," answered the Hedge, and was as smooth-tongued as if he had got melted butter in his mouth; but all the while he spread himself out, and made himself so big and tall, one had to think twice before crossing him. And so the old witch had no help for it but to turn round and go home again.

So when the man's daughter got home, her step-mother and her step-sister were more spiteful against her than ever; for now she was much neater, and so smart, it was a joy to look at her. Still she couldn't get leave to live with them, but they drove her out into a pig-sty. That was to be her house. So she scrubbed it out so neat and clean, and then she opened her casket, just to see

what she had got for her wages. But as soon as
ever she unlocked it, she saw inside so much gold
and silver, and lovely things, which came streaming
out till all the walls were hung with them, and at
last the pig-sty was far grander than the grandest
king's palace. And when the step-mother and
her daughter came to see this, they almost jumped
out of their skin, and began to ask what kind of
a place she had down there?

"Oh," said the lassie "can't you see when I
have got such good wages. 'Twas such a family,
and such a mistress to serve, you couldn't find
their like anywhere."

Yes! the woman's daughter made up her
mind to go out to serve too, that she might get
just such another gold casket. So they sat down
to spin again, and now the woman's daughter was
to spin bristles, and the man's daughter flax, and
she whose thread first snapped, was to go down
the well. It wasn't long, as you may fancy,
before the woman's daughter's thread snapped,
and so they threw her down the well.

So the same thing happened. She fell to the
bottom, but met with no harm, and found herself

on a lovely green meadow. When she had walked a bit she came to the hedge.

"Don't tread hard on me, pray, lassie, and I'll help you again," said the Hedge.

"Oh! said she, "what should I care for a bundle of twigs?" and tramped and stamped over the hedge till it cracked and groaned again.

A little farther on she came to the cow, which walked about ready to burst for want of milking.

"Be so good as to milk me, lassie," said the Cow, "and I'll help you again. Drink as much as you please, but throw the rest over my hoofs."

Yes? she did that; she milked the cow, and drank till she could drink no more; but when she left off, there was none left to throw over the cow's hoofs, and as for the pail, she tossed it down the hill and walked on.

When she had gone a bit further, she came to the sheep which walked along with his wool dragging after him.

"Oh, be so good as to clip me, lassie," said the Sheep, "And I'll serve you again. Take as much of the wool as you will, but twist the rest round my neck."

"Well! she did that; but she went so care-

lessly to work, that she cut great pieces out of the
poor sheep, and as for the wool, she carried it all
away with her.

A little while after she came to the apple-
tree, which stood there quite crooked with fruit
again.

" Be so good as to pluck the apples off me,
that my limbs may grow straight, for it's weary
work to stand all awry," said the Apple Tree.
" But please take care not to beat me too hard.
Eat as many as you will, but lay the rest neatly
round my root, and I'll help you again."

Well, she plucked those nearest to her, and
thrashed down those she couldn't reach with the
pole, but she didn't care how she did it, and broke
off and tore down great boughs, and ate till she
was as full as full could be, and then she threw
down the rest under the tree.

So when she had gone a good bit further, she
came to the farm where the old witch lived.
There she asked for a place, but the old hag said
she wouldn't have any more maids, for they were
either worth nothing, or were too clever, and
cheated her out of her goods. But the woman's
daughter was not to be put off, she *would* have a

place, so the old witch said she'd give her a trial, if she was fit for anything.

The first thing she had to do was to fetch water in a sieve. Well, off she went to the well, and drew water in a sieve, but as fast as she got it in it ran out again. So the little birds sung—

> "Daub in clay,
> Put in straw;
> Daub in clay,
> Put in straw!"

' But she didn't care to listen to the birds' song, and pelted them with clay, till they flew off, far away. And so she had to go home with the empty sieve, and got well scolded by the old witch.

Then she was to go into the byre to clean it, and milk the kine. But she was too good for such dirty work, she thought. Still, she went out into the byre, but when she got there, she couldn't get on at all with the pitchfork, it was so big. The birds said the same to her as they had said to her step-sister, and told her to take the broom-stick, and toss out a little dung, and then all the rest would fly after it; but all she did with the broomstick was to throw it at the birds. When she came to milk, the kine were so unruly, they kicked and pushed, and every time she got a little milk in the pail, over they kicked it. Then the birds sang again—

> "A little drop and a tiny sup
> For the little birds to drink it up."

But she beat and banged the cows about, and threw and pelted at the birds everything she could lay hold of, and made such a to do, 'twas awful to see. So she didn't make much either of her pitching or milking, and when she came in doors she got blows as well as hard words from the old witch, who sent her off to wash the black wool white; but that, too, she did no better.

Then the old witch thought this really too bad, so she set out the three caskets, one red, one green, and one blue, and said she'd no longer any need of her services, for she wasn't worth keeping, but for wages she should have leave to choose whichever casket she pleased.

Then sung the little birds,—

> "Don't take the red, don't take the green,
> But choose the blue, where may be seen
> Three little crosses, all in a row ;
> We saw the marks, and so we know."

She didn't care a pin for what the birds sang, but took the red, which caught her eye most.

And so she set out on her road home, and she went along quietly and easily enough ; there was no one who came after *her*.

So when she got home, her mother was ready to jump with joy, and the two went at once into the ingle, and put the casket up there, for they made up their minds there could be nothing in it but pure silver and gold, and they thought to have all the walls and roof gilded like the pig-sty. But lo ! when they opened the casket there came tumbling out nothing but toads, and frogs, and snakes ; and worse than that, whenever the woman's daughter opened her mouth, out popped a toad or a snake, and all the vermin one ever thought of, so that at last there was no living in the house with her.

That was all the wages *she* got for going out to service with the old witch.

BUTTERCUP.

ONCE on a time there was an old wife who sat and baked. Now you must know that this old wife had a little son, who was so plump and fat, and so fond of good things, that they called him Buttercup; she had a dog, too, whose name was Goldtooth, and as she was baking, all at once Goldtooth began to bark.

"Run out, Buttercup, there's a dear!" said the old wife, "and see what Goldtooth is barking at."

So the boy ran out, and came back crying out,—

"Oh, Heaven help us! here comes a great big witch, with her head under her arm, and a bag at her back."

"Jump under the kneading-trough and hide yourself," said his mother.

So in came the old hag!

"Good day," said she.

"God bless you," said Buttercup's mother.

"Isn't your Buttercup at home to-day?" asked the hag.

"No, that he isn't. He's out in the wood with his father, shooting ptarmigan."

"Plague take it," said the hag, "for I had such a nice little silver knife I wanted to give him."

· "Pip, pip! here I am," said Buttercup under the kneading-trough, and out he came.

"I'm so old and stiff in the back," said the hag, "you must creep into the bag and fetch it out for yourself."

But when Buttercup was well into the bag, the hag threw it over her back and strode off, and when they had gone a good bit of the way, the old hag got tired, and asked,—

"How far is it off to Snoring?"

"Half a mile," answered Buttercup.

So the hag put down the sack on the road and went aside by herself into the wood, and lay down to sleep. Meantime Buttercup set to work and cut a hole in the sack with his knife; then he crept out and put a great root of a fir-tree into the sack, and ran home to his mother.

When the hag got home and saw what there

was in the sack, you may fancy she was in a fine rage.

Next day the old wife sat and baked again, and her dog began to bark just as he did the day before.

"Run out, Buttercup, my boy," said she, "and see what Goldtooth is barking at."

"Well, I never!" cried Buttercup, as soon as he got out; "if there isn't that ugly old beast coming again 'with her head under her arm, and a great sack at her back."

"Under the kneading-trough with you and hide," said his mother.

"Good day," said the hag, "is your Buttercup at home to-day?"

"I'm sorry to say he isn't," said his mother; "he's out in the wood with his father shooting ptarmigan."

"What a bore," said the hag; "here I have a beautiful little silver spoon I want to give him."

"Pip, pip! here I am," said Buttercup, and crept out.

"I'm so stiff in the back said the old witch "you must creep into the sack and fetch it out for yourself."

So when Buttercup, was well into the sack, the hag swung it over her shoulders and set off home as fast as her legs could carry her. But when they had gone a good bit, she grew weary, and asked,—

" How far is it off to Snoring ?"

" A mile and a half," answered Buttercup.

So the hag set down the sack, and went aside into the wood to sleep a bit, but while she slept, Buttercup made a hole in the sack and got out, and put a great stone into it. Now, when the old witch got home, she made a great fire on the hearth, and put a big pot on it, and got everything ready to boil Buttercup; but when she took the sack, and thought she was going to turn out Buttercup into the pot, down plumped the stone and made a hole in the bottom of the pot, so that the water ran out and quenched the fire. Then the old hag was in a dreadful rage, and said, " If he makes himself ever so heavy next time, he shan't take me in again."

The third day everything went just as it had gone twice before; Goldtooth began to bark, and Buttercup's mother said to him,—

" Do run out and see what our dog is barking at."

So out he went, but he soon came back crying out,—

"Heaven save us! Here comes the old hag again with her head under her arm, and a sack at her back."

"Jump under the kneading-trough and hide," said his mother.

"Good day!" said the hag, as she came in at the door; "is your Buttercup at home to-day?"

"You're very kind to ask after him," said his mother; "but he's out in the wood with his father shooting ptarmigan."

"What a bore now," said the old hag; "here have I got such a beautiful little silver fork for him."

"Pip, pip! here I am," said Buttercup, as he came out from under the kneading-trough.

"I'm so stiff in the back," said the hag, "you must creep into the sack and fetch it out for yourself."

But when Buttercup was well inside the sack, the old hag swung it across her shoulders, and set off as fast as she could. This time she did not turn aside to sleep by the way, but went straight home with Buttercup in the sack, and when she reached her house it was Sunday.

So the old hag said to her daughter,—

"Now you must take Buttercup and kill him, and boil him nicely till I come back, for I'm off to church to bid my guests to dinner."

So, when all in the house were gone to church, the daughter was to take Buttercup and kill him, but then she didn't know how to set about it at all.

"Stop a bit," said Buttercup; "I'll soon shew you how to do it; just lay your head on the chopping-block, and you'll soon see."

So the poor silly thing laid her head down, and Buttercup took an axe and chopped her head off, just as if she had been a chicken. Then he laid her head in the bed, and popped her body into the pot, and boiled it so nicely; and when he had done that, he climbed up on the roof, and dragged up with him the fir-tree root and the stone, and put the one over the door, and the other at the top of the chimney.

So when the household came back from church, and saw the head on the bed, they thought it was the daughter who lay there asleep; and then they thought they would just taste the broth.

> "Good, by my troth!
> Buttercup broth,"

said the old hag.

> "Good by my troth!
> Daughter broth,"

said Buttercup down the chimney, but no one heeded him.

So the old hag's husband, who was every bit as bad as she, took the spoon to have a taste.

> "Good by my troth!
> Buttercup broth,"

said he.

> "Good, by my troth!
> Daughter broth,"

said Buttercup down the chimney pipe.

Then they all began to wonder who it could be that chattered so, and ran out to see. But when they came out at the door, Buttercup threw down on them the fir-tree root and the stone, and broke all their heads to bits. After that he took all the gold and silver that lay in the house, and went home to his mother, and became a rich man.

TAMING THE SHREW.

ONCE on a time there was a king, and he had a daughter who was such a scold, and whose tongue went so fast, there was no stopping it. So he gave out that the man who could stop her tongue should have the Princess to wife, and half his kingdom into the bargain. Now, three brothers, who heard this, made up their minds to go and try their luck; and first of all the two elder went, for they thought they were the cleverest; but they couldn't cope with her at all, and got well thrashed besides.

Then Boots, the youngest, set off, and when he had gone a little way he found an ozier band lying on the road, and he picked it up. When he had gone a little farther he found a piece of a broken plate, and he picked that up too. A little farther on he found a dead magpie, and a little farther on still, a crooked ram's horn; so he went on a bit and found the fellow to the horn; and at last, just as he was crossing the fields by the king's palace, where they were pitching out dung, he found a worn-out shoe-sole. All these things he took with him into the palace, and went before the Princess.

"Good day," said he.

"Good day," said she, and made a wry face.

"Can I get my magpie cooked here?" he asked.

"I'm afraid it will burst," answered the Princess.

"Oh! never fear! for I'll just tie this ozier band round it," said the lad, as he pulled it out.

"The fat will run out of it," said the Princess.

"Then I'll hold this under it," said the lad, and shewed her the piece of broken plate.

"You are so crooked in your words," said the Princess, "there's no knowing where to have you."

"No, I'm not crooked," said the lad; but "this is," as he held up one of the horns.

"Well!" said the Princess, "I never saw the match of this in all my days."

"Why, here you see the match to it," said the lad, as he pulled out the other ram's horn.

"I think," said the Princess, "you must have come here to wear out my tongue with your nonsense."

"No, I have not," said the lad; "but this is worn out," as he pulled out the shoe-sole.

To this the Princess hadn't a word to say, for she had fairly lost her voice with rage.

"Now you are mine," said the lad; and so he got the Princess to wife, and half the kingdom.

SHORTSHANKS.

ONCE on a time there was a poor couple who lived in a tumble-down hut, in which there was nothing but black want, so that they hadn't a morsel to eat, nor a stick to burn. But though they had next to nothing of other things, they had God's blessing in the way of children, and every year they had another babe. Now, when this story begins, they were just looking out for a new child; and to tell the truth, the husband was rather cross, and he was always going about grumbling and growling, and saying " For his part, he thought one might have too many of these God's gifts." So when the time came that the babe was to be born, he went off into the wood to fetch fuel, saying " he didn't care to stop and see the young squaller; he'd be sure to hear him soon enough, screaming for food."

Now when her husband was well out of the house, his wife gave birth to a beautiful boy, who

K

began to look about the room as soon as ever he came into the world.

"Oh! dear mother," he said, "give me some of my brother's cast-off clothes, and a few days' food, and I'll go out into the world and try my luck; you have children enough as it is, that I can see."

"God help you, my son!" answered his mother; "that can never be, you are far too young yet."

But the tiny one stuck to what he said, and begged and prayed till his mother was forced to let him have a few old rags, and a little food tied up in a bundle, and off he went right merrily and manfully into the wide world. But he was scarce out of the house before his mother had another boy, and he too looked about him, and said—

"Oh, dear mother! give me some of my brother's old clothes and a few days' food, and I'll go out into the world to find my twin brother; you have children enough already on your hands, that I can see."

"God help you, my poor little fellow!" said his mother; "you are far too little, this will never do."

But it was no good; the tiny one begged and prayed so hard, till he got some old tattered rags and a bundle of food; and so he wandered out into the world like a man, to find his twin-brother. Now, when the younger had walked a while, he saw his brother a good bit on before him, so he called out to him to stop.

"Holloa! can't you stop? why you lay legs to the ground as if you were running a race. But you might just as well have stayed to see your youngest brother before you set off into the world in such a hurry."

So the elder stopped and looked round; and when the younger had come up to him and told him the whole story, and how he was his brother, he went on to say,—

"But let's sit down here and see what our mother has given us for food." So they sat down together, and were soon great friends.

Now, when they had gone a bit further on their way, they came to a brook which ran through a green meadow, and the youngest said now the time was come to give one another names, "Since we set off in such a hurry that we hadn't time to do it at home, we may as well do it here."

"Well," said the elder, "and what shall your name be?"

"Oh!" said the younger, "my name shall be Shortshanks; and yours, what shall it be?"

"I will be called King Sturdy," answered the eldest.

So they christened each other in the brook, and went on; but when they had walked a while they came to a cross road, and agreed they should part there, and each take his own road. So they parted, but they hadn't gone half a mile before their roads met again. So they parted the second time, and took each a road; but in a little while the same thing happened, and they met again, they scarce knew how; and the same thing happened a third time also. Then they agreed that they should each choose a quarter of the heavens, and one was to go east and the other west; but before they parted, the elder said,—

"If you ever fall into misfortune or need, call three times on me, and I will come and help you; but mind you don't call on me till you are at the last pinch."

"Well!" said Shortshanks, "if that's to be the rule, I don't think we shall meet again very soon."

After that they bade each other good-bye, and Shortshanks went east, and King Sturdy west. Now, you must know, when Shortshanks had gone a good bit alone, he met an old, old crook-backed hag, who had only one eye, and Shortshanks snapped it up.

"Oh! oh!" screamed the hag, "what has become of my eye?"

"What will you give me," asked Shortshanks, "if you get your eye back?"

"I'll give you a sword, and such a sword! It will put a whole army to flight, be it ever so great," answered the old woman.

"Out with it, then!" said Shortshanks.

So the old hag gave him the sword, and got her eye back again. After that, Shortshanks wandered on a while, and another old, old crook-backed hag met him who had only one eye, which Shortshanks stole before she was aware of him.

"Oh, oh! whatever has become of my eye," screamed the hag.

"What will you give me to get your eye back?" asked Shortshanks.

"I'll give you a ship," said the woman, "which

can sail over fresh water and salt water, and over high hills and deep dales."

"Well! out with it," said Shortshanks.

So the old woman gave him a little tiny ship, no bigger than he could put in his pocket, and she got her eye back again, and they each went their way. But when he had wandered on a long, long way, he met a third time an old, old crook-backed hag, with only one eye. This eye, too, Shortshanks stole; and when the hag screamed and made a great to-do, bawling out what had become of her eye, Shortshanks said,—

"What will you give me to get back your eye?"

Then she answered,—

"I'll give you the art how to brew a hundred lasts of malt at one strike."

Well! for teaching that art the old hag got back her eye, and they each went their way.

But when Shortshanks had walked a little way, he thought it might be worth while to try his ship; so he took it out of his pocket, and put first one foot into it, and then the other; and as soon as ever he set one foot into it, it began to grow bigger and bigger, and by the time he set the other foot into it, it was as big as other ships that sail on the sea. Then Shortshanks said,—

"Off and away, over fresh water and salt water, over high hills and deep dales, and don't stop till you come to the king's palace."

And lo! away went the ship as swiftly as a bird through the air, till it came down a little below the king's palace, and there it stopped. From the palace windows people had stood and seen Shortshanks come sailing along, and they were all so amazed that they ran down to see who it could be that came sailing in a ship through the air. But while they were running down, Shortshanks had stepped out of his ship and put it into his pocket again; for as soon as he stepped out of it, it became as small as it was when he got it from the old woman. So those who had run down from the palace saw no one but a ragged little boy standing down there by the strand. Then the king asked whence he came, but the boy said he didn't know, nor could he tell them how he had got there. There he was, and that was all they could get out of him; but he begged and prayed so prettily to get a place in the king's palace; saying, if there was nothing else for him to do, he could carry in wood and water for the kitchen-maid, that their hearts were touched, and he got leave to stay there.

Now when Shortshanks came up to the palace, he saw how it was all hung with black, both outside and in, wall and roof; so he asked the kitchen-maid what all that mourning meant?

"Don't you know?" said the kitchen-maid; "I'll soon tell you: the king's daughter was promised away a long time ago to three ogres, and next Thursday evening one of them is coming to fetch her. Ritter Red, it is true, has given out that he is man enough to set her free, but God knows if he can do it; and now you know why we are all in grief and sorrow."

So when Thursday evening came, Ritter Red led the Princess down to the strand, for there it was she was to meet the Ogre, and he was to stay by her there and watch; but he wasn't likely to do the Ogre much harm, I reckon, for as soon as ever the Princess had sat down on the strand, Ritter Red climbed up into a great tree that stood there, and hid himself as well as he could among the boughs. The Princess begged and prayed him not to leave her, but Ritter Red turned a deaf ear to her, and all he said was,—

"'Tis better for one to lose life than for two."

That was what Ritter Red said.

Meantime Shortshanks went to the kitchen-maid, and asked her so prettily if he mightn't go down to the strand for a bit?

"And what should take you down to the strand," asked the kitchen-maid? "You know you've no business there."

"Oh, dear friend," said Shortshanks, "do let me go? I should so like to run down there and play a while with the other children; that I should."

"Well, well!" said the kitchen-maid, "off with you; but don't let me catch you staying there a bit over the time when the brose for supper must be set on the fire, and the roast put on the spit; and let me see; when you come back, mind you bring a good armful of wood with you."

Yes! Shortshanks would mind all that; so off he ran down to the strand.

But just as he reached the spot where the Princess sat, what should come but the Ogre tearing along in his ship, so that the wind roared and howled after him. He was so tall and stout it was awful to look on him, and he had five heads of his own.

"Fire and flame!" screamed the Ogre.

"Fire and flame yourself!" said Shortshanks.

"Can you fight?" roared the Ogre.

"If I can't, I can learn," said Shortshanks.

So the Ogre struck at him with a great thick iron club which he had in his fist, and the earth and stones flew up five yards into the air after the stroke.

"My!" said Shortshanks, "that was something like a blow, but now you shall see a stroke of mine."

Then he grasped the sword he had got from the old crook-backed hag, and cut at the Ogre; and away went all his five heads flying over the sand. So when the Princess saw she was saved, she was so glad that she scarce knew what to do, and she jumped and danced for joy. "Come, lie down, and sleep a little in my lap," she said to Shortshanks, and as he slept she threw over him a tinsel robe.

Now you must know, it wasn't long before Ritter Red crept down from the tree, as soon as he saw there was nothing to fear in the way, and he went up to the Princess and threatened her until she promised to say it was he who had saved her life; for if she wouldn't say so, he said he would kill her on the spot. After that he cut out the Ogre's lungs and tongue, and wrapped them up in his handkerchief, and so led the Princess back to the palace, and whatever honours he had not before he got then, for the king did not know how to find honour enough for him, and made him sit every day on his right hand at dinner.

As for Shortshanks, he went first of all on board the Ogre's ship, and took a whole heap of gold and silver rings, as large as hoops, and trotted off with them as hard as he could to the palace. When the kitchen-maid set her eyes on all that gold and silver, she was quite scared, and asked him,—

" But dear, good, Shortshanks, wherever did you get all this from ?" for she was rather afraid he hadn't come rightly by it.

"Oh !" answered Shortshanks, " I went home for a bit, and there I found these hoops, which had fallen off some old pails of ours, so I laid hands on them for you, if you must know."

Well ! when the kitchen-maid heard they were

for her, she said nothing more about the matter, but thanked Shortshanks, and they were good friends again.

The next Thursday evening it was the same story over again; all were in grief and trouble, but Ritter Red said, as he had saved the Princess from one Ogre, it was hard if he couldn't save her from another; and down he led her to the strand as brave as a lion. But he didn't do this Ogre much harm either, for when the time came that they looked for the Ogre, he said, as he had said before,—

"'Tis better one should lose life than two," and crept up into his tree again. But Shortshanks begged the kitchen-maid to let him go down to the strand for a little.

"Oh!" asked the kitchen-maid, "and what business have you down there?"

"Dear friend," said Shortshanks, "do pray let me go. I long so to run down and play a while with the other children."

Well! the kitchen-maid gave him leave to go, but he must promise to be back by the time the roast was turned, and he was to mind and bring a big bundle of wood with him. So Shortshanks had scarce got down to the strand, when the Ogre came tearing along in his ship, so that the wind howled and roared around him ; he was twice as big as the other Ogre, and he had ten heads on his shoulders.

" Fire and flame !" screamed the Ogre.

" Fire and flame yourself !" answered Short-shanks.

" Can you fight ?" roared the Ogre.

" If I can't, I can learn," said Shortshanks.

Then the Ogre struck at him with his iron club ; it was even bigger than that which the first Ogre had, and the earth and stones flew up ten yards into the air.

" My !" said Shortshanks, " that was something like a blow ; now you shall see a stroke of mine." Then he grasped his sword, and cut off all the Ogre's ten heads at one blow, and sent them dancing away over the sand.

Then the Princess said again to him, " Lie down and sleep a little while on my lap ;" and while Shortshanks lay there, she threw over him a silver robe. But as soon as Ritter Red marked that there was no more danger in the way, he crept down from the tree, and threatened the Princess, till she was forced to give her word, to say it was he who had set her free; after that, he cut the lungs and tongue out of the Ogre, and wrapped them in his handkerchief, and led the Princess back to the palace. Then you may fancy what mirth and joy there was, and the King was at his wit's end to know how to shew Ritter Red honour and favour enough.

This time, too, Shortshanks took a whole armful of gold and silver rings from the Ogre's ship, and when he came back to the palace the kitchen-maid clapped her hands in wonder, asking wherever he got all that gold and silver from. But Shortshanks answered that he had been home a while, and that the hoops had fallen off some old pails, so he had laid his hands on them for his friend the kitchen-maid.

So when the third Thursday evening came, everything happened as it had happened twice before; the whole palace was hung with black, and all went about mourning and weeping. But Ritter Red said he couldn't see what need they had to be so afraid; he had freed the Princess from two Ogres, and he could very well free her from a third; so he led her down to the strand, but when the time drew near for the Ogre to come up, he crept into his tree again, and hid himself. The Princess begged and prayed, but it was no good, for Ritter Red said again,—

"'Tis better that one should lose life than two."

That evening, too, Shortshanks begged for leave to go down to the strand.

"Oh!" said the kitchen-maid, "what should take you down there?"

But he begged and prayed so, that at last he got leave to go, only he had to promise to be back in the kitchen again when the roast was to be turned. So off he went, but he had scarce reached the strand when the Ogre came with the wind howling and roaring after him. He was much, much bigger than either of the other two, and he had fifteen heads on his shoulders.

"Fire and flame!" roared out the Ogre.

"Fire and flame yourself," said Shortshanks.

"Can you fight?" screamed the Ogre.

"If I can't, I can learn," said Shortshanks.

"I'll soon teach you," screamed the Ogre, and struck at him with his iron club, so that the earth and stones flew up fifteen yards into the air.

"My!" said Shortshanks, "that was something like a blow; but now you shall see a stroke of mine."

As he said that, he grasped his sword, and cut off all the Ogre's fifteen heads at one blow, and sent them all dancing over the sand.

So the Princess was freed from all the Ogres, and she both blessed and thanked Shortshanks for saving her life.

"Sleep now a while on my lap," she said ; and he laid his head on her lap, and while he slept, she threw over him a golden robe.

"But how shall we let it be known that it is you that have saved me?" she asked, when he awoke.

"Oh, I'll soon tell you," answered Shortshanks. When Ritter Red has led you home again, and given himself out as the man who has saved you, you know he is to have you to wife, and half the kingdom. Now, when they ask you, on your wedding-day, whom you will have to be your cup-bearer, you must say, 'I will have the ragged boy who does odd jobs in the kitchen, and carries in wood and water for the kitchen-maid.' So when I am filling your cups, I will spill a drop on his plate, but none on yours; then he will be wroth, and give me a blow, and the same thing will happen three times. But the third time you must mind and say, 'Shame on you! to strike my heart's darling; he it is who set me free, and him will I have!'"

After that Shortshanks ran back to the palace, as he had done before; but he went first on board the Ogre's ship, and took a whole heap of gold, silver, and precious stones, and out of them he gave the kitchen-maid another great armful of gold and silver rings.

Well! as for Ritter Red, as soon as ever he saw that all risk was over, he crept down from his tree, and threatened the Princess till she was forced to promise she would say it was he who had saved her. After that he led her back to the palace, and all the honour shown him before was nothing to what he got now, for the king thought of nothing else than how he might best honour the man who had saved his daughter from the three Ogres. As for his marrying her, and having half the kingdom, that was a settled thing, the king said. But when the wedding-day came, the Princess begged she might have the ragged boy

L

who carried in wood and water for the cook to be
her cup-bearer at the bridal-feast.

"I can't think why you should want to bring
that filthy beggar boy in here," said Ritter Red;
but the Princess had a will of her own, and said
she would have him, and no one else, to pour out
her wine; so she had her way at last.   Now everything went as it had been agreed between Shortshanks and the Princess; he spilled a drop on
Ritter Red's plate, but none on her's, and each
time Ritter Red got wroth and struck him.   At
the first blow Shortshank's rags fell off which he
had worn in the kitchen; at the second the tinsel
robe fell off; and at the third the silver robe;
and then he stood in his golden robe, all gleaming
and glittering in the light.   Then the Princess
said,—

"Shame on you! to strike my heart's darling!
he has saved me, and him will I have!"

Ritter Red cursed and swore it was he who
had set her free; but the king put in his word,
and said,—

"The man who saved my daughter must have
some token to show for it."

"Yes! Ritter Red had something to show,

and he ran off at once after his handkerchief with
the lungs and tongues in it, and Shortshanks
fetched all the gold and silver, and precious things,
he had taken out of the Ogres' ships. So each
laid his tokens before the king, and the king
said,—

"The man who has such precious stores of
gold, and silver, and diamonds, must have slain
the Ogre, and spoiled his goods, for such things
are not to be had elsewhere."

So Ritter Red was thrown into a pit full of
snakes, and Shortshanks was to have the Princess
and half the kingdom.

One day Shortshanks and the king were out
walking, and Shortshanks asked the king if he
hadn't any more children?

"Yes," said the king, "I had another daughter;
but the Ogre has taken her away, because there
was no one who could save her. Now you are
going to have one daughter, but if you can set the
other free whom the Ogre has carried off, you
shall have her too with all my heart, and the other
half of my kingdom."

"Well," said Shortshanks, "I may as well try;
but I must have an iron cable, five hundred fathoms

long, and five hundred men, and food for them to last fifteen weeks, for I have a long voyage before me."

Yes! the king said he should have them, but he was afraid there wasn't a ship in his kingdom big enough to carry such a freight.

"Oh! if that's all," said Shortshanks, "I have a ship of my own."

With that he whipped out of his pocket the ship he had got from the old hag.

The king laughed, and thought it was all a joke; but Shortshanks begged him only to give him what he asked, and he should soon see if it was a joke. So they got together what he wanted, and Shortshanks bade him put the cable on board the ship first of all; but there was no one man who could lift it, and there wasn't room for more than one at a time round the tiny ship. Then Shortshanks took hold of the cable by one end, and laid a link or two into the ship; and as he threw in the links, the ship grew bigger and bigger, till at last it got so big, that there was room enough and to spare in it for the cable, and the five hundred men, and their food, and Shortshanks, and all. Then he said to the ship,—

" Off and away, over fresh water and salt

water, over high hill and deep dale, and don't stop till you come to where the king's daughter is." And away went the ship over land and sea, till the wind whistled after it.

So when they had sailed far, far away, the ship stood stock still in the middle of the sea.

"Ah!" said Shortshanks, "now we have got so far; but how we are to get back is another story."

Then he took the cable and tied one end of it round his waist, and said,—

"Now, I must go to the bottom, but when I give the cable a good tug, and want to come up again, mind you all hoist away with a will, or your lives will be lost as well as mine;" and with these words overboard he leapt, and dived down, so that yellow waves rose round him in an eddy.

Well, he sank and sank, and at last he came to the bottom, and there he saw a great rock rising up with a door in it, so he opened the door and went in. When he got inside, he saw another Princess, who sat and sewed, but when she saw Shortshanks, she clasped her hands together and cried out,—

"Now, God be thanked! you are the first

Christian man I've set eyes on since I came here."

"Very good," said Shortshanks; "but do you know I've come to fetch you?"

"Oh!" she cried, "you'll never fetch me; you'll never have that luck, for if the Ogre sees you, he'll kill you on the spot."

"I'm glad you spoke of the Ogre," said Shortshanks; "'twould be fine fun to see him; whereabouts is he?"

Then the Princess told him the Ogre was out looking for some one who could brew a hundred lasts of malt at one strike, for he was going to give a great feast, and less drink wouldn't do.

"Well! I can do that," said Shortshanks.

"Ah!" said the Princess; "if only the Ogre wasn't so hasty, I might tell him about you; but he's so cross; I'm afraid he'll tear you to pieces as soon as he comes in, without waiting to hear my story. Let me see what is to be done. Oh! I have it; just hide yourself in the side-room yonder, and let us take our chance."

Well! Shortshanks did as she told him, and he had scarce crept into the side-room before the Ogre came in.

"HUF!" said the Ogre; "what a horrid smell of Christian man's blood!"

"Yes!" said the Princess, "I know there is, for a bird flew over the house with a Christian man's bone in his bill and let it fall down the chimney. I made all the haste I could to get it out again, but I daresay it's that you smell."

"Ah!" said the Ogre, "like enough."

Then the Princess asked the Ogre if he had laid hold of any one who could brew a hundred lasts of malt at one strike?

"No," said the Ogre, "I can't hear of any one who can do it."

"Well," she said, "a while ago, there was a chap in here who said he could do it."

"Just like you with your wisdom!" said the Ogre; "why did you let him go away then, when you knew he was the very man I wanted?"

"Well then, I didn't let him go," said the Princess; "but father's temper is a little hot, so I hid him away in the side-room yonder; but if father hasn't hit upon any one, here he is."

"Well," said the Ogre, "let him come in then."

So Shortshanks came in, and the Ogre asked

him if it were true that he could brew a hundred lasts of malt at a strike?

"Yes it is," said Shortshanks.

"'Twas good luck then to lay hands on you," said the Ogre "and now fall to work this minute; but heaven help you if you don't brew the ale strong enough."

"Oh," said Shortshanks, "never fear, it shall be stinging stuff;" and with that he began to brew without more fuss, but all at once he cried out,––

"I must have more of you Ogres to help in the brewing, for these I have got a'nt half strong enough."

Well, he got more — so many that there was a whole swarm of them, and then the brewing went on bravely. Now when the sweet-wort was ready, they were all eager to taste it, you may guess; first of all the Ogre, and then all his kith and kin. But Shortshanks had brewed the wort so strong that they all fell down dead, one after another, like so many flies, as soon as they had tasted it. At last there wasn't one of them left alive but one vile old hag, who lay bed-ridden in the chimney-corner.

"Oh, you poor old wretch," said Shortshanks,

"you may just as well taste the wort along with the rest."

So he went and scooped up a little from the bottom of the copper in a scoop, and gave her a drink, and so he was rid of the whole pack of them.

As he stood there and looked about him, he cast his eye on a great chest, so he took it and filled it with gold and silver; then he tied the cable round himself and the Princess and the chest, and gave it a good tug, and his men pulled them all up, safe and sound. As soon as ever Shortshanks was well up, he said to the ship.

"Off and away, over fresh water and salt water, high hill and deep dale, and don't stop till you come to the king's palace;" and straightway the ship held on her course, so that the yellow billows foamed round her. When the people in the palace saw the ship sailing up, they were not slow in meeting them with songs and music, welcoming Shortshanks with great joy; but the gladdest of all was the king, who had now got his other daughter back again.

But now Shortshanks was rather down-hearted for you must know that both the princesses wanted to have him, and he would have no other than the one he had first saved, and she was the youngest. So he walked up and down, and thought and thought what he should do to get her, and yet do something to please her sister. Well, one day as he was turning the thing over in his mind, it struck him if he only had his brother King Sturdy, who was so like him that no one could tell the one from the other, he would give up to him the other princess and half the kingdom, for he thought one-half was quite enough.

Well, as soon as ever this came into his mind he went outside the palace and called on King Sturdy, but no one came. So he called a second time a little louder, but still no one came. Then he called out the third time " King Sturdy" with all his might, and there stood his brother before him.

" Didn't I say !" he said to Shortshanks, " didn't I say you were not to call me except in your utmost need ? and here there is not so much as a gnat to do you any harm," and with that he gave him such a box on the ear that Shortshanks tumbled head over heels on the grass.

" Now shame on you to hit so hard !" said Shortshanks. " First of all I won a princess and half the kingdom, and then I won another princess and the other half of the kingdom ; and now I'm thinking to give you one of the princesses and half the kingdom. Is there any rhyme or reason in giving me such a box on the ear ?"

When King Sturdy heard that, he begged his brother to forgive him, and they were soon as good friends as ever again.

"Now," said Shortshanks, "you know we are so much alike that no one can tell the one from the other ; so just change clothes with me and go into the palace ; then the princesses will think it is I that am coming in, and the one that kisses you first you shall have for your wife, and I will have the other for mine."

And he said this because he knew well enough that the elder king's daughter was the stronger, and so he could very well guess how things would go. As for King Sturdy, he was willing enough, so he changed clothes with his brother and went into the palace. But when he came into the princesses' bower they thought it was Shortshanks, and both ran up to him to kiss him ; but the elder, who was stronger and bigger, pushed her sister on one side, and threw her arms round King Sturdy's neck, and gave him a kiss; and so he got her for his wife, and Shortshanks got the younger Princess. Then they made ready for the wedding, and you may fancy what a grand one it was, when I tell you that the fame of it was noised abroad over seven kingdoms.

GUDBRAND ON THE HILL-SIDE.

ONCE on a time there was a man whose name was Gudbrand ; he had a farm which lay far, far away upon a hill-side, and so they called him Gudbrand on the Hill-side.

Now, you must know this man and his good-wife lived so happily together, and understood one another so well, that all the husband did the wife thought so well done there was nothing like it in the world, and she was always glad whatever he turned his hand to. The farm was their own land, and they had a hundred dollars lying at the bottom of their chest, and two cows tethered up in a stall in their farm-yard.

So one day his wife said to Gudbrand,—

" Do you know, dear, I think we ought to take one of our cows into town and sell it ; that's what I think ; for then we shall have some money in hand, and such well to-do people as we ought to have ready money like the rest of the world. As for the hundred dollars at the bottom of the

chest yonder, we can't make a hole in them, and
I'm sure I don't know what we want with more
than one cow. Besides, we shall gain a little in
another way, for then I shall get off with only
looking after one cow, instead of having, as now,
to feed and litter and water two."

Well, Gudbrand thought his wife talked right
good sense, so he set off at once with the cow
on his way to town to sell her ; but when he got
to the town, there was no one who would buy his
cow.

"Well! well! never mind," said Gudbrand,
"at the worst, I can only go back home again with
my cow. I've both stable and tether for her, I
should think, and the road is no farther out than
in ;" and with that he began to toddle home with
his cow.

But when he had gone a bit of the way, a
man met him who had a horse to sell, so Gudbrand
thought 'twas better to have a horse than a cow,
so he swopped with the man. A little farther on,
he met a man walking along, and driving a fat
pig before him, and he thought it better to have a
fat pig than a horse, so he swopped with the man.
After that he went a little farther, and a man met

him with a goat ; so he thought it better to have
a goat than a pig, and he swopped with the man
that owned the goat. Then he went on a good
bit till he met a man who had a sheep, and he
swopped with him too, for he thought it always
better to have a sheep than a goat. After a
while he met a man with a goose, and he swopped
away the sheep for the goose ; and when he had
walked a long, long time, he met a man with a
cock, and he swopped with him, for he thought in
this wise, "'Tis surely better to have a cock than
a goose." Then he went on till the day was far
spent, and he began to get very hungry, so he
sold the cock for a shilling, and bought food with
the money, for, thought Gudbrand on the Hill-side,
"'Tis always better to save one's life than to have
a cock."

After that he went on home till he reached
his nearest neighbour's house, where he turned in.

"Well," said the owner of the house, "how
did things go with you in town ?"

" Rather so so," said Gudbrand ; " I can't praise
my luck, nor do I blame it either," and with that
he told the whole story from first to last.

" Ah !" said his friend, " you'll get nicely called

over the coals, that one can see, when you get home to your wife. Heaven help you, I wouldn't stand in your shoes for something."

"Well!" said Gudbrand on the Hill-side, "I think things might have gone much worse with me; but now, whether I have done wrong or not, I have so kind a goodwife, she never has a word to say against anything that I do."

"Oh!" answered his neighbour, "I hear what you say, but I don't believe it for all that."

"Shall we lay a bet upon it?" asked Gudbrand on the Hill-side. "I have a hundred dollars at the bottom of my chest at home; will you lay as many against them?"

Yes! the friend was ready to bet; so Gudbrand stayed there till evening, when it began to get dark, and then they went together to his house, and the neighbour was to stand outside the door and listen, while the man went in to see his wife.

"Good evening!" said Gudbrand on the Hill-side.

"Good evening!" said the goodwife. "Oh! is that you? now, God be praised."

Yes! it was he. So the wife asked how things had gone with him in town?

"Oh! only so so," answered Gudbrand; "not much to brag of. When I got to the town there was no one who would buy the cow, so you must know I swopped it away for a horse."

"For a horse!" said his wife; "well that is good of you; thanks with all my heart. We are so well to do that we may drive to church, just as well as other people; and if we choose to keep a horse we have a right to get one, I should think. So run out, child, and put up the horse."

" Ah !" said Gudbrand, " but you see I've not got the horse after all; for when I got a bit farther on the road, I swopped it away for a pig."

"Think of that, now!" said the wife; "you did just as I should have done myself; a thousand thanks! Now I can have a bit of bacon in the house to set before people when they come to see me, that I can. What do we want with a horse? People would only say we had got so proud that we couldn't walk to church. Go out, child, and put up the pig in the stye."

" But I've not got the pig either," said Gudbrand; " for when I got a little farther on, I swopped it away for a milch goat."

" Bless us !" cried his wife, " how well you

M

manage every thing! Now I think it over, what should I do with a pig? People would only point at us and say, 'Yonder they eat up all they have got.' No! now I have got a goat, and I shall have milk and cheese, and keep the goat too. Run out, child, and put up the goat."

"Nay, but I haven't got the goat either," said Gudbrand, "for a little farther on I swopped it away, and got a fine sheep instead."

"You don't say so!" cried his wife; "why you do everything to please me, just as if I had been with you; what do we want with a goat? If I had it I should lose half my time in climbing up the hills to get it down. No! if I have a sheep, I shall have both wool and clothing, and fresh meat in the house. Run out, child, and put up the sheep."

"But I haven't got the sheep any more than the rest," said Gudbrand, "for when I had gone a bit farther, I swopped it away for a goose."

"Thank you! thank you! with all my heart," cried his wife; "what should I do with a sheep? I have no spinning-wheel, nor carding-comb, nor should I care to worry myself with cutting, and shaping, and sewing clothes. We can buy clothes

now, as we have always done; and now I shall
have roast goose, which I have longed for so
often; and, besides, down to stuff my little pillow
with.   Run out, child, and put up the goose."

"Ah!" said Gudbrand, "but I haven't the
goose either; for when I had gone a bit farther
I swopped it away for a cock."

"Dear me!" cried his wife, "how you think
of everything! just as I should have done myself.   A cock! think of that! why it's as good
as an eight-day clock, for every morning the cock
crows at four o'clock, and we shall be able to stir
our stumps in good time.   What should we do
with a goose?   I don't know how to cook it;
and as for my pillow, I can stuff it with cotton-
grass.   Run out, child, and put up the cock."

"But, after all, I haven't got the cock," said
Gudbrand; "for when I had gone a bit farther, I
got as hungry as a hunter, so I was forced to sell
the cock for a shilling, for fear I should starve."

"Now, God be praised that you did so!" cried his
wife; "whatever you do, you do it always just after
my own heart.   What should we do with the
cock?   We are our own masters, I should think, and
can lie a-bed in the morning as long as we like.

Heaven be thanked that I have got you safe back again; you who do everything so well that I want neither cock nor goose; neither pigs nor kine."

Then Gudbrand opened the door and said,—

" Well, what do you say now? Have I won the hundred dollars?" and his neighbour was forced to allow that he had.

THE BLUE BELT.

ONCE on a time there was an old beggar-woman, who had gone out to beg. She had a little lad with her, and when she had got her bag full, she struck across the hills towards her own home. So when they had gone a bit up the hill-side, they came upon a little blue belt, which lay where two paths met, and the lad asked his mother's leave to pick it up.

"No," said she, "may be there's witchcraft in it;" and so with threats she forced him to follow her. But when they had gone a bit farther, the lad said he must turn aside a moment out of the road, and meanwhile his mother sat down on a tree-stump. But the lad was a long time gone, for as soon as he got so far into the wood, that the old dame could not see him, he ran off to where the belt lay, took it up, tied it round his waist, and lo! he felt as strong as if he could lift the whole hill. When he got back, the old dame was in a great rage, and wanted to know what he had

been doing all that while. You don't care how
much time you waste, and yet you know the night
is drawing on, and we must cross the hill before
it is dark!" So on they tramped; but when they
had got about half-way, the old dame grew weary,
and said she must rest under a bush.

"Dear mother," said the lad, "mayn't I just
go up to the top of this high crag while you rest,
and try if I can't see some sign of folk hereabouts?"

Yes! he might do that; so when he had got
to the top, he saw a light shining from the north.
So he ran down and told his mother.

"We must get on mother; we are near a house,
for I see a bright light shining quite close to us in the
north." Then she rose and shouldered her bag,
and set off to see; but they hadn't gone far, before
there stood a steep spur of the hill, right across
their path.

"Just as I thought!" said the old dame; "now
we can't go a step farther; a pretty bed we shall
have here!"

But the lad took the bag under one arm, and
his mother under the other, and ran straight up
the steep crag with them.

"Now, don't you see! don't you see that we

are close to a house! don't you see the bright light?"

But the old dame said those were no Christian folk, but Trolls, for she was at home in all that forest far and near, and knew there was not a living soul in it, until you were well over the ridge, and had come down on the other side. But they went on, and in a little while they came to a great house which was all painted red.

"What's the good?" said the old dame, "we daren't go in, for here the Trolls live."

"Don't say so; we must go in. There must be men where the lights shine so," said the lad. So in he went, and his mother after him, but he had scarce opened the door before she swooned away, for there she saw a great stout man, at least twenty feet high, sitting on the bench.

"Good evening, grandfather!" said the lad.

"Well, here I've sat three hundred years," said the man who sat on the bench, "and no one has ever come and called me grandfather before." Then the lad sat down by the man's side, and began to talk to him as if they had been old friends.

"But what's come over your mother?" said

the man, after they had chattered a while. "I
think she swooned away; you had better look
after her."

So the lad went and took hold of the old
dame; and dragged her up the hall along the
floor. That brought her to herself, and she kicked,
and scratched, and flung herself about, and at last
sat down upon a heap of firewood in the corner;
but she was so frightened that she scarce dared
to look one in the face.

After a while, the lad asked if they could
spend the night there.

"Yes, to be sure," said the man.

So they went on talking again, but the lad
soon got hungry, and wanted to know if they could
get food as well as lodging.

"Of course," said the man, "that might be got
too." And after he had sat a while longer, he
rose up and threw six loads of dry pitch-pine on
the fire. This made the old hag still more afraid.

"Oh! now he's going to roast us alive," she
said, in the corner where she sat.

And when the wood had burned down to
glowing embers, up got the man and strode out of
his house.

"Heaven bless and help us! what a stout heart you have got," said the old dame; "don't you see we have got amongst Trolls?"

"Stuff and nonsense!" said the lad; "no harm if we have."

In a little while back came the man with an ox so fat and big, the lad had never seen its like, and he gave it one blow with his fist under the ear, and down it fell dead on the floor. When that was done, he took it up by all the four legs, and laid it on the glowing embers, and turned it and twisted it about till it was burnt brown outside. After that, he went to a cupboard and took out a great silver dish, and laid the ox on it; and the dish was so big that none of the ox hung over on any side. This he put on the table, and then he went down into the cellar, and fetched a cask of wine, knocked out the head, and put the cask on the table, together with two knives, which were each six feet long. When this was done, he bade them go and sit down to supper and eat. So they went, the lad first and the old dame after, but she began to whimper and wail, and to wonder how she should ever use such knives. But her son seized one, and began to cut slices out of the

thigh of the ox, which he placed before his
mother.   And when they had eaten a bit, he took
up the cask with both hands, and lifted it down to
the floor; then he told his mother to come and
drink, but it was still so high she couldn't reach
up to it; so he caught her up, and held her up to
the edge of the cask while she drank; as for him·
self, he clambered up and hung down like a cat
inside the cask while he drank.   So when he had
quenched his thirst, he took up the cask and put
it back on the table, and thanked the man for the
good meal, and told his mother to come and
thank him too, and a-feared though she was, she
dared do nothing else but thank the man.   Then
the lad sat down again alongside the man and
began to gossip, and after they had sat a while,
the man said—

"Well! I must just go and get a bit of supper
too;" and so he went to the table and ate up
the whole ox—hoofs, and horns, and all—and
drained the cask to the last drop, and then went
back and sat on the bench.

"As for beds," he said, "I don't know what's
to be done.   I've only got one bed and a cradle;
but we could get on pretty well if you would sleep

in the cradle, and then your mother might lie in the bed yonder."

"Thank you kindly, that'll do nicely," said the lad; and with that he pulled off his clothes and lay down in the cradle; but, to tell you the truth it was quite as big as a four-poster. As for the old dame, she had to follow the man who showed her to bed, though she was out of her wits for fear.

"Well!" thought the lad to himself, "'twill never do to go to sleep yet. I'd best lie awake and listen how things go as the night wears on."

So after a while the man began to talk to the old dame, and at last he said—

"We two might live here so happily together, could we only be rid of this son of yours."

"But do you know how to settle him? Is that what you're thinking of?" said she.

"Nothing easier," said he; at any rate he would try. He would just say he wished the old dame would stay and keep house for him a day or two, and then he would take the lad out with him up the hill to quarry corner-stones, and roll down a great rock on him. All this the lad lay and listened to.

Next day the Troll—for it was a Troll as clear as day—asked if the old dame would stay and keep house for him a few days; and as the day went on he took a great iron crowbar, and asked the lad if he had a mind to go with him up the hill and quarry a few corner-stones. With all his heart, he said, and went with him; and so, after they had split a few stones, the Troll wanted him to go down below and look after cracks in the rock; and while he was doing this, the Troll worked away, and wearied himself with his crowbar till he moved a whole crag out of its bed, which came rolling right down on the place where the lad was; but he held it up till he could get on one side, and then let it roll on.

"Oh!" said the lad to the Troll, "now I see what you mean to do with me. You want to crush me to death; so just go down yourself and look after the cracks and refts in the rock, and I'll stand up above."

The Troll did not dare to do otherwise than the lad bade him, and the end of it was that the lad rolled down a great rock, which fell upon the Troll, and broke one of his thighs.

"Well! you *are* in a sad plight," said the lad,

as he strode down, lifted up the rock, and set the man free. After that he had to put him on his back and carry him home; so he ran with him as fast as a horse, and shook him so that the Troll screamed and screeched as if a knife were run into him. And when he got home, they had to put the Troll to bed, and there he lay in a sad pickle.

When the night wore on the Troll began to talk to the old dame again, and to wonder how ever they could be rid of the lad.

" Well," said the old dame, " if you can't hit on a plan to get rid of him, I'm sure I can't."

" Let me see," said the Troll; " I've got twelve lions in a garden; if they could only get hold of the lad they'd soon tear him to pieces."

So the old dame said it would be easy enough to get him there. She would sham sick, and say she felt so poorly, nothing would do her any good but lion's milk. All that the lad lay and listened to; and when he got up in the morning his mother said. she was worse than she looked, and she thought she should never be right again unless she could get some lion's milk.

" Then I'm afraid you'll be poorly a long time,

mother," said the lad, "for I'm sure I don't know where any is to be got."

"Oh! if that be all," said the Troll, "there's no lack of lion's milk, if we only had the man to fetch it;" and then he went on to say how his brother had a garden with twelve lions in it, and how the lad might have the key if he had a mind to milk the lions.   So the lad took the key and a milking pail, and strode off; and when he unlocked the gate and got into the garden, there stood all the twelve lions on their hind-paws, rampant and roaring at him.   But the lad laid hold of the biggest, and led him about by the fore-paws, and dashed him against stocks and stones, till there wasn't a bit of him left but the two paws.   So when the rest saw that, they were so afraid that they crept up and lay at his feet like so many curs.   After that they followed him about where-ever he went, and when he got home, they lay down outside the house, with their fore-paws on the door sill.

"Now, mother, you'll soon be well," said the lad, when he went in, "for here is the lion's milk."

He had just milked a drop in the pail.

But the Troll, as he lay in bed, swore it was

all a lie. He was sure the lad was not the man to milk lions.

When the lad heard that, he forced the Troll to get out of bed, threw open the door, and all the lions rose up and seized the Troll, and at last the lad had to make them leave their hold.

That night the Troll began to talk to the old dame again. "I'm sure I can't tell how to put this lad out of the way—he is so awfully strong; can't you think of some way?"

"No!" said the old dame, "if you can't tell, I'm sure I can't."

"Well!" said the Troll, "I have two brothers in a castle; they are twelve times as strong as I am, and that's why I was turned out and had to put up with this farm. They hold that castle, and round it there is an orchard with apples in it, and whoever eats those apples sleeps for three days and three nights. If we could only get the lad to go for the fruit, he wouldn't be able to keep from tasting the apples, and as soon as ever he fell asleep my brothers would tear him in pieces."

The old dame said she would sham sick, and say she could never be herself again unless she tasted those apples; for she had set her heart on them.

All this the lad lay and listened to.

When the morning came the old dame was so poorly that she couldn't utter a word but groans and sighs. She was sure she should never be well again, unless she had some of those apples that grew in the orchard near the castle where the man's brothers lived; only she had no one to send for them.

Oh! the lad was ready to go that instant; but the eleven lions went with him. So when he came to the orchard, he climbed up into the apple tree' and ate as many apples as he could, and he had scarce got down before he fell into a deep sleep; but the lions all lay round him in a ring. The third day came the Troll's brothers, but they did not come in man's shape. They came snort-ing like man-eating steeds, and wondered who it was that dared to be there, and said they would tear him to pieces, so small that there should not be a bit of him left. But up rose the lions and tore the Trolls into small pieces, so that the place looked as if a dungheap had been tossed about it; and when they had finished the Trolls they lay down again. The lad did not wake till late in the afternoon, and when he got on his knees and rubbed the sleep out of his eyes, he began to wonder what had been going on, when he saw the marks of hoofs. But when he went towards the castle, a maiden looked out of a window who had seen all that had happened, and she said,—

"You may thank your stars you weren't in that tussle, else you must have lost your life."

"What! I lose my life! no fear of that, I think," said the lad.

So she begged him to come in that she might talk with him, for she hadn't seen a Christian soul ever since she came there. But when she opened the door the lions wanted to go in too, but she got so frightened, that she began to scream, and so the lad let them lie outside. Then the two talked and talked, and the lad asked how it came that she, who was so lovely, could put up with those ugly Trolls. She never wished it, she said; 'twas quite against her will. They had seized her by force, and she was the King of Arabia's daughter. So they talked on, and at last she asked him what he would do; whether she should go back home, or whether he would have her to wife. Of course he would have her, and she shouldn't go home.

After that they went round the castle, and at last they came to a great hall, where the Trolls' two great swords hung high up on the wall.

" I wonder if you are man enough to wield one of these," said the Princess.

" Who ?—I ?" said the lad. " 'Twould be a pretty thing if I couldn't wield one of these."

With that he put two or three chairs one a-top of the other, jumped up, and touched the biggest sword with his finger tips, tossed it up in the air, and caught it again by the hilt ; leapt down, and at the same time dealt such a blow with it on the floor, that the whole hall shook. After he had thus got down, he thrust the sword under his arm, and carried it about with him.

So, when they had lived a little while in the castle, the Princess thought she ought to go home to her parents, and let them know what had become of her; so they loaded a ship, and she set sail from the castle.

After she had gone, and the lad had wandered about a little, he called to mind that he had been sent on an errand thither, and had come to fetch

something for his mother's health; and though he
said to himself, "After all, the old dame was not
so bad but she's all right by this time,"——still
he thought he ought to go and just see how she
was. So he went and found both the man and
his mother quite fresh and hearty.

"What wretches you are to live in this beg-
garly hut," said the lad. "Come with me up to my
castle, and you shall see what a fine fellow I am."

Well! they were both ready to go, and on the
way his mother talked to him, and asked, "How
it was he had got so strong?"

"If you must know, it came of that blue belt
which lay on the hill-side that time when you and
I were out begging," said the lad.

"Have you got it still!" asked she.

"Yes,"— he had. It was tied round his waist.

"Might she see it?"

"Yes, she might;" and with that he pulled
open his waistcoat and shirt to show it her.

Then she seized it with both hands, tore it off,
and twisted it round her fist.

"Now," she cried, "what shall I do with such
a wretch as you? I'll just give you one blow,
and dash your brains out!"

"Far too good a death for such a scamp," said the Troll. "No! let's first burn out his eyes, and then turn him adrift in a little boat."

So they burned out his eyes and turned him adrift, in spite of his prayers and tears; but, as the boat drifted, the lions swam after, and at last they laid hold of it and dragged it ashore on an island, and placed the lad under a fir tree. They caught game for him, and they plucked the birds and made him a bed of down; but he was forced to eat his meat raw, and he was blind. At last, one day the biggest lion was chasing a hare which was blind, for it ran straight over stock and stone, and the end was, it ran right up against a fir stump and tumbled head over heels across the field right into a spring; but lo! when it came out of the spring it saw its way quite plain, and so saved its life.

"So, so!" thought the lion, and went and dragged the lad to the spring, and dipped him over head and ears in it. So, when he had got his sight again, he went down to the shore and made signs to the lions that they should all lie close together like a raft; then he stood upon their backs while they swam with him to the mainland. When he had reached the shore he went up into a

birchen copse, and made the lions lie quiet. Then
he stole up to the castle, like a thief, to see if he
couldn't lay hands on his belt; and when he got
to the door, he peeped through the keyhole, and
there he saw his belt hanging up over a door in
the kitchen. So he crept softly in across the floor,
for there was no one there; but as soon as he had
got hold of the belt, he began to kick and stamp
about as though he were mad. Just then his
mother came rushing out,—

"Dear heart, my darling little boy! do give
me the belt again," she said.

"Thank you kindly," said he. "Now you
shall have the doom you passed on me," and he
fulfilled it on the spot. When the old Troll heard
that, he came in and begged and prayed so
prettily that he might not be smitten to death.

"Well, you may live," said the lad, "but you
shall undergo the same punishment you gave me;"
and so he burned out the Troll's eyes, and turned
him adrift on the sea in a little boat, but he had
no lions to follow him.

Now the lad was all alone, and he went about
longing and longing for the Princess; at last he
could bear it no longer; he must set out to seek

her, his heart was so bent on having her. So he loaded four ships and set sail for Arabia. For some time they had fair wind and fine weather, but after that they lay wind-bound under a rocky island. So the sailors went ashore and strolled about to spend the time, and there they found a huge egg, almost as big as a little house. So they began to knock it about with large stones, but after all, they couldn't crack the shell. Then the lad came up with his sword to see what all the noise was about, and when he saw the egg, he thought it a trifle to crack it; so he gave it one blow and the egg split, and out came a chicken as big as an elephant.

"Now we have done wrong," said the lad; "this can cost us all our lives;" and then he asked his sailors if they were men enough to sail to Arabia in four-and-twenty hours, if they got a fine breeze. Yes! they were good to do that, they said, so they set sail with a fine breeze, and got to Arabia in three-and-twenty hours. As soon as they landed, the lad ordered all the sailors to go and bury themselves up to the eyes in a sandhill, so that they could barely see the ships. The lad and the captains climbed a high crag and sate down under a fir. In a little while came a great bird flying with an island in its claws and let it fall down on the fleet, and sunk every ship. After it had done that, it flew up to the sand-hill and flapped its wings, so that the wind nearly took off the heads of the sailors, and it flew past the fir with such force that it turned the lad right about, but he was ready with his sword, and gave the bird one blow and brought it down dead.

After that he went to the town, where every one was glad because the king had got his daughter back; but now the king had hidden her away somewhere himself, and promised her hand as a reward to any one who could find her, and this though she was betrothed before. Now as the lad went along he met a man who had white bear-skins for sale, so he bought one of the hides and put it on; and one of the captains was to take an iron chain and lead him about, and so he went into the town and began to play pranks. At last the news came to the king's ears, that there never had been such fun in the town before, for here was a white bear that danced and cut capers just as it was bid. So a messenger came to say the bear must come to the castle at once, for the king wanted to see its tricks. So when it got to the castle every one was afraid, for such a beast they had never seen before; but the captain said there was no danger unless they laughed at it. They mustn't do that, else it would tear them to pieces. When the king heard that, he warned all the court not to laugh. But while the fun was going on, in came one of the king's maids, and began to laugh and make game of the bear, and the bear flew at her and tore her, so that there was scarce a rag of her left. Then all the court began to bewail, and the captain most of all.

"Stuff and nonsense!" said the king; "she's only a maid, besides its more my affair than yours."

When the show was over, it was late at night. "It's no good your going away, when it's so late," said the king. "The bear had best sleep here."

"Perhaps it might sleep in the ingle by the kitchen fire," said the captain.

"Nay," said the king, "it shall sleep up here, and it shall have pillows and cushions to sleep on." So a whole heap of pillows and cushions was brought, and the captain had a bed in a side-room.

But at midnight the king came with a lamp in his hand, and a big bunch of keys, and carried off the white bear. He passed along gallery after gallery, through doors and rooms, up-stairs and down-stairs, till at last he came to a pier which ran out into the sea. Then the king began to pull and haul at posts and pins, this one up and that one down, till at last a little house floated up to the water's edge. There he kept his daughter, for she was so dear to him, that he had hid her, so that no one could find her out. He left the white bear outside while he went in and told her how it had danced and played its pranks. She said she was afraid and dared not look at it; but he talked her over, saying there was no danger, if she only wouldn't laugh. So they brought the bear in, and locked the door, and it danced and played its tricks; but just when the fun was at its height, the Princess's maid began to laugh. Then the lad flew at her and tore her to bits, and the Princess began to cry and sob.

"Stuff and nonsense," cried the king; "all this fuss about a maid! I'll get you just as good a one again. But now I think the bear had best stay here till morning, for I don't care to have to go and lead it along all those galleries and stairs at this time of night."

"Well!" said the Princess, "if it sleeps here, I'm sure I won't."

But just then the bear curled himself up and lay down by the stove; and it was settled at last that the Princess should sleep there too, with a light burning. But as soon as the king was well gone, the white bear came and begged her to undo his collar. The Princess was so scared she almost swooned away; but she felt about till she found the collar, and she had scarce undone it before the bear pulled his head off. Then she knew him again, and was so glad there was no end to her joy, and she wanted to tell her father at once that her deliverer was come. But the lad would not hear of it; he would earn her once more, he said. So in the morning, when they heard the king rattling at the posts outside, the lad drew on the hide and lay down by the stove.

"Well, has it lain still?" the king asked.

"I should think so," said the Princess; "it hasn't so much as turned or stretched itself once."

When they got up to the castle again, the captain took the bear and led it away, and then the lad threw off the hide, and went to a tailor and ordered clothes fit for a prince; and when they were fitted on he went to the king, and said he wanted to find the Princess.

"You're not the first who has wished the same thing," said the king, "but they have all lost their lives; for if any one who tries can't find her in four-and-twenty hours his life is forfeited."

Yes; the lad knew all that. Still he wished to try, and if he couldn't find her, 'twas his look-out. Now in the castle there was a band that played sweet tunes, and there were fair maids to dance with, and so the lad danced away. When twelve hours were gone, the king said,—

"I pity you with all my heart. You're so poor a hand at seeking; you will surely lose your life."

"Stuff!" said the lad; "while there's life there's hope! So long as there's breath in the body there's no fear; we have lots of time;" and so he went on dancing till there was only one hour left.

Then he said he would begin to search.

"It's no use now," said the king; "time's up."

"Light your lamp; out with your big bunch of keys," said the lad, "and follow me whither I wish to go. There is still a whole hour left."

So the lad went the same way which the king

had led him the night before, and he bade the
king unlock door after door till they came down
to the pier which ran out into the sea.

"It's all no use, I tell you," said the king;
"time's up, and this will only lead you right out
into the sea."

"Still five minutes more," said the lad, as he
pulled and pushed at the posts and pins, and the
house floated up.

"Now the time IS up," bawled the king; "come
hither, headsman, and take off his head."

"Nay, nay!" said the lad; "stop a bit, there
are still three minutes! Out with the key, and
let me get into this house."

But there stood the king and fumbled with
his keys, to draw out the time. At last he said
he hadn't any key.

"Well, if you haven't, I *have*," said the lad,
as he gave the door such a kick that it flew to
splinters inwards on the floor.

At the door the Princess met him, and told
her father this was her deliverer, on whom her
heart was set. So she had him; and this was
how the beggar boy came to marry the king's
daughter of Arabia.

WHY THE BEAR IS STUMPY-TAILED.

ONE day the Bear met the Fox, who came slinking along with a string of fish he had stolen.

"Whence did you get those from?" asked the Bear.

"Oh! my Lord Bruin, I've been out fishing and caught them," said the Fox.

So the Bear had a mind to learn to fish too, and bade the Fox tell him how he was to set about it.

"Oh! it's an easy craft for you," answered the Fox, "and soon learnt. You've only got to go upon the ice, and cut a hole and stick your tail down into it; and so you must go on holding it there as long as you can. You're not to mind if your tail smarts a little; that's when the fish bite. The longer you hold it there the more fish you'll get; and then all at once out with it, with a cross pull sideways, and with a strong pull too."

Yes; the Bear did as the Fox had said, and held his tail a long, long time down in the hole, till it was fast frozen in. Then he pulled it out with a cross pull, and it snapped short off. That's why Bruin goes about with a stumpy tail this very day.

NOT A PIN TO CHOOSE BETWEEN THEM.

ONCE on a time there was a man, and he had a wife. Now this couple wanted to sow their fields, but they had neither seed-corn nor money to buy it with. But they had a cow, and the man was to drive it into town and sell it, to get money to buy corn for seed. But when it came to the pinch, the wife dared not let her husband start for fear he should spend the money in drink, so she set off herself with the cow, and took besides a hen with her.

Close by the town she met a butcher, who asked,—

"Will you sell that cow, Goody?"

"Yes, that I will," she answered.

"Well, what do you want for her?"

"Oh! I must have five shillings for the cow, but you shall have the hen for ten pound."

"Very good!" said the man; "I don't want the hen, and you'll soon get it off your hands in the town, but I'll give you five shillings for the cow."

Well, she sold her cow for five shillings, but there was no one in the town who would give ten pound for a lean tough old hen, so she went back to the butcher, and said,—

"Do all I can, I can't get rid of this hen, master! you must take it too, as you took the cow."

"Well," said the butcher, "come along and we'll see about it." Then he treated her both with meat and drink, and gave her so much brandy that she lost her head, and didn't know what she was about, and fell fast asleep. But while she slept, the butcher took and dipped her into a tar-barrel, and then laid her down on a heap of feathers; and when she woke up, she was feathered all over, and began to wonder what had befallen her.

"Is it me, or is it not me? No, it can never be me; it must be some great strange bird. But what shall I do to find out whether it is me or not. Oh! I know how I shall be able to tell whether it is me; if the calves come and lick me, and our dog Tray doesn't bark at me when

I get home, then it must be me, and no one else."

Now, Tray, her dog, had scarce set his eyes on the strange monster which came through the gate, than he set up such a barking, one would have thought all the rogues and robbers in the world were in the yard.

"Ah, deary me," said she, "I thought so; it can't be me surely." So she went to the straw-yard, and the calves wouldn't lick her, when they snuffed in the strong smell of tar.

"No, no!" she said, "it can't be me; it must be some strange outlandish bird."

So she crept up on the roof of the safe, and began to flap her arms, as if they had been wings, and was just going to fly off.

When her husband saw all this, out he came with his rifle, and began to take aim at her.

"Oh!" cried his wife, "don't shoot, don't shoot! it is only me."

"If it's you," said her husband, "don't stand up there like a goat on a house-top, but come down and let me hear what you have to say for yourself."

So she crawled down again, but she hadn't a

shilling to shew, for the crown she had got from
the butcher she had thrown away in her drunken-
ness.   When her husband heard her story, he
said, "You're only twice as silly as you were
before," and he got so angry that he made up
his mind to go away from her altogether, and
never to come back till he had found three other
Goodies as silly as his own.

So he toddled off, and when he had walked a
little way he saw a Goody, who was running in
and out of a newly-built wooden cottage with an
empty sieve, and every time she ran in, she threw
her apron over the sieve just as if she had something in it, and when she got in she turned it
upside down on the floor.

"Why, Goody!" he asked, "what are you
doing!"

"Oh," she answered, "I'm only carrying in a
little sun; but I don't know how it is, when I'm
outside, I have the sun in my sieve, but when I
get inside, somehow or other I've thrown it away.
But in my old cottage I had plenty of sun, though
I never carried in the least bit.   I only wish I
knew some one who would bring the sun inside;
I'd give him three hundred dollars and welcome."

" Have you got an axe?" asked the man. " If you have, I'll soon bring the sun inside."

So he got an axe, and cut windows in the cottage, for the carpenters had forgotten them : then the sun shone in, and he got his three hundred dollars.

" That was one of them," said the man to himself, as he went on his way.

After a while he passed by a house, out of which came an awful screaming and bellowing ; so he turned in and saw a Goody, who was hard at work banging her husband across the head with a beetle, and over his head she had drawn a shirt without any slit for the neck.

"Why, Goody!" he asked, "will you beat your husband to death?"

" No," she said, " I only must have a hole in this shirt for his neck to come through."

All the while the husband kept on screaming and calling out,----

" Heaven help and comfort all who try on new shirts. If any one would teach my Goody another way of making a slit for the neck in my new shirts, I'd give him three hundred dollars down and welcome."

"I'll do it in the twinkling of an eye," said the man, "if you'll only give me a pair of scissors."

So he got a pair of scissors, and snipped a hole in the neck, and went off with his three hundred dollars.

"That was another of them," he said to himself, as he walked along.

Last of all, he came to a farm, where he made up his mind to rest a bit. So when he went in, the mistress asked him,—

"Whence do you come, master?"

"Oh!" said he, "I come from Paradise Place," for that was the name of his farm.

"From Paradise Place!" she cried, "you don't say so! Why, then you must know my second husband Peter, who is dead and gone, God rest his soul."

For you must know this Goody had been married three times, and as her first and last husbands had been bad, she had made up her mind that the second only was gone to heaven.

"Oh yes," said the man; "I know him very well."

"Well," asked the Goody, "how do things go with him, poor dear soul?"

"Only middling," was the answer; "he goes about begging from house to house, and has neither food nor a rag to his back. As for money, he hasn't a sixpence to bless himself with."

"Mercy on me!" cried out the Goody; "he never ought to go about such a figure when he left so much behind him. Why, there's a whole cupboard full of old clothes up-stairs which belonged to him, besides a great chest full of money yonder. Now, if you will take them with you, you shall have a horse and cart to carry them. As for the horse, he can keep it, and sit on the cart, and drive about from house to house, and then he needn't trudge on foot."

So the man got a whole cart-load of clothes, and a chest full of shining dollars, and as much meat and drink as he would; and when he had got all he wanted, he jumped into the cart and drove off.

"That was the third," he said to himself, as he went along.

Now this Goody's third husband was a little way off in a field ploughing, and when he saw a strange man driving off from the farm with his horse and cart, he went home and asked his wife who that was that had just started with the black horse.

" Oh, do you mean him ? " said the Goody; " why, that was a man from Paradise, who said that Peter, my dear second husband, who is dead and gone, is in a sad plight, and that he goes from house to house begging, and has neither clothes nor money; so I just sent him all those old clothes he left behind him, and the old money-box with the dollars in it."

The man saw how the land lay in a trice, so he saddled his horse and rode off from the farm at full gallop. It wasn't long before he was close behind the man who sat and drove the cart ; but when the latter saw this he drove the cart into a thicket by the side of the road, pulled out a hand-full of hair from the horse's tail, jumped up on a little rise in the wood, where he tied the hair fast to a birch, and then lay down under it, and began to peer and stare up at the sky.

"Well, well, if I ever !" he said, as Peter the third came riding up. "No! I never saw the like of this in all my born days !"

Then Peter stood and looked at him for some time, wondering what had come over him ; but at last he asked,—

"What do you lie there staring at?"

"No," kept on the man, "I never did see anything like it!—here is a man going straight up to heaven on a black horse, and here you see his horse's tail still hanging in this birch; and yonder up in the sky you see the black horse."

Peter looked first at the man, and then at the sky, and said,—

"I see nothing but the horse hair in the birch; that's all I see!"

"Of course you can't where you stand," said the man; "but just come and lie down here, and stare straight up, and mind you don't take your eyes off the sky; and then you shall see what you shall see."

But while Peter the third lay and stared up at the sky till his eyes filled with tears, the man from Paradise Place took his horse and jumped on its back, and rode off both with it and the cart and horse.

When the hoofs thundered along the road Peter the third jumped up; but he was so taken aback when he found the man had gone off with his horse that he hadn't the sense to run after him till it was too late.

He was rather down in the mouth when he got home to his Goody ; but when she asked him what he had done with the horse, he said,—

" I gave it to the man too for Peter the second, for I thought it wasn't right he should sit in a cart, and scramble about from house to house; so now he can sell the cart and buy himself a coach to drive about in."

" Thank you heartily !" said his wife ; " I never thought you could be so kind."

Well, when the man reached home, who had got the six hundred dollars and the cart-load of clothes and money, he saw that all his fields were ploughed and sown, and the first thing he asked his wife was, where she had got the seed-corn from.

" Oh," she said, " I have always heard that what a man sows he shall reap, so I sowed the salt which our friends the north-country men laid up here with us, and if we only have rain I fancy it will come up nicely."

" Silly you are," said her husband, " and silly you will be so long as you live ; but that is all one now, for the rest are not a bit wiser than you. There is not a pin to choose between you."

ONE'S OWN CHILDREN ARE ALWAYS PRETTIEST.

A SPORTSMAN went out once into a wood to shoot, and he met a Snipe.

"Dear friend," said the Snipe, "don't shoot my children!"

"How shall I know your children?" asked the Sportsman; "what are they like?"

"Oh!" said the Snipe, "mine are the prettiest children in all the wood."

"Very well," said the Sportsman, "I'll not shoot them; don't be afraid."

But for all that, when he came back, there he had a whole string of young snipes in his hand which he had shot.

"Oh, oh!" said the Snipe, "why did you shoot my children after all?"

"What! these your children!" said the Sportsman; "why, I shot the ugliest I could find, that I did!"

"Woe is me!" said the Snipe; "don't you know that each one thinks his own children the prettiest in the world?"

THE THREE PRINCESSES OF WHITELAND.

ONCE on a time there was a fisherman who lived close by a palace, and fished for the king's table. One day when he was out fishing he just caught nothing. Do what he would—however he tried with bait and angle—there was never a sprat on his hook. But when the day was far spent a head bobbed up out of the water, and said,—

"If I may have what your wife bears under her girdle, you shall catch fish enough."

So the man answered boldly, "Yes;" for he did not know that his wife was going to have a child. After that, as was like enough, he caught plenty of fish of all kinds. But when he got home at night, and told his story, how he had got all that fish, his wife fell a weeping and moaning, and was beside herself for the promise which her husband had made, for she said, "I bear a babe under my girdle."

Well the story soon spread, and came up to

THE THREE PRINCESSES OF WHITELAND

the castle; and when the king heard the woman's grief and its cause, he sent down to say he would take care of the child, and see if he couldn't save it.

So the months went on and on, and when her time came the fisher's wife had a boy; so the king took it at once, and brought it up as his own son, until the lad grew up. Then he begged leave one day to go out fishing with his father; he had such a mind to go, he said. At first the king wouldn't hear of it, but at last the lad had his way, and went. So he and his father were out the whole day, and all went right and well till they landed at night. Then the lad remembered he had left his handkerchief, and went to look for it; but as soon as ever he got into the boat, it began to move off with him at such speed that the water roared under the bow, and all the lad could do in rowing against it with the oars was no use; so he went and went the whole night, and at last he came to a white strand, far, far away.

There he went ashore, and when he had walked about a bit, an old, old man met him, with a long white beard.

"What's the name of this land?" asked the lad.

"Whiteland," said the man, who went on to

ask the lad whence he came, and what he was going to do. So the lad told him all.

"Ay, ay!" said the man; "now when you have walked a little farther along the strand here, you'll come to three Princesses, whom you will see standing in the earth up to their necks, with only their heads out. Then the first—she is the eldest—will call out and beg you so prettily to come and help her; and the second will do the same; to neither of these shall you go; make haste past them, as if you neither saw nor heard anything. But the third you shall go to, and do what she asks. If you do this you'll have good luck—that's all."

When the lad came to the first Princess, she called out to him, and begged him so prettily to come to her, but he passed on as though he saw her not. In the same way he passed by the second; but to the third he went straight up.

"If you'll do what I bid you," she said, "you may have which of us you please."

"Yes;" he was willing enough; so she told him how three Trolls had set them down in the earth there; but before they had lived in the castle up among the trees.

" Now," she said, " you must go into that castle, and let the Trolls whip you each one night for each of us. If you can bear that you'll set us free."

Well, the lad said he was ready to try.

" When you go in," the Princess went on to say, " you'll see two lions standing at the gate ; but if you'll only go right in the middle between them they'll do you no harm. Then go straight on into a little dark room, and make your bed. Then the Troll will come to whip you ; but if you take the flask which hangs on the wall, and rub yourself with the ointment that's in it wherever his lash falls, you'll be as sound as ever. Then grasp the sword that hangs by the side of the flask and strike the Troll dead."

Yes, he did as the Princess told him ; he passed in the midst between the lions, as if he hadn't seen them, and went straight into the little room, and there he lay down to sleep. The first night there came a Troll with three heads and three rods, and whipped the lad soundly ; but he stood it till the Troll was done ; then he took the flask and rubbed himself, and grasped the sword and slew the Troll.

So, when he went out next morning, the Princesses stood out of the earth up to their waists.

The next night 'twas the same story over again, only this time the Troll had six heads and six rods, and he whipped him far worse than the first; but when he went out next morning, the Princesses stood out of the earth as far as the knee.

The third night there came a Troll that had nine heads and nine rods, and he whipped and flogged the lad so long that he fainted away; then the Troll took him up and dashed him against the wall; but the shock brought down the flask, which fell on the lad, burst, and spilled the ointment all over him, and so he became as strong and sound as ever again. Then he wasn't slow; he grasped the sword and slew the Troll; and next morning when he went out of the castle the Princesses stood before him with all their bodies out of the earth. So he took the youngest for his Queen, and lived well and happily with her for some time.

At last he began to long to go home for a little to see his parents. His Queen did not like this; but at last his heart was so set on it, and he longed and longed so much, there was no holding him back, so she said,—

"One thing you must promise me. This.— Only to do what your father begs you to do, and not what your mother wishes;" and that he promised.

Then she gave him a ring, which was of that kind that any one who wore it might wish two wishes. So he wished himself home, and when he got home his parents could not wonder enough what a grand man their son had become.

Now, when he had been at home some days, his mother wished him to go up to the palace and shew the king what a fine fellow he had come to be. But his father said,- --

"No! don't let him do that; if he does, we shan't have any more joy of him this time."

But it was no good, the mother begged and prayed so long, that at last he went. So when he got up to the palace, he was far braver, both in clothes and array, than the other king, who didn't quite like this, and at last he said,—

"All very fine; but here you can see my queen, what like she is, but I can't see yours, that I can't. Do you know, I scarce think she's so good-looking as mine."

"Would to Heaven," said the young king, "she were standing here, then you'd see what she was like." And that instant there she stood before them.

But she was very woeful, and said to him,—

"Why did you not mind what I told you; and why did you not listen to what your father said? Now, I must away home, and as for you, you have had both your wishes."

With that she knitted a ring among his hair, with her name on it, and wished herself home, and was off.

Then the young king was cut to the heart, and went, day out day in, thinking and thinking how he should get back to his queen. "I'll just try," he thought, "if I can't learn where Whiteland lies;" and so he went out into the world to ask. So when he had gone a good way, he came to a high hill, and there he met one who was lord over all the beasts of the wood, for they all came home to him when he blew his horn; so the king asked if he knew where Whiteland was?

"No, I don't," said he, "but I'll ask my beasts." Then he blew his horn and called them, and asked if any of them knew where Whiteland lay? but there was no beast that knew.

So the man gave him a pair of snow-shoes.

"When you get on these," he said, "you'll come to my brother, who lives hundreds of miles off; he is lord over all the birds of the air. Ask him. When you reach his house, just turn the shoes, so that the toes point this way, and they'll come home of themselves." So when the king reached the house, he turned the shoes as the lord of the beasts had said, and away they went home of themselves.

So he asked again after Whiteland, and the man called all the birds with a blast of his horn, and asked if any of them knew where Whiteland lay; but none of the birds knew. Now, long, long after the rest of the birds, came an old eagle, which had been away ten round years, but he couldn't tell any more than the rest.

"Well! well!" said the man, "I'll lend you a pair of snow-shoes, and when you get them on, they'll carry you to my brother, who lives hundreds of miles off; he's lord of all the fish in the sea; you'd better ask him. But don't forget to turn the toes of the shoes this way."

The king was full of thanks, got on the shoes, and when he came to the man who was lord over

P

the fish of the sea, he turned the toes round, and
so off they went home like the other pair.   After
that, he asked again after Whiteland.

So the man called the fish with a blast, but
no fish could tell where it lay.   At last came an
old pike which they had great work to call home,
he was such a way off.   So when they asked him
he said,—

"Know it! I should think I did.   I've been
cook there ten years, and to-morrow I'm going
there again; for now, the queen of Whiteland,
whose king is away, is going to wed another
husband."

"Well!" said the man, "as this is so, I'll
give you a bit of advice.   Hereabouts, on a moor,
stand three brothers, and here they have stood
these hundred years, fighting about a hat, a cloak,
and a pair of boots.   If any one has these three
things, he can make himself invisible, and wish
himself anywhere he pleases.   You can tell them
you wish to try the things, and after that, you'll
pass judgment between them, whose they shall be."

Yes! the king thanked the man, and went and
did as he told him.

"What's all this?" he said to the brothers.

"Why do you stand here fighting for ever and a day? Just let me try these things, and I'll give judgment whose they shall be."

They were very willing to do this; but as soon as he had got the hat, cloak, and boots, he said,—

"When we meet next time I'll tell you my judgment," and with these words he wished himself away.

So as he went along up in the air, he came up with the North Wind.

"Whither away?" roared the North Wind.

"To Whiteland," said the king; and then he told him all that had befallen him.

"Ah," said the North Wind, "you go faster than I—you do; for you can go straight, while I have to puff and blow round every turn and corner. But when you get there, just place yourself on the stairs by the side of the door, and then I'll come storming in, as though I were going to blow down the whole castle. And then when the prince, who is to have your queen, comes out to see what's the matter, just you take him by the collar and pitch him out of doors; then I'll look after him, and see if I can't carry him off."

Well—the king did as the North Wind said.
He took his stand on the stairs, and when the
North Wind came, storming and roaring, and took
hold of the castle wall, so that it shook again, the
prince came out to see what was the matter.
But as soon as ever he came, the king caught him
by the collar and pitched him out of doors, and
then the North Wind caught him up, and carried
him off.   So when there was an end of him, the
king went into the castle, and at first his queen
didn't know him, he was so wan and thin, through
wandering so far and being so woeful ; but when
he shewed her the ring, she was as glad as glad
could be ; and so the rightful wedding was held,
and the fame of it spread far and wide.

THE LASSIE AND HER GODMOTHER.

ONCE on a time a poor couple lived far, far away in a great wood. The wife was brought to bed, and had a pretty girl, but they were so poor they did not know how to get the babe christened, for they had no money to pay the parson's fees. So one day the father went out to see if he could find any one who was willing to stand for the child and pay the fees; but though he walked about the whole day from one house to another, and though all said they were willing enough to stand, no one thought himself bound to pay the fees. Now, when he was going home again, a lovely lady met him, dressed so fine, and who looked so thoroughly good and kind; she offered to get the babe christened, but after that, she said, she must keep it for her own. The husband answered, he must first ask his wife what she wished to do; but when he got home and told his story, the wife said, right out, "No!"

Next day the man went out again, but no one

would stand if they had to pay the fees; and though he begged and prayed, he could get no help. And again as he went home, towards evening the same lovely lady met him, who looked so sweet and good, and she made him the same offer. So he told his wife again how he had fared, and this time she said, if he couldn't get any one to stand for his babe next day, they must just let the lady have her way, since she seemed so kind and good.

The third day, the man went about, but he couldn't get any one to stand; and so when, towards evening, he met the kind lady again, he gave his word she should have the babe if she would only get it christened at the font. So next morning she came to the place where the man lived, followed by two men to stand godfathers, took the babe and carried it to church, and there it was christened. After that she took it to her own house, and there the little girl lived with her several years, and her foster-mother was always kind and friendly to her.

Now, when the lassie had grown to be big enough to know right and wrong, her foster-mother got ready to go on a journey.

"You have my leave," she said, "to go all

over the house, except those rooms which I shew you ;" and when she had said that, away she went.

But the lassie could not forbear just to open one of the doors a little bit, when—POP! out flew a Star.

When her foster-mother came back, she was very vexed to find that the star had flown out, and she got very angry with her foster-daughter, and threatened to send her away ; but the child cried and begged so hard that she got leave to stay.

Now, after a while, the foster-mother had to go on another journey ; and, before she went, she forbade the lassie to go into those two rooms into which she had never been. She promised to beware ; but when she was left alone, she began to think and to wonder what there could be in the second room, and at last she could not help setting the door a little a-jar, just to peep in, when—POP! out flew the Moon.

When her foster-mother came home and found the Moon let out, she was very downcast, and said to the lassie she must go away, she could not stay with her any longer. But the lassie wept so bitterly, and prayed so heartily for forgiveness, that this time, too, she got leave to stay.

Some time after, the foster-mother had to go
away again, and she charged the lassie, who by
this time was half grown up, most earnestly that
she mustn't try to go into, or to peep into, the
third room.   But when her foster-mother had been
gone some time, and the lassie was weary of walking about alone, all at once she thought, "Dear
me, what fun it would be just to peep a little into
that third room."   Then she thought she mustn't
do it for her foster-mother's sake; but when the
bad thought came the second time, she could hold
out no longer; come what might, she must and
would look into the room; so she just opened the
door a tiny bit, when—POP! out flew the Sun.

But when her foster-mother came back and
saw that the sun had flown away, she was cut to
the heart, and said, "Now, there was no help for
it, the lassie must and should go away; she
couldn't hear of her staying any longer."   Now
the lassie cried her eyes out, and begged and
prayed so prettily; but it was all no good.

"Nay! but I must punish you!" said her
foster-mother; "but you may have your choice,
either to be the loveliest woman in the world, and
not to be able to speak, or to keep your speech,

and be the ugliest of all women ; but away from me you must go."

And the lassie said, " I would sooner be lovely." So she became all at once wondrous fair ; but from that day forth she was dumb.

So, when she went away from her foster-mother, she walked and wandered through a great, great wood ; but the farther she went, the farther off the end seemed to be. So, when the evening came on, she clomb up into a tall tree, which grew over a spring, and there she made herself up to sleep that night. Close by lay a castle, and from that castle came early every morning a maid to draw water, to make the Prince's tea, from the spring over which the lassie was sitting. So the maid looked down into the spring, saw the lovely face in the water, and thought it was her own ; then she flung away the pitcher, and ran home ; and, when she got there, she tossed up her head and said, " If I'm so pretty, I'm far too good to go and fetch water."

So another maid had to go for the water, but the same thing happened to her ; she went back and said she was far too pretty and too good to fetch water from the spring for the Prince. Then

the Prince went himself, for he had a mind to see
what all this could mean. So, when he reached
the spring, he too saw the image in the water;
but he looked up at once, and became aware of
the lovely lassie who sate there up in the tree.
Then he coaxed her down and took her home;
and at last made up his mind to have her for his
queen, because she was so lovely; but his mother,
who was still alive, was against it.

"She can't speak," she said, "and maybe
she's a wicked witch."

But the Prince could not be content till he got
her. So after they had lived together a while,
the lassie was to have a child, and when the child
came to be born, the Prince set a strong watch round
her; but at the birth one and all fell into a deep
sleep, and her foster-mother came, cut the babe on
its little finger, and smeared the Queen's mouth
with the blood; and said,—

"Now you shall be as grieved as I was when
you let out the star;" and with these words she
carried off the babe.

But when those who were on the watch woke,
they thought the Queen had eaten her own child,
and the old queen was all for burning her alive.

but the Prince was so fond of her that at last he begged her off, but he had hard work to set her free.

So the next time the young Queen was to have a child, twice as strong a watch was set as the first time, but the same thing happened over again, only this time her foster-mother said,--

"Now you shall be as grieved as I was when you let the moon out."

And the Queen begged, and prayed, and wept; for when her foster-mother was there, she could speak—but it was all no good.

And now the old queen said she must be burnt, but the Prince found means to beg her off. But when the third child was to be born, a watch was set three times as strong as the first, but just the same thing happened. Her foster-mother came while the watch slept, took the babe and cut its little finger, and smeared the Queen's mouth with the blood, telling her now she should be as grieved as she had been when the lassie let out the sun.

And now the Prince could not save her any longer. She must and should be burnt. But just as they were leading her to the stake, all at once they saw her foster mother, who came with all three children—two she led by the hand, and the third she had on her arm; and so she went up to the young Queen and said,—

"Here are your children; now you shall have them again. I am the Virgin Mary, and so grieved as you have been, so grieved was I when you let out sun, and moon, and star. Now you have been punished for what you did, and henceforth you shall have your speech."

How glad the Queen and Prince now were, all may easily think, but no one can tell. After that they were always happy; and from that day even the Prince's mother was very fond of the young Queen.

THE THREE AUNTS.

ONCE on a time there was a poor man who lived in a hut far away in the wood, and got his living by shooting. He had an only daughter who was very pretty, and as she had lost her mother when she was a child, and was now half grown up, she said she would go out into the world and earn her bread.

"Well, lassie!" said the father, "true enough you have learnt nothing here but how to pluck birds and roast them, but still you may as well · try to earn your bread."

So the girl went off to seek a place, and when she had gone a little while, she came to a palace. There she stayed and got a place, and the queen liked her so well, that all the other maids got envious of her. So they made up their minds to tell the queen how the lassie said she was good to spin a pound of flax in four and twenty hours, for you must know the queen was a great house-wife, and thought much of good work.

" Have you said this ? then you shall do it,"
said the queen; "but you may have a little longer
time if you choose."

Now, the poor lassie dared not say she had
never spun in all her life, but she only begged for
a room to herself.   That she got, and the wheel
and the flax were brought up to her.   There she
sat sad and weeping, and knew not how to help
herself.   She pulled the wheel this way and that,
and twisted and turned it about, but she made a
poor hand of it, for she had never even seen a
spinning-wheel in her life.

But all at once, as she sat there, in came an
old woman to her.

" What ails you child ?" she said.

" Ah !" said the lassie, with a deep sigh, " it's
no good to tell you, for you'll never be able to
help me."

" Who knows ?" said the old wife.   " May be
I know how to help you after all."

Well, thought the lassie to herself, I may as
well tell her, and so she told her how her fellow-
servants had given out that she was good to spin
a pound of flax in four and twenty hours.

" And here am I, wretch that I am, shut up

to spin all that heap in a day and a night, when I have never even seen a spinning-wheel in all my born days."

"Well, never mind, child," said the old woman, " if you'll call me Aunt on the happiest day of your life, I'll spin this flax for you, and so you may just go away and lie down to sleep."

Yes the lassie was willing enough, and off she went and lay down to sleep.

Next morning when she awoke, there lay all the flax spun on the table, and that so clean and fine, no one had ever seen such even and pretty yarn. The queen was very glad to get such nice yarn, and she set greater store by the lassie than ever. But the rest were still more envious, and agreed to tell the queen how the lassie had said she was good to weave the yarn she had spun in four and twenty hours. So the queen said again, as she had said it she must do it; but if she couldn't quite finish it in four and twenty hours, she wouldn't be too hard upon her, she might have a little more time. This time, too, the lassie dared not say No, but begged for a room to herself, and then she would try. There she sat again, sobbing and crying, and not knowing which way to turn, when another old woman came in and asked,—

"What ails you, child?"

At first the lassie wouldn't say, but at last she told her the whole story of her grief.

"Well, well!" said the old wife, "never mind. If you'll call me Aunt on the happiest day of your life, I'll weave this yarn for you, and so you may just be off, and lie down to sleep."

Yes, the lassie was willing enough; so she went away and lay down to sleep. When she awoke, there lay the piece of linen on the table, woven so neat and close, no woof could be better. So the lassie took the piece and ran down to the queen, who was very glad to get such beautiful linen, and set greater store than ever by the lassie. But as for the others, they grew still more bitter against her, and thought of nothing but how to find out something to tell about her.

At last they told the queen the lassie had said she was good to make up the piece of linen into shirts in four and twenty hours. Well, all happened as before; the lassie dared not say she couldn't sew; so she was shut up again in a room by herself, and there she sat in tears and grief.

But then another old wife came, who said she
would sew the shirts for her if she would call her
Aunt on the happiest day of her life. The lassie
was only too glad to do this, and then she did as
the old wife told her, and went and lay down to
sleep.

Next morning when she woke she found the
piece of linen made up into shirts, which lay on
the table—and such beautiful work no one had
ever set eyes on; and more than that, the shirts
were all marked and ready for wear. So when
the queen saw the work, she was so glad at the
way in which it was sewn, that she clapped her
hands and said,—

"Such sewing I never had, nor even saw in
all my born days;" and after that she was as fond
of the lassie as of her own children; and she said
to her,—

"Now, if you like to have the Prince for your
husband, you shall have him; for you will never
need to hire workwomen. You can sew, and spin,
and weave all yourself."

So as the lassie was pretty, and the Prince
was glad to have her, the wedding soon came on.
But just as the Prince was going to sit down with

Q

the bride to the bridal feast, in came an ugly old hag with a long nose—I'm sure it was three ells long.

So up got the bride and made a curtsey, and said,—

" Good-day, Auntie."

" *That* Auntie to my bride," said the Prince.

" Yes, she was !"

" Well, then, she'd better sit down with us to the feast," said the Prince ; but, to tell you the truth, both he and the rest thought she was a loathsome woman to have next you.

But just then in came another ugly old hag. She had a back so humped and broad, she had hard work to get through the door. Up jumped the bride in a trice, and greeted her with " Good-day, Auntie !"

And the Prince asked again if that were his bride's aunt. They both said Yes ; so the Prince said, if that were so, she too had better sit down with them to the feast.

But they had scarce taken their seats before another ugly old hag came in, with eyes as large as saucers, and so red and bleared, 'twas grue-some to look at her. But up jumped the bride

again, with her "Good-day, Auntie," and her, too,
the Prince asked to sit down; but I can't say he
was very glad, for he thought to himself,—

"Heaven shield me from such Aunties as my
bride has!" So when he had sat a while, he
could not keep his thoughts to himself any longer,
but asked,—

"But how, in all the world, can my bride, who
is such a lovely lassie, have such loathsome, mis-
shapen Aunts?"

"I'll soon tell you how it is," said the first.
"I was just as good-looking when I was her age;
but the reason why I've got this long nose is,
because I was always kept sitting, and poking,
and nodding over my spinning, and so my nose
got stretched and stretched, until it got as long as
you now see it."

"And I," said the second, "ever since I was
young, I have sat and scuttled backwards and
forwards over my loom, and that's how my back
has got so broad and humped, as you now see
it."

"And I," said the third, "ever since I was
little, I have sat, and stared, and sewn, and sewn
and stared, night and day; and that's why my

eyes have got so ugly and red, and now there's no help for them."

"So! so!" said the Prince, "'twas lucky I came to know this; for if folk can get so ugly and loathsome by all this, then my bride shall neither spin, nor weave, nor sew, all her life long."

THE COCK, THE CUCKOO, AND THE BLACK-COCK.

[This is another of those tales in which the birds' notes must be imitated.]

ONCE on a time the Cock, the Cuckoo, and the Black-cock bought a cow between them. But when they came to share it, and couldn't agree which should buy the others out, they settled that he who woke first in the morning should have the cow.

So the Cock woke first.

"Now the cow's mine! Now the cow's mine! Hurrah! hurrah!" he crew, and as he crew, up woke the Cuckoo.

"Half cow! Half cow!" sang the Cuckoo, and woke up the Black-cock.

"A like share, a like share; dear friends, that's only fair! Saw see! See saw!"

That's what the Black-cock said.

And now, can you tell me which of them ought to have the cow?

ONCE on a time there was a man whom they called Rich Peter the Pedlar, because he used to travel about with a pack, and got so much money, that he became quite rich. This Rich Peter had a daughter, whom he held so dear that all who came to woo her, were sent about their business, for no one was good enough for her, he thought. Well, this went on and on, and at last no one came to woo her, and as years rolled on, Peter began to be afraid that she would die an old maid.

"I wonder now," he said to his wife, "why suitors no longer come to woo our lass, who is so rich. 'Twould be odd if nobody cared to have her, for money she has, and more she shall have. I think I'd better just go off to the Stargazers, and ask them whom she shall have, for not a soul comes to us now."

"But how," asked the wife, "can the Stargazers answer that?"

ELF FETTER HE PE...

"Can't they?" said Peter; "why! they read all things in the stars."

So he took with him a great bag of money, and set off to the Stargazers, and asked them to be so good as to look at the stars, and tell him the husband his daughter was to have.

Well! the Stargazers looked and looked, but they said they could see nothing about it. But Peter begged them to look better, and to tell him the truth; he would pay them well for it. So the Stargazers looked better, and at last they said that his daughter's husband was to be the miller's son, who was only just born, down at the mill below Rich Peter's house. Then Peter gave the Stargazers a hundred dollars, and went home with the answer he had got.

Now, he thought it too good a joke that his daughter should wed one so newly born, and of such poor estate. He said this to his wife, and added,--

"I wonder now if they would sell me the boy; then I'd soon put him out of the way?"

"I daresay they would," said his wife; "you know they're very poor."

So Peter went down to the mill, and asked

the miller's wife whether she would sell him her son; she should get a heap of money for him.

"No!" that she wouldn't.

"Well!" said Peter, "I'm sure I can't see why you shouldn't; you've hard work enough as it is to keep hunger out of the house, and the boy won't make it easier, I think."

But the mother was so proud of the boy, she couldn't part with him. So when the miller came home, Peter said the same thing to him, and gave his word to pay six hundred dollars for the boy, so that they might buy themselves a farm of their own, and not have to grind other folks' corn, and to starve when they ran short of water. The miller thought it was a good bargain, and he talked over his wife; and the end was, that Rich Peter got the boy. The mother cried and sobbed, but Peter comforted her by saying, the boy should be well cared for; only they had to promise never to ask after him, for he said he meant to send him far away to other lands, so that he might learn foreign tongues.

So when Peter the Pedlar got home with the boy, he sent for a carpenter, and had a little chest made, which was so tidy and neat, 'twas a joy to see. This he made water-tight with pitch, put the miller's boy into it, locked it up, and threw it into the river, where the stream carried it away.

"Now, I'm rid of him," thought Peter the Pedlar.

But when the chest had floated ever so far down the stream, it came into the mill-head of another mill, and ran down and hampered the shaft of the wheel, and stopped it. Out came the miller to see what stopped the mill, found the chest, and took it up. So when he came home to dinner to his wife, he said,—

" I wonder now whatever there can be inside this chest which came floating down the mill-head, and stopped our mill to-day?"

" That we'll soon know," said his wife; " see there's the key in the lock, just turn it."

So they turned the key and opened the chest, and lo! there lay the prettiest child you ever set eyes on. So they were both glad, and were ready to keep the child, for they had no children of their own, and were so old, they could now hope for none.

" Now, after a little while Peter the Pedlar began to wonder how it was no one came to

woo his daughter, who was so rich in land, and
had so much ready money.   At last, when no one
came, off he went again to the Stargazers, and
offered them a heap of money if they could tell
him whom his daughter was to have for a husband.

"Why! we have told you already, that she is
to have the miller's son down yonder," said the
Stargazers.

"All very true I daresay," said Peter the
Pedlar; "but it so happens he's dead; but if you
can tell me whom she's to have, I'll give you two
hundred dollars, and welcome."

So the Stargazers looked at the stars again,
but they got quite cross, and said,—

"We told you before, and we tell you now,
she is to have the miller's son, whom you threw
into the river, and wished to make an end of; for
he is alive, safe and sound, in such and such a
mill, far down the stream."

So Peter the Pedlar gave them two hundred
dollars for this news, and thought how he could
best be rid of the miller's son.   The first thing
Peter did when he got home, was to set off for
the mill.   By that time the boy was so big that
he had been confirmed, and went about the mill

and helped the miller. Such a pretty boy you
never saw.

"Can't you spare me that lad yonder?" said
Peter the Pedlar to the miller.

" No! that I can't," he answered; " I've brought
him up as my own son, and he has turned out so
well, that now he's a great help and aid to me in
the mill, for I'm getting old and past work."

" It's just the same with me," said Peter the
Pedlar; " that's why I'd like to have some one to
learn my trade. Now, if you'll give him up to
me, I'll give you six hundred dollars, and then you
can buy yourself a farm, and live in peace and
quiet the rest of your days."

Yes ! when the miller heard that, he let Peter
the Pedlar have the lad.

Then the two travelled about far and wide
with their packs and wares, till they came to an
inn, which lay by the edge of a great wood.
From this Peter the Pedlar sent the lad home
with a letter to his wife, for the way was not so
long if you took the short cut across the wood,
and told him to tell her she was to be sure and do
what was written in the letter as quickly as she
could. But it was written in the letter, that she

was to have a great pile made there and then, fire it, and cast the miller's son into it. If she didn't do that, he'd burn her alive himself when he came back. So the lad set off with the letter across the wood, and when evening came on he reached a house far, far away in the wood, into which he went; but inside he found no one. In one of the rooms was a bed ready made, so he threw himself across it and fell asleep. The letter he had stuck into his hat-band, and the hat he pulled over his face. So when the robbers came back—for in that house twelve robbers had their abode—and saw the lad lying on the bed, they began to wonder who he could be, and one of them took the letter and broke it open and read it.

"Ho! ho!" said he; "this comes from Peter the Pedlar, does it? Now we'll play him a trick. It would be a pity if the old niggard made an end of such a pretty lad."

So the robbers wrote another letter to Peter the Pedlar's wife, and fastened it under his hat-band while he slept; and in that they wrote, that as soon as ever she got it she was to make a wedding for her daughter and the miller's boy, and give them horses and cattle, and household stuff, and set them up for themselves in the farm which he had under the hill; and if he didn't find all this done by the time he came back, she'd smart for it —that was all.

Next day the robbers let the lad go, and when he came home and delivered the letter, he said he was to greet her kindly from Peter the Pedlar, and to say that she was to carry out what was written in the letter as soon as ever she could.

" You must have behaved very well then," said Peter the Pedlar's wife to the miller's boy, " if he can write so about you now, for when you set off, he was so mad against you, he didn't know how to put you out of the way." So she married them on the spot, and set them up for themselves, with horses, and cattle, and household stuff, in the farm up under the hill.

No long time after Peter the Pedlar came home, and the first thing he asked was, if she had done what he had written in his letter.

" Ay! ay!" she said; " I thought it rather odd, but I dared not do anything else;" and so Peter asked where his daughter was.

" Why, you know well enough where she is," said his wife. " Where should she be but up at the farm under the hill, as you wrote in the letter."

So when Peter the Pedlar came to hear the whole story, and came to see the letter, he got so angry he was ready to burst with rage, and off he ran up to the farm to the young couple.

"It's all very well, my son, to say you have got my daughter," he said to the miller's lad; "but if you wish to keep her, you must go to the Dragon of Deepferry, and get me three feathers out of his tail; for he who has them may get anything he chooses."

"But where shall I find him?" said his son-in-law.

"I'm sure I can't tell," said Peter the Pedlar; "that's your look out, not mine."

So the lad set off with a stout heart, and after he had walked some way, he came to a king's palace.

"Here I'll just step in and ask," he said to himself; "for such great folk know more about the world than others, and perhaps I may here learn the way to the Dragon."

Then the King asked him whence he came, and whither he was going?

"Oh!" said the lad, "I'm going to the Dragon of Deepferry to pluck three feathers out of his tail, if I only knew where to find him."

"You must take luck with you, then," said the King, "for I never heard of any one who came back from that search. But if you find him, just ask him from me why I can't get clear water in my well; for I've dug it out time after time, and still I can't get a drop of clear water."

"Yes, I'll be sure to ask him," said the lad. So he lived on the fat of the land at the palace, and got money and food when he left it.

At even he came to another king's palace, and when he went into the kitchen, the King came out of the parlour, and asked whence he came, and on what errand he was bound?

"Oh!" said the lad, "I'm going to the Dragon of Deepferry to pluck three feathers out of his tail."

"Then you must take luck with you," said the King, "for I never yet heard that any one came back who went to look for him. But if you find him, be so good as to ask him from me where my daughter is, who has been lost so many years. I have hunted for her, and had her name given out in every church in the country, but no one can tell me anything about her."

"Yes, I'll mind and do that," said the lad; and in that palace too he lived on the best, and when he went away he got both money and food.

So when evening drew on again he came at last to another king's palace. Here who should come out into the kitchen but the Queen and she asked him whence he came, and on what errand he was bound?

"I'm going to the Dragon of Deepferry to pluck three feathers out of his tail," said the lad.

"Then you'd better take a good piece of luck with you," said the Queen, "for I never heard of any one that came back from him. But if you find him, just be good enough to ask him from me where I shall find my gold keys which I have lost."

"Yes! I'll be sure to ask him," said the lad.

Well! when he left the palace he came to a great broad river; and while he stood there and wondered whether he should cross it, or go down along the bank, an old hunchbacked man came up, and asked whither he was going?

"Oh, I'm going to the Dragon of Deepferry,

if I could only find any one to tell where I can find him."

"I can tell you that," said the man; "for here I go backwards and forwards, and carry those over who are going to see him. He lives just across, and when you climb the hill you'll see his castle; but mind, if you come to talk with him, to ask him from me how long I'm to stop here and carry folk over.

"I'll be sure to ask him," said the lad.

So the man took him on his back and carried him over the river; and when he climbed the hill, he saw the castle, and went in.

He found there a Princess who lived with the Dragon all alone; and she said,—

"But, dear friend, how can Christian folk dare to come hither? None have been here since I came, and you'd best be off as fast as you can; for as soon as the Dragon comes home, he'll smell you out, and gobble you up in a trice, and that'll make me so unhappy."

"Nay! nay!" said the lad; "I can't go before I've got three feathers out of his tail."

"You'll never get them," said the Princess; "you'd best be off."

R

But the lad wouldn't go; he would wait for the Dragon, and get the feathers, and an answer to all his questions.

"Well, since you're so steadfast, I'll see what I can do to help you," said the Princess; "just try to lift that sword that hangs on the wall yonder."

No; the lad could not even stir it.

"I thought so," said the Princess; "but just take a drink out of this flask."

So when the lad had sat a while, he was to try again; and then he could just stir it.

"Well! you must take another drink," said the Princess, "and then you may as well tell me your errand hither."

So he took another drink, and then he told her how one king had begged him to ask the Dragon, how it was he couldn't get clean water in his well?—how another had bidden him ask, what had become of his daughter, who had been lost many years since?—and how a queen had begged him to ask the Dragon what had become of her gold keys?—and, last of all, how the ferryman had begged him to ask the Dragon, how long he was to stop there and carry folk over? When he had done his story, and took hold of the sword, he

could lift it; and when he had taken another
drink, he could brandish it.

"Now," said the Princess, "if you don't want
the Dragon to make an end of you, you'd best
creep under the bed, for night is drawing on, and
he'll soon be home, and then you must lie as still
as you can, lest he should find you out. And
when we have gone to bed, I'll ask him, but you
must keep your ears open, and snap up all that he
says; and under the bed you must lie till all is
still, and the Dragon falls asleep; then creep out
softly and seize the sword, and as soon as he rises,
look out to hew off his head at one stroke, and at
the same time pluck out the three feathers, for
else he'll tear them out himself, that no one may
get any good by them."

So the lad crept under the bed, and the Dragon
came home.

"What a smell of Christian flesh," said the
Dragon.

"Oh yes," said the Princess, "a raven came
flying with a man's bone in his bill, and perched
on the roof. No doubt it's that you smell."

"So it is, I daresay," said the Dragon.

So the Princess served supper; and after they

had eaten, they went to bed. But after they had lain a while, the Princess began to toss about, and all at once she started up and said,—

"Ah! ah!"

"What's the matter?" said the Dragon.

"Oh," said the Princess, "I can't rest at all, and I've had such a strange dream."

"What did you dream about? Let's hear?" said the Dragon.

"I thought a king came here, and asked you what he must do to get clear water in his well."

"Oh," said the Dragon, "he might just as well have found that out for himself. If he dug the well out, and took out the old rotten stump which lies at the bottom, he'd get clean water fast enough. But be still now, and don't dream any more."

When the Princess had lain a while, she began to toss about, and at last she started up with her

"Ah! ah!"

"What's the matter now?" said the Dragon.

"Oh! I can't get any rest at all, and I've had such a strange dream," said the Princess.

"Why, you seem full of dreams to-night," said the Dragon; "what was your dream now?"

"I thought a king came here, and asked you what had become of his daughter who had been lost many years since," said the Princess.

"Why, you are she," said the Dragon; "but he'll never set eyes on you again. But now, do pray be still, and let me get some rest, and don't let's have any more dreams, else I'll break your ribs."

Well, the Princess hadn't lain much longer before she began to toss about again. At last she started up with her

"Ah! ah!"

"What! Are you at it again?" said the Dragon. "What's the matter now?" for he was wild and sleep-surly, so that he was ready to fly to pieces.

"Oh, don't be angry," said the Princess; "but I've had such a strange dream."

"The deuce take your dreams," roared the Dragon; "what did you dream this time?"

"I thought a queen came here, who asked you to tell her where she would find her gold keys, which she has lost."

"Oh," said the Dragon, "she'll find them soon enough if she looks among the bushes where she lay that time she wots of. But do now let me have no more dreams, but sleep in peace."

So they slept a while; but then the Princess was just as restless as ever, and at last she screamed out—

"Ah! ah!"

"You'll never behave till I break your neck," said the Dragon, who was now so wroth that sparks of fire flew out of his eyes. What's the matter now?"

"Oh, don't be so angry," said the Princess; "I can't bear that; but I've had such a strange dream."

"Bless me!" said the Dragon, "if I ever heard the like of these dreams—there's no end to them. And pray, what did you dream now?"

"I thought the ferryman down at the ferry came and asked how long he was to stop there and carry folk over," said the Princess.

"The dull fool!" said the Dragon; "he'd soon be free, if he chose. When any one comes who wants to go across, he has only to take and throw him into the river, and say, 'Now, carry folk over yourself till some one sets you free.' But now, pray let's have an end of these dreams, else I'll lead you a pretty dance."

So the Princess let him sleep on. But as soon as all was still, and the miller's lad heard that the Dragon snored, he crept out. Before it was light the Dragon rose; but he had scarce set both his feet on the floor before the lad cut off his head, and plucked three feathers out of his tail. Then came great joy, and both the lad and the Princess took as much gold and silver, and money, and precious things as they could carry; and when they came down to the ford, they so puzzled the ferryman with all they had to tell, that he quite forgot to ask what the Dragon had said about him till they had got across.

"Halloa, you sir," he said, as they were going off, "did you ask the Dragon what I begged you to ask?"

"Yes I did," said the lad, "and he said, 'When any one comes and wants to go over, you must throw him into the midst of the river, and say, 'Now, carry folk over yourself till some one comes to set you free,'' and then you'll be free."

"Ah, bad luck to you," said the ferryman; "had you told me that before, you might have set me free yourself."

So, when they got to the first palace, the

Queen asked if he had spoken to the Dragon about her gold keys?

"Yes," said the lad, and whispered in the Queen's ear, "he said you must look among the bushes where you lay the day you wot of."

"Hush! hush! Don't say a word," said the Queen, and gave the lad a hundred dollars.

When they came to the second palace, the King asked if he had spoken to the Dragon of what he begged him?

"Yes," said the lad, "I did; and see, here is your daughter."

At that the King was so glad, he would gladly have given the Princess to the miller's lad to wife, and half the kingdom beside; but as he was married already, he gave him two hundred dollars, and coaches and horses, and as much gold and silver as he could carry away.

When he came to the third King's palace, out came the King and asked if he had asked the Dragon of what he begged him?

"Yes," said the lad, "and he said you must dig out the well, and take out the rotten old stump which lies at the bottom, and then you'll get plenty of clear water."

Then the King gave him three hundred dollars, and he set out home; but he was so loaded with gold and silver, and so grandly clothed, that it gleamed and glistened from him, and he was now far richer than Peter the Pedlar.

When Peter got the feathers he hadn't a word more to say against the wedding; but when he saw all that wealth, he asked if there was much still left at the Dragon's castle.

"Yes, I should think so," said the lad; "there was much more than I could carry with me—so much, that you might load many horses with it; and if you choose to go, you may be sure there'll be enough for you."

So his son-in-law told him the way so clearly, that he hadn't to ask it of any one.

"But the horses," said the lad, "you'd best leave this side the river; for the old ferryman, he'll carry you over safe enough."

So Peter set off, and took with him great store of food and many horses; but these he left behind him on the river's brink, as the lad had said. And the old ferryman took him upon his back; but when they had come a bit out into the stream, he cast him into the midst of the river, and said,—

"Now you may go backwards and forwards, here, and carry folk over till you are set free."

And unless some one has set him free, there goes Rich Peter the Pedlar backwards and forwards, and carries folk across this very day.

ONCE on a time there was a poor man who had three sons. When he died, the two elder set off into the world to try their luck, but the youngest they wouldn't have with them at any price.

"As for you," they said, "you're fit for nothing but to sit and poke about in the ashes."

So the two went off and got places at a palace —the one under the coachman, and the other under the gardener. But Boots, he set off too, and took with him a great kneading-trough, which was the only thing his parents left behind them, but which the other two would not bother themselves with. It was heavy to carry, but he did not like to leave it behind, and so, after he had trudged a bit, he too came to the palace, and asked for a place. So they told him they did not want him, but he begged so prettily that at last he got leave to be in the kitchen, and carry in wood and water for the kitchen-maid. He was quick and ready, and in a little while every one liked him; but the two others were dull, and so they got more kicks than halfpence, and grew quite envious of Boots, when they saw how much better he got on.

Just opposite the Palace, across a lake, lived a Troll, who had seven silver ducks which swam on the lake, so that they could be seen from the palace. These the king had often longed for; and so the two elder brothers told the coachman,—

"If our brother only chose, he has said he could easily get the king those seven silver ducks."

You may fancy it wasn't long before the coachman told this to the king; and the king called Boots before him, and said,—

"Your brothers say you can get me the silver ducks; so now go and fetch them."

"I'm sure I never thought or said anything of the kind," said the lad.

"You did say so, and you shall fetch them," said the king, who would hold his own.

"Well! well!" said the lad; "needs must, I suppose; but give me a bushel of rye, and a bushel of wheat, and I'll try what I can do."

So he got the rye and the wheat, and put them

into the kneading trough he had brought with
him from home, got in, and rowed across the lake.
When he reached the other side he began to walk
along the shore, and to sprinkle and strew the
grain, and at last he coaxed the ducks into his
kneading-trough, and rowed back as fast as ever
he could.

When he got half over, the Troll came out of
his house, and set eyes on him.

"HALLOA!" roared out the Troll; "is it you
that has gone off with my seven silver ducks?"

"AYE! AYE!" said the lad.

"Shall you be back soon?" asked the Troll.

"Very likely," said the lad.

So when he got back to the king, with the
seven silver ducks, he was more liked than ever,
and even the king was pleased to say, "Well
done!" But at this his brothers grew more and
more spiteful and envious; and so they went and
told the coachman that their brother had said, if
he chose, he was man enough to get the king the
Troll's bed-quilt, which had a gold patch and a
silver patch, and a silver patch and a gold patch;
and this time, too, the coachman was not slow in
telling all this to the king. So the king said to

the lad, how his brothers had said he was good to steal the Troll's bed-quilt, with gold and silver patches ; so now he must go and do it, or lose his life.

Boots answered, he had never thought or said any such thing ; but when he found there was no help for it, he begged for three days to think over the matter.

So when the three days were gone, he rowed over in his kneading-trough, and went spying about. At last he saw those in the Troll's cave come out and hang the quilt out to air, and as soon as ever they had gone back into the face of the rock, Boots pulled the quilt down, and rowed away with it as fast as he could.

And when he was half across, out came the Troll and set eyes on him, and roared out,—

" HALLOA ! It is you who took my seven silver ducks ?"

" AYE ! AYE !" said the lad.

" And now, have you taken my bed-quilt, with silver patches and gold patches, and gold patches and silver patches ?"

" Aye ! aye !" said the lad.

" Shall you come back again ?"

" Very likely," said the lad.

But when he got back with the gold and silver patch-work quilt, every one was fonder of him than ever, and he was made the king's body-servant.

At this, the other two were still more vexed, and to be revenged they went and told the coachman,—

" Now, our brother has said, he is man enough to get the king the gold harp which the Troll has, and that harp is of such a kind, that all who listen when it is played grow glad, however sad they may be."

Yes! the coachman went and told the king, and he said to the lad,—

" If you have said this, you shall do it. If you do it, you shall have the Princess and half the kingdom. If you don't, you shall lose your life."

" I'm sure I never thought or said anything of the kind," said the lad; " but if there's no help for it, I may as well try; but I must have six days to think about it."

Yes! he might have six days, but when they were over he must set out.

Then he took a tenpenny nail, a birch-pin, and

a waxen taper-end in his pocket, and rowed across, and walked up and down before the Troll's cave, looking stealthily about him. So when the Troll came out, he saw him at once.

"HO, HO!" roared the Troll; "is it you who took my seven silver ducks?"

"AYE! AYE!" said the lad.

"And it is you who took my bed-quilt, with the gold and silver patches?" asked the Troll.

"Aye! aye!" said the lad.

So the Troll caught hold of him at once, and took him off into the cave in the face of the rock.

"Now, daughter dear," said the Troll, "I've caught the fellow who stole the silver ducks and my bed-quilt with gold and silver patches; put him into the fattening coop; and when he's fat we'll kill him, and make a feast for our friends."

She was willing enough, and put him at once into the fattening coop, and there he stayed eight days, fed on the best, both in meat and drink, and as much as he could cram. So, when the eight days were over, the Troll said to his daughter to go down and cut him in his little finger, that they might see if he were fat. Down she came to the coop.

"Out with your little finger!" she said.

But Boots stuck out his tenpenny-nail, and she cut at it.

"Nay! nay! he's as hard as iron still," said the Troll's daughter, when she got back to her father; "we can't take him yet."

After another eight days the same thing happened, and this time Boots stuck out his birchen pin.

"Well, he's a little better," she said, when she got back to the Troll; "but still he'll be as hard as wood to chew."

But when another eight days were gone, the Troll told his daughter to go down and see if he wasn't fat now.

"Out with your little finger," said the Troll's daughter, when she reached the coop, and this time Boots stuck out the taper end.

"Now he'll do nicely," she said.

"Will he?" said the Troll. "Well, then, I'll just set off and ask the guests; meantime you must kill him, and roast half and boil half."

So when the Troll had been gone a little while, the daughter began to sharpen a great long knife.

S

"Is that what you're going to kill me with?" asked the lad.

"Yes it is," said she.

"But it isn't sharp," said the lad. "Just let me sharpen it for you, and then you'll find it easier work to kill me."

So she let him have the knife, and he began to rub and sharpen it on the whetstone.

"Just let me try it on one of your hair plaits; I think it's about right now."

So he got leave to do that; but at the same time that he grasped the plait of hair, he pulled back her head, and at one gash, cut off the Troll's daughter's head; and half of her he roasted and half of her he boiled, and served it all up.

After that he dressed himself in her clothes, and sat away in the corner.

So when the Troll came home with his guests, he called out to his daughter—for he thought all the time it was his daughter—to come and take a snack.

"No thank you," said the lad, "I don't care for food, I'm so sad and downcast."

"Oh!" said the Troll, "if that's all, you know the cure; take the harp and play a tune on it."

"Yes!" said the lad; "but where has it got to; I can't find it."

"Why, you know well enough," said the Troll; "you used it last; where should it be but over the door yonder?"

The lad did not wait to be told twice; he took down the harp, and went in and out playing tunes; but, all at once he shoved off the kneading trough, jumped into it, and rowed off, so that the foam flew around the trough.

After a while the Troll thought his daughter was a long while gone, and went out to see what ailed her; and then he saw the lad in the trough, far, far out on the lake.

"HALLOA! Is it you," he roared, "that took my seven silver ducks?"

"AYE, AYE!" said the lad.

"Is it you that took my bed-quilt with the gold and silver patches?"

"Yes!" said the lad.

"And now you have taken off my gold harp?" screamed the Troll.

"Yes!" said the lad; "I've got it, sure enough."

"And haven't I eaten you up after all, then?"

"No, no! 'twas your own daughter you ate," answered the lad.

But when the Troll heard that, he was so sorry, he burst; and then Boots rowed back, and took a whole heap of gold and silver with him, as much as the trough could carry. And so, when he came to the palace with the gold harp, he got the Princess and half the kingdom as the king had promised him; and, as for his brothers, he treated them well, for he thought they had only wished his good when they said what they had said.

THE LAD WHO WENT TO THE NORTH WIND.

ONCE on a time there was an old widow who had one son; and as she was poorly and weak, her son had to go up into the safe to fetch meal for cooking; but when he got outside the safe and was just going down the steps, there came the North Wind, puffing and blowing, caught up the meal, and so away with it through the air. Then the lad went back into the safe for more; but when he came out again on the steps, if the North Wind didn't come again and carry off the meal with a puff; and more than that, he did so the third time. At this the lad got very angry; and as he thought it hard that the North Wind should behave so, he thought he'd just look him up, and ask him to give up his meal.

So off he went, but the way was long, and he walked and walked; but at last he came to the North Wind's house.

"Good day!" said the lad, "and thank you for coming to see us yesterday."

"GOOD DAY!" answered the North Wind, for his voice was loud and gruff, "AND THANKS FOR COMING TO SEE ME. WHAT DO YOU WANT?"

"Oh!" answered the lad, "I only wished to ask you to be so good as to let me have back that meal you took from me on the safe steps, for we haven't much to live on; and if you're to go on snapping up the morsel we have, there'll be nothing for it but to starve."

"I haven't got your meal," said the North Wind; "but if you are in such need, I'll give you a cloth which will get you everything you want, if you only say 'Cloth, spread yourself, and serve up all kind of good dishes!'"

With this the lad was well content. But, as the way was so long he couldn't get home in one day, so he turned into an inn on the way; and when they were going to sit down to supper he laid the cloth on a table which stood in the corner, and said,—

"Cloth, spread yourself, and serve up all kinds of good dishes."

He had scarce said so before the cloth did as

it was bid; and all who stood by thought it a fine thing, but most of all the landlady. So, when all were fast asleep, at dead of night, she took the lad's cloth, and put another in its stead, just like the one he had got from the North Wind, but which couldn't so much as serve up a bit of dry bread.

So, when the lad woke, he took his cloth and went off with it, and that day he got home to his mother.

"Now," said he, "I've been to the North Wind's house, and a good fellow he is, for he gave me this cloth, and when I only say to it, 'Cloth, spread yourself, and serve up all kind of good dishes,' I get any sort of food I please."

"All very true, I dare say," said his mother; "but seeing is believing, and I shan't believe it till I see it."

So the lad made haste, drew out a table, laid the cloth on it, and said,—

"Cloth, spread yourself, and serve up all kind of good dishes."

But never a bit of dry bread did the cloth serve up.

"Well!" said the lad, "there's no help for it

but to go to the North Wind again;" and away he went.

So he came to where the North Wind lived late in the afternoon.

"Good evening!" said the lad.

"Good evening!" said the North Wind.

"I want my rights for that meal of ours which you took," said the lad; "for, as for that cloth I got, it isn't worth a penny."

"I've got no meal," said the North Wind; "but yonder you have a ram which coins nothing but golden ducats as soon as you say to it,—

"Ram, ram! make money!"

So the lad thought this a fine thing; but as it was too far to get home that day, he turned in for the night to the same inn where he had slept before.

Before he called for anything, he tried the truth of what the North Wind had said of the ram, and found it all right; but, when the landlord saw that, he thought it was a famous ram, and, when the lad had fallen asleep, he took another which couldn't coin gold ducats, and changed the two.

Next morning off went the lad; and when he got home to his mother, he said,—

"After all, the North Wind is a jolly fellow; for now he has given me a ram which can coin golden ducats if I only say, 'Ram, ram! make money.'"

"All very true, I daresay," said his mother; "but I shan't believe any such stuff until I see the ducats made."

"Ram, ram! make money!" said the lad! but if the ram made anything it wasn't money.

So the lad went back again to the North Wind and blew him up, and said the ram was worth nothing, and he must have his rights for the meal.

"Well!" said the North Wind; "I've nothing else to give up but that old stick in the corner yonder; but it's a stick of that kind that if you say,—

"'Stick, stick! lay on!' it lays on till you say,—

"'Stick, stick! now stop!'"

So, as the way was long, the lad turned in this night too to the landlord; but as he could pretty well guess how things stood as to the cloth and the ram, he lay down at once on the bench and began to snore as if he were asleep.

Now the landlord, who easily saw that the

stick must be worth something, hunted up one which was like it, and when he heard the lad snore was going to change the two; but, just as the landlord was about to take it, the lad bawled out,-

"Stick, stick! lay on!"

So the stick began to beat the landlord, till he jumped over chairs, and tables, and benches, and yelled and roared,—

"Oh my! oh my! bid the stick be still, else it will beat me to death, and you shall have back both your cloth and your ram."

When the lad thought the landlord had got enough, he said,

"Stick, stick! now stop."

Then he took the cloth and put it into his pocket, and went home with his stick in his hand, leading the ram by a cord round its horns; and so he got his rights for the meal he had lost.

THE BEST WISH.

ONCE on a time there were three brothers; I
don't quite know how it happened, but
each of them had got the right to wish one thing,
whatever he chose. So the two elder were not
long a-thinking; they wished that every time they
put their hands in their pockets they might pull
out a piece of money; for, said they,—

"The man who has as much money as he
wishes for is always sure to get on in the world."

But the youngest wished something better still.
He wished that every woman he saw might fall in
love with him as soon as she saw him; and you
shall soon hear how far better this was than gold
and goods.

So, when they had all wished their wishes, the
two elder were for setting out to see the world;
and Boots, their youngest brother, asked if he
mightn't go along with them; but they wouldn't
hear of such a thing.

"Wherever we go," they said, "we shall be

treated as counts and kings; but you, you starveling wretch, who haven't a penny, and never will have one, who do you think will care a bit about you?"

" Well, but in spite of that, I'd like to go with you," said Boots; " perhaps a dainty bit may fall to my share too off the plates of such high and mighty lords,"

At last, after begging and praying, he got leave to go with them, if he would be their servant, else they wouldn't hear of it.

So when they had gone a day or so, they came to an inn, where the two who had the money alighted, and called for fish, and flesh, and fowl, and brandy and mead, and everything that was good; but Boots, poor fellow, had to look after their luggage and all that belonged to the two great people. Now, as he went to and fro outside, and loitered about in the inn-yard, the innkeeper's wife looked out of window and saw the servant of the gentlemen up stairs; and, all at once, she thought she had never set eyes on such a handsome chap. So she stared and stared, and the longer she looked the handsomer he seemed.

" Why what, by the Deil's skin and bones, is

it that you are standing there gaping at out of the window?" said her husband. " I think 'twould be better if you just looked how the sucking pig is getting on, instead of hanging out of window in that way. Don't you know what grand folk we have in the house to-day?"

"Oh!" said his old dame, "I don't care a farthing about such a pack of rubbish; if they don't like it they may lump it, and be off; but just do come and look at this lad out in the yard, se handsome a fellow I never saw in all my born days; and, if you'll do as I wish, we'll ask him to step in and treat him a little, for, poor lad, he seems to have a hard fight of it."

"Have you lost the little brains you had Goody?" said the husband, whose eyes glistened with rage; "into the kitchen with you, and mind the fire; but don't stand there glowering after strange men."

So the wife had nothing left for it but to go into the kitchen, and look after the cooking; as for the lad outside, she couldn't get leave to ask him in, or to treat him either; but just as she was about spitting the pig in the kitchen, she made an excuse for running out into the yard, and then and there she gave Boots a pair of scissors, of such a kind that they cut of themselves out of the air the loveliest clothes any one ever saw, silk and satin, and all that was fine.

"This you shall have because you are so handsome," said the innkeeper's wife.

So when the two elder brothers had crammed themselves with roast and boiled, they wished to be off again, and Boots had to stand behind their carriage, and be their servant; and so they travelled a good way, till they came to another inn.

There the two brothers again alighted and went in-doors, but Boots, who had no money, they wouldn't have inside with them; no, he must wait outside and watch the luggage.

"And mind," they said, "if any one asks whose servant you are, say we are two foreign Princes."

But the same thing happened now as it happened before; while Boots stood hanging about out in the yard, the innkeeper's wife came to the window and saw him, and she too fell in love with him, just like the first innkeeper's wife; and there she stood and stared, for she thought she could never have her fill of looking at him. Then her husband came running through the room with something the two Princes had ordered.

"Don't stand there staring like a cow at a barn-door, but take this into the kitchen, and look after your fish-kettle, Goody," said the man; "don't you see what grand people we have in the house to-day?"

"I don't care a farthing for such a pack of rubbish," said the wife; "if they don't like what they get they may lump it, and eat what they brought with them. But just do come here, and see what you shall see! Such a handsome fellow as walks here, out in the yard, I never saw in all my born days. Shan't we ask him in and treat him a little; he looks as if he needed it, poor chap?" and then she went on,—

"Such a love! such a love!"

"You never had much wit, and the little you had is clean gone, I can see," said the man, who was much more angry than the first innkeeper, and chased his wife back, neck and crop, into the kitchen.

"Into the kitchen with you, and don't stand glowering after lads," he said.

So she had to go in and mind her fish-kettle,

and she dared not treat Boots, for she was afraid
of her old man ; but as she stood there making up
the fire, she made an excuse for running out into
the yard, and then and there she gave Boots a
tablecloth, which was such that it covered itself
with the best dishes you could think of, as soon as
it was spread out.

"This you shall have," she said, "because
you're so handsome."

So when the two brothers had eaten and drank
of all that was in the house, and had paid the bill
in hard cash, they set off again, and Boots stood
up behind their carriage. But when they had
gone so far that they grew hungry again, they
turned into a third inn, and called for the best and
dearest they could think of.

"For," said they, "we are two kings on our
travels, and as for our money, it grows like
grass."

Well, when the innkeeper heard that, there
was such a roasting, and baking, and boiling; why!
you might smell the dinner at the next neighbour's
house, though it wasn't so very near; and the
innkeeper was at his wit's end to find all he wished
to put before the two kings. But Boots, he had

to stand outside here too, and look after the things in the carriage.

So it was the same story over again. The innkeeper's wife came to the window and peeped out, and there she saw the servant standing by the carriage. Such a handsome chap she had never set eyes on before; so she looked and looked, and the more she stared the handsomer he seemed to the innkeeper's wife. Then out came the innkeeper, scampering through the room, with some dainty which the travelling kings had ordered, and he wasn't very soft-tongued when he saw his old dame standing and glowering out of the window.

"Don't you know better than to stand gaping and staring there, when we have such great folk in the house," he said; "back into the kitchen with you this minute, to your custards."

"Well! well!" she said, "as for them, I don't care a pin. If they can't wait till the custards are baked, they may go without— that's all. But do, pray, come here, and you'll see such a lovely lad standing out here in the yard. Why, I never saw such a pretty fellow in my life. Shan't we ask him in now, and treat him a little,

T

for he looks as if it would do him good. Oh!
what a darling !   What a darling !"

"A wanton gadabout you've been all your
days, and so you are still," said her husband, who
was in such a rage he scarce knew which leg to
stand on ; but if you don't be off to your custards
this minute, I'll soon find out how to make you
stir your stumps ; see if I don't."

So the wife had off to her custards as fast as
she could, for she knew that her husband would
stand no nonsense ; but as she stood there over the
fire she stole out into the yard, and gave Boots a
tap.

"If you only turn this tap," she said ; "you'll
get the finest drink of whatever kind you choose,
both mead, and wine, and brandy ; and this you
shall have because you are so handsome."

So when the two brothers had eaten and
drunk all they could, they started from the inn,
and Boots stood up behind again as their servant,
and thus they drove far and wide till they came to
a king's palace.   There the two elder gave themselves out for two emperor's sons, and as they had
plenty of money, and were so fine that their clothes
shone again ever so far off, they were well treated.

They had rooms in the palace, and the king couldn't tell how to make enough of them. But Boots, who went about in the same rags he stood in when he left home, and who had never a penny in his pocket, he was taken up by the king's guard, and put across to an island, whither they used to row over all the beggars and rogues that came to the palace. This the king had ordered, because he wouldn't have the mirth at the palace spoilt by those dirty blackguards; and thither, too, only just as much food as would keep body and soul together was sent over every day. Now Boots' brothers saw very well that the guard was rowing him over to the island, but they were glad to be rid of him, and didn't pay the least heed to him.

But when Boots got over there, he just pulled out his scissors and began to snip and cut in the air; so the scissors cut out the finest clothes any one would wish to see; silk and satin both, and all the beggars on the island were soon dressed far finer than the king and all his guests in the palace. After that, Boots pulled out his table-cloth, and spread it out, and so they got food too, the poor beggars. Such a feast had never been seen at

the king's palace, as was served that day at the
Beggar's Isle.

"Thirsty, too, I'll be bound you all are," said
Boots, and out with his tap, gave it a turn, and so
the beggars got all a drop to drink; and such ale
and mead the king himself had never tasted in all
his life.

So, next morning, when those who were to
bring the beggars their food on the island, came
rowing over with the scrapings of the porridge-
pots and cheese-parings—that was what the poor
wretches had—the beggars wouldn't so much as
taste them, and the king's men fell to wondering
what it could mean; but they wondered much more
when they got a good look at the beggars, for they
were so fine the guard thought they must be Em-
perors or Popes at least, and that they must have
rowed to a wrong island; but when they looked
better about them, they saw they were come to
the old place.

Then they soon found out it must be he whom
they had rowed out the day before who had
brought the beggars on the island all this state
and bravery; and as soon as they got back to the
palace, they were not slow to tell how the man,

whom they had rowed over the day before, had dressed out all the beggars so fine and grand that precious things fell from their clothes.

"And as for the porridge and cheese we took, they wouldn't even taste them, so proud have they got," they said.

One of them, too, had smelt out that the lad had a pair of scissors which he cut out the clothes with.

"When he only snips with those scissors up in the air he snips and cuts out nothing but silk and satin," said he.

So, when the Princess heard that, she had neither peace nor rest till she saw the lad and his scissors that cut out silk and satin from the air; such a pair was worth having, she thought, for with its help she would soon get all the finery she wished for. Well, she begged the king so long and hard, he was forced to send a messenger for the lad who owned the scissors; and when he came to the palace, the Princess asked him if it were true that he had such and such a pair of scissors, and if he would sell it to her. Yes, it was all true he had such a pair, said Boots, but sell it he wouldn't; and with that he took the scissors out of his pocket, and snipped and snipped with them in the air till strips of silk and satin flew all about him.

"Nay, but you must sell me these scissors," said the Princess. "You may ask what you please · for them, but have them I must."

No ! such a pair of scissors he wouldn't sell at any price, for he could never get such a pair again; and while they stood and haggled for the scissors, the Princess had time to look better at Boots, and she too thought with the innkeepers' wives that she had never seen such a handsome fellow before. So she began to bargain for the scissors over again, and begged and prayed Boots to let her have them ; he might ask many, many hundred dollars for them, 'twas all the same to her, so she got them.

"No! sell them I won't," said Boots; "but all the same, if I can get leave to sleep one night on the floor of the Princess' bed-room, close by the door, I'll give her the scissors. I'll do her no harm, but if she's afraid, she may have two men to watch inside the room."

Yes! the Princess was glad enough to give him leave, for she was ready to grant him any-thing if she only got the scissors. So Boots lay

on the floor inside the Princess' bedroom that
night, and two men stood watch there too; but
the Princess didn't get much rest after all; for
when she ought to have been asleep, she must
open her eyes to look at Boots, and so it went on
the whole night. If she shut her eyes for a
minute, she peeped out at him again the next, such
a handsome fellow he seemed to her to be.

Next morning Boots was rowed over to the
Beggar's Isle again; but when they came with the
porridge scrapings and cheese parings from the
palace, there was no one who would taste them
that day either, and so those who brought the
food were more astonished than ever. But one
of those who brought the food contrived to smell
out that the lad who had owned the scissors owned
also a table-cloth, which he only needed to spread
out, and it was covered with all the good things
he could wish for. So when he got back to the
palace, he wasn't long before he said,—

" Such hot joints and such custards I never
saw the like of in the king's palace."

And when the Princess heard that, she told it
to the king, and begged and prayed so long, that
he was forced to send a messenger out to the

island to fetch the lad who owned the table-cloth ; and so Boots came back to the palace. The Princess must and would have the cloth of him, and offered him gold and green woods for it, but Boots wouldn't sell it at any price.

"But if I may have leave to lie on the bench by the Princess' bed-side to night, she shall have the cloth ; but if she's afraid, she is welcome to set four men to watch inside the room."

Yes ! the Princess agreed to this, so Boots lay down on the bench by the bed-side, and the four men watched ; but if the Princess hadn't much sleep the night before, she had much less this, for she could scarce get a wink of sleep ; there she lay wide awake looking at the lovely lad the whole night through, and after all, the night seemed too short.

Next morning Boots was rowed off again to the Beggars' Island, though sorely against the Princess' will, so happy was she to be near him ; but it was past praying for ; to the island he must go, and there was an end of it. But when those who brought the food to the beggars came with the porridge scrapings and cheese parings, there wasn't one of them who would even look at what

the king sent, and those who brought it didn't
wonder either; though they all thought it strange
that none of them were thirsty. But just then
one of the king's guard smelled out that the lad
who had owned the scissors and the table-cloth
had a tap besides, which, if one only turned it a
little, gave out the rarest drink, both ale, and
mead, and wine. So when he came back to the
palace, he couldn't keep his mouth shut this time
any more than before; he went about telling high
and low about the tap, and how easy it was to
draw all sorts of drink out of it.

"And as for that mead and ale, I've never
tasted the like of them in the king's palace;
honey and syrup are nothing to them for sweet-
ness."

So when the Princess heard that, she was all
for getting the tap, and was nothing loath to strike
a bargain with the owner either. So she went
again to the king, and begged him to send a
messenger to the Beggars' Isle after the lad who
had owned the scissors and cloth, for now he had
another thing worth having, she said; and when
the king heard it was a tap, that was good to give
the best ale and wine any one could drink, when

one gave it a turn, he wasn't long in sending the
messenger, I should think.

So when Boots came up to the palace, the
Princess asked whether it were true he had a tap
which could do such and such things?   "Yes! he
had such a tap in his waistcoat pocket," said Boots;
but when the Princess wished with all her might
to buy it, Boots said, as he had said twice before,
he wouldn't sell it, even if the Princess bade half
the kingdom for it.

"But all the same," said Boots; "if I may
have leave to sleep on the Princess' bed to-night,
outside the quilt, she shall have my tap.   I'll not
do her any harm ; but, if she's afraid, she may set
eight men to watch in her room."

"Oh, no !" said the Princess, "there was no
need of that, she knew him now so well ;" and so
Boots lay outside the Princess' bed that night.
But if she hadn't slept much the two nights before,
she had less sleep that night; for she couldn't
shut her eyes the livelong night, but lay and
looked at Boots, who lay alongside her outside
the quilt.

So, when she got up in the morning, and they
were going to row Boots back to the island, she

begged them to hold hard a little bit; and in she ran to the king, and begged him so prettily to let her have Boots for a husband, she was so fond of him, and, unless she had him, she did not care to live.

" Well, well!" said the king, "you shall have him if you must; for he who has such things is just as rich as you are."

So Boots got the Princess and half the kingdom—the other half he was to have when the king died; and so everything went smooth and well; but as for his brothers, who had always been so bad to him, he packed them off to the Beggars' Island.

" There," said Boots, " perhaps they may find out which is best off, the man who has his pockets full of money, or the man whom all women fall in love with."

Nor, to tell you the truth, do I think it would help them much to wander about upon the Beggars' Island pulling pieces of money out of their pockets; and so, if Boots hasn't taken them off the island, there they are still walking about to this very day, eating cheese parings and the scrapings of the porridge-pots.

THE THREE BILLY-GOATS GRUFF.

ONCE on a time there were three Billy-goats, who were to go up to the hill-side to make themselves fat, and the name of all three was "Gruff."

On the way up was a bridge over a burn they had to cross; and under the bridge lived a great ugly Troll, with eyes as big as saucers, and a nose as long as a poker.

So first of all came the youngest billy-goat Gruff to cross the bridge.

"Trip, trap; trip, trap!" went the bridge.

"WHO'S THAT tripping over my bridge?" roared the Troll.

"Oh! it is only I, the tiniest billy-goat Gruff; and I'm going up to the hill-side to make myself fat," said the billy-goat, with such a small voice.

"Now, I'm coming to gobble you up," said the Troll.

THE THREE BILLY-GOATS GRUFF.

"Oh, no! pray don't take me.   I'm too little, that I am," said the billy-goat; "wait a bit till the second billy-goat Gruff comes, he's much bigger."

"Well! be off with you," said the Troll.

A little while after came the second billy-goat Gruff to cross the bridge.

"TRIP, TRAP! TRIP, TRAP! TRIP, TRAP!" went the bridge.

"WHO'S THAT tripping over my bridge?" roared the Troll.

"Oh! it's the second billy-goat Gruff, and I'm going up to the hill-side to make myself fat," said the billy-goat, who hadn't such a small voice.

"Now, I'm coming to gobble you up," said the Troll.

"Oh, no! don't take me, wait a little till the big billy-goat Gruff comes, he's much bigger,"

"Very well! be off with you," said the Troll.

But just then up came the big billy-goat Gruff.

"TRIP, TRAP! TRIP, TRAP! TRIP, TRAP!" went the bridge, for the billy-goat was so heavy that the bridge creaked and groaned under him.

"WHO'S THAT tramping over my bridge?" roared the Troll.

"IT'S I! THE BIG BILLY-GOAT GRUFF," said the billy-goat, who had an ugly hoarse voice of his own.

"Now, I'm coming to gobble you up," roared the Troll.

> "Well, come along! I've got two spears,
> And I'll poke your eyeballs out at your ears;
> I've got besides two curling stones,
> And I'll crush you to bits, body and bones."

That was what the big billy-goat said; and so he flew at the Troll and poked his eyes out with his horns, and crushed him to bits, body and bones, and tossed him out into the burn, and after that he went up to the hill-side. There the billy-goats got so fat they were scarce able to walk home again; and if the fat hasn't fallen off them, why they're still fat; and so,—

> "Snip, snap, snout,
> This tale's told out."

WELL DONE AND ILL PAID.

ONCE on a time there was a man who had to drive his sledge to the wood for fuel. So a bear met him.

"Out with your horse," said the Bear, "or I'll strike all your sheep dead by summer."

"Oh! heaven help me then," said the man; "there's not a stick of firewood in the house; you must let me drive home a load of fuel, else we shall be frozen to death. I'll bring the horse to you to-morrow morning."

Yes! on those terms he might drive the wood home, that was a bargain; but Bruin said, "if he didn't come back, he should lose all his sheep by summer."

So the man got the wood on the sledge and rattled homewards, but he wasn't over pleased at the bargain you may fancy. So just then a fox met him.

"Why, what's the matter?" said the Fox; "why are you so down in the mouth?"

"Oh, if you want to know," said the man; " I met a bear up yonder in the wood, and I had to give my word to him to bring Dobbin back to-morrow, at this very hour; for if he didn't get him, he said he would tear all my sheep to death by summer."

" Stuff, nothing worse than that," said the Fox; "if you'll give me your fattest wether, I'll soon set you free; see if I don't."

Yes! the man gave his word, and swore he would keep it too.

" Well, when you come with Dobbin to-morrow for the bear," said the Fox, " I'll make a clatter up in that heap of stones yonder, and so when the bear asks what that noise is, you must say 'tis Peter the Marksman, who is the best shot in the world; and after that you must help yourself."

Next day off set the man, and when he met the Bear, something began to make a clatter up in the heap of stones.

" Hist! what's that?" said the Bear.

"Oh! that's Peter the Marksman, to be sure," said the man; "he's the best shot in the world. I know him by his voice."

"Have you seen any bears about here, Eric?" shouted out a voice in the wood.

"Say, no!" said the Bear.

"No, I haven't seen any," said Eric.

"What's that, then, that stands alongside your sledge?" bawled out the voice in the wood.

"Say it's an old fir-stump," said the Bear.

"Oh, it's only an old fir-stump," said the man.

"Such fir-stumps we take in our country and roll them on our sledges," bawled out the voice; "if you can't do it yourself, I'll come and help you."

"Say you can help yourself, and roll me up on the sledge," said the Bear.

"No, thank ye, I can help myself well enough," said the man, and rolled the Bear on to the sledge.

"Such fir-stumps we always bind fast on our sledges in our part of the world," bawled out the voice; "shall I come and help you?"

"Say you can help yourself, and bind me fast, do," said the Bear.

"No, thanks, I can help myself well enough," said the man, who set to binding Bruin fast with

U

all the ropes he had, so that at last the bear couldn't stir a paw.

"Such fir-stumps we always drive our axes into, in our part of the world," bawled out the voice; "for then we guide them better going down the steep pitches."

"Pretend to drive your axe into me, do now," said the bear.

Then the man took up his axe, and at one blow split the bear's skull, so that Bruin lay dead in a trice, and so the man and the Fox were great friends, and on the best terms. But when they came near the farm, the Fox said,—

"I've no mind to go right home with you, for I can't say I like your tykes; so I'll just wait here, and you can bring the wether to me, but mind and pick out one nice and fat.

Yes! the man would be sure to do that, and thanked the Fox much for his help. So when he had put up Dobbin, he went across to the sheep-stall.

"Whither away, now?" asked his old dame.

"Oh!" said the man, "I'm only going to the sheep-stall to fetch a fat wether for that cunning

Fox, who set our Dobbin free. I gave him my word I would."

"Wether, indeed," said the old dame; "never a one shall that thief of a Fox get. Haven't we got Dobbin safe, and the bear into the bargain; and as for the Fox, I'll be bound he's stolen more of our geese than the wether is worth; and even if he hasn't stolen them, he will. No, no; take a brace of your swiftest hounds in a sack, and slip them loose after him; and then perhaps we shall be rid of this robbing Reynard."

Well, the man thought that good advice; so he took two fleet red hounds, put them into a sack and set off with them.

"Have you brought the wether?" said the Fox.

"Yes, come and take it," said the man, as he untied the sack and let slip the hounds.

"HUF," said the Fox, and gave a great spring; "true it is what the old saw says, 'Well done is often ill paid;' and now, too, I see the truth of another saying, 'The worst foes are those of one's own house.'" That was what the Fox said as he ran off, and saw the red foxy hounds at his heels.

THE HUSBAND WHO WAS TO MIND
THE HOUSE.

ONCE on a time, there was a man so surly and cross, he never thought his wife did anything right in the house. So, one evening, in hay-making time, he came home, scolding and swearing, and showing his teeth and making a dust.

"Dear love, don't be so angry; there's a good man," said his goody; "to-morrow let's change our work. I'll go out with the mowers and mow, and you shall mind the house at home."

Yes! the husband thought that would do very well. He was quite willing, he said.

So, early next morning, his goody took a scythe over her neck, and went out into the hay-field with the mowers, and began to mow; but the man was to mind the house, and do the work at home.

First of all, he wanted to churn the butter; but when he had churned a while, he got thirsty, and went down to the cellar to tap a barrel of ale. So, just when he had knocked in the bung, and was putting the tap into the cask, he heard overhead the pig come into the kitchen. Then off he ran up the cellar steps, with the tap in his hand, as fast as he could, to look after the pig lest it should upset the churn; but when he got up, and saw the pig had already knocked the churn over, and stood there, routing and grunting amongst the cream which was running all over the floor, he got so wild with rage that he quite forgot the ale-barrel, and ran at the pig as hard as he could. He caught it, too, just as it ran out of doors, and gave it such a kick, that piggy lay for dead on the spot. Then all at once he remembered he had the tap in his hand; but when he got down to the cellar, every drop of ale had run out of the cask.

Then he went into the dairy and found enough cream left to fill the churn again, and so he began to churn, for butter they must have at dinner. When he had churned a bit, he remembered that their milking cow was still shut up in the byre and hadn't had a bit to eat or a drop to drink all the morning, though the sun was high. Then all at once he thought 'twas too far to take her down to the meadow, so he'd just get her up on the house top—for the house, you must know, was thatched with sods, and a fine crop of grass was growing there. Now their house lay close up against a steep down, and he thought if he laid a plank across to the thatch at the back he'd easily get the cow up.

But still he couldn't leave the churn, for there was his little babe crawling about on the floor, and "if I leave it," he thought, "the child is safe to upset it." So he took the churn on his back, and went out with it; but then he thought he'd better first water the cow before he turned her out on the thatch; so he took up a bucket to draw water out of the well; but as he stooped down at the well's brink, all the cream ran out of the churn over his shoulders, and so down into the well.

Now it was near dinner-time, and he hadn't even got the butter yet; so he thought he'd best boil the porridge, and filled the pot with water, and hung it over the fire. When he had done that, he thought the cow might perhaps fall off the thatch and break her legs or her neck. So he got up on the house to tie her up. One end of the rope he made fast to the cow's neck, and the other he slipped down the chimney and tied round his own thigh ; and he had to make haste, for the water now began to boil in the pot, and he had still to grind the oatmeal.

So he began to grind away ; but while he was hard at it, down fell the cow off the house-top after all, and as she fell, she dragged the man up the chimney by the rope. There he stuck fast ; and as for the cow, she hung half way down the wall, swinging between heaven and earth, for she could neither get down nor up.

And now the goody had waited seven lengths and seven breadths for her husband to come and call them home to dinner ; but never a call they had. At last she thought she'd waited long enough, and went home. But when she got there and saw the cow hanging in such an ugly place, she ran up and cut the rope in two with her scythe. But as she did this, down came her husband out of the chimney ; and so when his old dame came inside the kitchen, there she found him standing on his head in the porridge pot.

DAPPLEGRIM.

ONCE on a time there was a rich couple who had twelve sons; but the youngest, when he was grown up, said he wouldn't stay any longer at home, but be off into the world to try his luck. His father and mother said he did very well at home, and had better stay where he was. But no, he couldn't rest; away he must and would go. So at last they gave him leave. And when he had walked a good bit, he came to a king's palace, where he asked for a place, and got it.

Now the daughter of the king of that land had been carried off into the hill by a Troll, and the king had no other children; so he and all his land were in great grief and sorrow, and the king gave his word that any one who could set her free, should have the Princess and half the kingdom. But there was no one who could do it, though many tried.

So when the lad had been there a year or so, he longed to go home again and see his father and

DAPPLEGRIM

mother, and back he went; but when he got home his father and mother were dead, and his brothers had shared all that the old people owned between them, and so there was nothing left for the lad.

"Shan't I have anything at all, then, out of father's and mother's goods?" said the lad.

"Who could tell you were still alive, when you went gadding and wandering about so long?" said his brothers. "But all the same; there are twelve mares up on the hill, which we haven't yet shared among us; if you choose to take them for your share, you're quite welcome."

Yes! the lad was quite content; so he thanked his brothers, and went at once up on the hill, where the twelve mares were out at grass. And when he got up there and found them, each of them had a foal at her side, and one of them had besides, along with her, a big dapple-gray foal, which was so sleek that the sun shone from its coat.

"A fine fellow you are, my little foal," said the lad.

"Yes," said the foal; "but if you'll only kill all the other foals, so that I may run and suck all the mares one year more, you'll see how big and sleek I'll be then."

Yes! the lad was ready to do that; so he killed all those twelve foals, and went home again.

So when he came back the next year to look after his foal and mares, the foal was so fat and sleek, that the sun shone from its coat, and it had grown so big, the lad had hard work to mount it. As for the mares, they had each of them another foal.

"Well, it's quite plain I lost nothing by letting you suck all my twelve mares," said the lad to the yearling, " but now you're big enough to come along with me."

" No," said the colt, " I must bide here a year longer; and now kill all the twelve foals, that I may suck all the mares this year too, and you'll see how big and sleek I'll be by summer."

Yes! the lad did that; and next year when he went up on the hill to look after his colt and the mares, each mare had her foal, but the dapple colt was so tall the lad couldn't reach up to his crest when he wanted to feel how fat he was; and so sleek he was too, that his coat glistened in the sunshine.

" Big and beautiful you were last year, my

colt," said the lad, "but this year you're far grander. There's no such horse in the king's stable. But now you must come along with me."

"No," said Dapple again, "I must stay here one year more. Kill the twelve foals as before, that I may suck the mares the whole year, and then just come and look at me when the summer comes."

Yes! the lad did that; he killed the foals, and went away home.

But when he went up next year to look after Dapple and the mares, he was quite astonished. So tall, and stout, and sturdy, he never thought a horse could be; for Dapple had to lay down on all fours before the lad could bestride him, and it was hard work to get up even then, although he lay flat; and his coat was so smooth and sleek, the sunbeams shone from it as from a looking-glass.

This time Dapple was willing enough to follow the lad, so he jumped up on his back and when he came riding home to his brothers, they all clapped their hands and crossed themselves, for such a horse they had never heard of nor seen before.

"If you will only get me the best shoes you can for my horse, and the grandest saddle and bridle that are to be found," said the lad, "you may have my twelve mares that graze up on the hill yonder, and their twelve foals into the bargain." For you must know that this year too every mare had her foal.

Yes, his brothers were ready to do that, and so the lad got such strong shoes under his horse, that the stones flew high aloft as he rode away across the hills; and he had a golden saddle and a golden bridle, which gleamed and glistened a long way off.

"Now we're off to the king's palace," said Dapplegrim—that was his name; "but mind you ask the king for a good stable and good fodder for me."

Yes! the lad said he would mind; he'd be sure not to forget; and when he rode off from his brothers' house, you may be sure it wasn't long, with such a horse under him, before he got to the king's palace.

When he came there the king was standing on the steps, and stared and stared at the man who came riding along.

"Nay, nay!" said he, "such a man and such a horse I never yet saw in all my life."

But when the lad asked if he could get a place in the king's household, the king was so glad he was ready to jump and dance as he stood on the steps.

Well, they said, perhaps he might get a place there.

"Aye," said the lad, "but I must have good stable-room for my horse, and fodder that one can trust."

Yes! he should have meadow-hay and oats, as much as Dapple could cram, and all the other knights had to lead their horses out of the stable that Dapplegrim might stand alone, and have it all to himself.

But it wasn't long before all the others in the king's household began to be jealous of the lad, and there was no end to the bad things they would have done to him, if they had only dared. At last they thought of telling the king he had said he was man enough to set the king's daughter free—whom the Troll had long since carried away into the hill—if he only chose. The King called the lad before him, and said he had heard the lad

said he was good to do so and so; so now he must
go and do it. If he did it he knew how the king
had promised his daughter and half the kingdom,
and that promise would be faithfully kept; if he
didn't, he should be killed.

The lad kept on saying he never said any
such thing; but it was no good,—the king
wouldn't even listen to him; and so the end of it
was, he was forced to say he'd go and try.

So he went into the stable, down in the mouth
and heavy-hearted, and then Dapplegrim asked
him at once why he was in such dumps.

Then the lad told him all, and how he
couldn't tell which way to turn,—

"For as for setting the Princess free, that's
downright stuff."

"Oh! but it might be done, perhaps," said
Dapplegrim. "I'll help you through; but you
must first have me well shod. You must go and
ask for ten pound of iron and twelve pound of steel
for the shoes, and one smith to hammer and
another to hold."

Yes, the lad did that, and got for answer
"Yes!" He got both the iron and the steel, and
the smiths, and so Dapplegrim was shod both

strong and well, and off went the lad from the court-yard in a cloud of dust.

But when he came to the hill into which the Princess had been carried, the pinch was how to get up the steep wall of rock where the Troll's cave was, in which the Princess had been hid. For you must know the hill stood straight up and down right on end, as upright as a house-wall, and as smooth as a sheet of glass.

The first time the lad went at it he got a little way up; but then Dapple's forelegs slipped, and down they went again, with a sound like thunder on the hill.

The second time he rode at it he got some way further up; but then one foreleg slipped, and down they went with a crash like a landslip.

But the third time Dapple said,—

"Now we must show our mettle;" and went at it again till the stones flew heaven-high about them, and so they got up.

Then the lad rode right into the cave at full speed and caught up the Princess, and threw her over his saddle-bow, and out and down again before the Troll had time even to get on his legs; and so the Princess was freed.

When the lad came back to the palace, the king was both happy and glad to get his daughter back; that you may well believe; but some how or other, though I don't know how, the others about the court had so brought it about that the king was angry with the lad after all.

"Thanks you shall have for freeing my Princess," said he to the lad, when he brought the Princess into the hall, and made his bow.

"She ought to be mine as well as yours; for you're a word-fast man, I hope," said the lad.

"Aye, aye!" said the king, "have her you shall, since I said it; but first of all, you must make the sun shine into my palace hall."

Now you must know there was a high steep ridge of rock close outside the windows, which threw such a shade over the hall that never a sunbeam shone into it.

"That wasn't in our bargain," answered the lad; "but I see this is past praying against; I must e'en go and try my luck, for the Princess I must and will have."

So down he went to Dapple, and told him what the king wanted, and Dapplegrim thought it might easily be done, but first of all he must be new shod; and for that ten pound of iron, and twelve pound of steel besides, were needed, and two smiths, one to hammer and the other to hold, and then they'd soon get the sun to shine into the palace hall.

So when the lad asked for all these things, he got them at once—the king couldn't say nay for very shame; and so Dapplegrim got new shoes, and such shoes! Then the lad jumped upon his back, and off they went again; and for every leap that Dapplegrim gave, down sank the ridge fifteen ells into the earth, and so they went on till there was nothing left of the ridge for the king to see.

When the lad got back to the king's palace, he asked the king if the Princess were not his now; for now no one could say that the sun didn't shine into the hall. But then the others set the king's back up again, and he answered the lad should have her of course, he had never thought of any thing else; but first of all he must get as grand a horse for the bride to ride on to church as the bridegroom had himself.

The lad said the king hadn't spoken a word about this before, and that he thought he had now fairly earned the Princess; but the king held

X

to his own; and more, if the lad couldn't do that he should lose his life; that was what the king said. So the lad went down to the stable in doleful dumps, as you may well fancy, and there he told Dapplegrim all about it; how the king had laid that task on him, to find the bride as good a horse as the bridegroom had himself, else he would lose his life.

"But that's not so easy," he said, "for your match isn't to be found in the wide world."

"Oh yes, I have a match," said Dapplegrim; "but 'tisn't so easy to find him, for he abides in Hell. Still, we'll try. And now you must go up to the king and ask for new shoes for me, ten pound of iron, and twelve pound of steel; and two smiths, one to hammer and one to hold; and mind you see that the points and ends of these shoes are sharp; and twelve sacks of rye, and twelve sacks of barley, and twelve slaughtered oxen, we must have with us; and mind, we must have the twelve ox-hides, with twelve hundred spikes driven into each; and, let me see, a big tar-barrel;—that's all we want."

So the lad went up to the king and asked for all that Dapplegrim had said, and the king again thought he couldn't say nay, for shame's sake, and so the lad got all he wanted.

Well, he jumped up on Dapplegrim's back, and rode away from the palace, and when he had ridden far far over hill and heath, Dapple asked,—

"Do you hear anything?"

"Yes, I hear an awful hissing and rustling up in the air," said the lad; "I think I'm getting afraid."

"That's all the wild birds that fly through the wood. They are sent to stop us; but just cut a hole in the corn-sacks, and then they'll have so much to do with the corn, they'll forget us quite."

Yes! the lad did that; he cut holes in the corn-sacks, so that the rye and barley ran out on all sides. Then all the wild birds that were in the wood came flying round them so thick that the sunbeams grew dark; but as soon as they saw the corn, they couldn't keep to their purpose, but flew down and began to pick and scratch at the rye and barley, and after that, they began to fight among themselves. As for Dapplegrim and the lad, they forgot all about them, and did them no harm.

So the lad rode on and on—far far over mountain and dale, over sand-hills and moor. Then Dapplegrim began to prick up his ears again, and at last he asked the lad if he heard anything?

"Yes! now I hear such an ugly roaring and howling in the wood all round, it makes me quite afraid."

"Ah!" said Dapplegrim, "that's all the wild beasts that range through the wood, and they're sent out to stop us. But just cast out the twelve carcasses of the oxen, that will give them enough to do, and so they'll forget us outright."

Yes! the lad cast out the carcasses, and then all the wild beasts in the wood, both bears, and wolves, and lions—all fell beasts of all kinds— came after them. But when they saw the carcasses, they began to fight for them among themselves, till blood flowed in streams; but Dapplegrim and the lad they quite forgot.

So the lad rode far away, and they changed the landscape many, many times, for Dapplegrim did n't let the grass grow under him, as you may fancy. At last Dapple gave a great neigh.

"Do you hear anything?" he said.

"Yes, I hear something like a colt neighing loud, a long, long way off," answered the lad.

"That's a full-grown colt then," said Dapplegrim, "if we hear him neigh so loud such a long
way off."

After that they travelled a good bit, changing
the landscape once or twice, maybe. Then Dapplegrim gave another neigh.

"Now listen, and tell me if you hear anything," he said.

"Yes, now I hear a neigh like a full-grown
horse," answered the lad.

"Aye! aye!" said Dapplegrim, "you'll hear
him once again soon, and then you'll hear he's got
a voice of his own."

So they travelled on and on, and changed the
landscape once or twice, perhaps, and then Dapplegrim neighed the third time; but before he could
ask the lad if he heard anything, something gave
such a neigh across the heathy hill-side, the lad
thought hill and rock would surely be rent
asunder.

"Now he's here!" said Dapplegrim; "make
haste, now, and throw the ox hides, with the spikes
in them, over me, and throw down the tar-barrel
on the plain; then climb up into that great spruce-
fir yonder. When it comes, fire will flash out of

both nostrils, and then the tar-barrel will catch
fire. Now, mind what I say. If the flame rises,
I win; if it falls, I lose; but if you see me win-
ning, take and cast the bridle—you must take it
off me—over its head, and then it will be tame
enough."

So just as the lad had done throwing the ox
hides, with the spikes, over Dapplegrim, and had
cast down the tar-barrel on the plain, and had
got well up into the spruce-fir, up galloped a
horse, with fire flashing out of his nostrils, and the
flame caught the tar-barrel at once. Then
Dapplegrim and the strange horse began to fight
till the stones flew heaven high. They fought,
and bit, and kicked, both with fore-feet and hind-
feet, and sometimes the lad could see them, and
sometimes he couldn't; but at last the flame
began to rise; for wherever the strange horse
kicked or bit, he met the spiked hides, and at last
he had to yield. When the lad saw that, he
wasn't long in getting down from the tree, and in
throwing the bridle over its head, and then it was
so tame you could hold it with a pack-thread.

And what do you think? that horse was
dappled too, and so like Dapplegrim, you couldn't

tell which was which. Then the lad bestrode the new Dapple he had broken, and rode home to the palace, and old Dapplegrim ran loose by his side. So when he got home, there stood the king out in the yard.

"Can you tell me now," said the lad, "which is the horse I have caught and broken, and which is the one I had before. If you can't, I think your daughter is fairly mine."

Then the king went and looked at both Dapples, high and low, before and behind, but there wasn't a hair on one which wasn't on the other as well.

"No," said the king, "that I can't; and since you've got my daughter such a grand horse for her wedding, you shall have her with all my heart. But still we'll have one trial more, just to see whether you're fated to have her. First, she shall hide herself twice, and then you shall hide yourself twice. If you can find out her hiding-place, and she can't find out yours, why then you're fated to have her, and so you shall have her."

"That's not in the bargain either," said the lad; "but we must just try, since it must be so ;" and so the Princess went off to hide herself first.

So she turned herself into a duck, and lay swimming on a pond that was close to the palace. But the lad only ran down to the stable, and asked Dapplegrim what she had done with herself.

"Oh, you only need to take your gun," said Dapplegrim, "and go down to the brink of the pond, and aim at the duck which lies swimming about there, and she'll soon show herself."

So the lad snatched up his gun and ran off to the pond. "I'll just take a pop at this duck," he said, and began to aim at it.

"Nay, nay, dear friend, don't shoot. It's I," said the Princess.

So he had found her once.

The second time the Princess turned herself into a loaf of bread, and laid herself on the table among four other loaves ; and so like was she to the others, no one could say which was which.

But the lad went again down to the stable to Dapplegrim, and said how the Princess had hidden herself again, and he couldn't tell at all what had become of her.

"Oh, just take and sharpen a good bread-knife," said Dapplegrim, "and do as if you were going to cut in two the third loaf on the left hand of those four loaves which are lying on the dresser in the king's kitchen, and you'll find her soon enough."

Yes! the lad was down in the kitchen in no time, and began to sharpen the biggest bread-knife he could lay hands on; then he caught hold of the third loaf on the left hand, and put the knife to it, as though he was going to cut it in two.

"I'll just have a slice off this loaf," he said.

"Nay, dear friend," said the Princess, "don't cut. It's I."

So he had found her twice.

Then he was to go and hide; but he and Dapplegrim had settled it all so well beforehand, it wasn't easy to find him. First he turned himself into a tick, and hid himself in Dapplegrim's left nostril; and the Princess went about hunting him everywhere, high and low; at last she wanted to go into Dapplegrim's stall, but he began to bite and kick, so that she daren't go near him, and so she couldn't find the lad.

"Well," she said, "since I can't find you, you must show where you are yourself;" and in a trice the lad stood there on the stable floor.

The second time Dapplegrim told him again what to do; and then he turned himself into a clod of earth, and stuck himself between Dapple's hoof and shoe on the near forefoot. So the Princess hunted up and down, out and in, everywhere; at last she came into the stable, and wanted to go into Dapplegrim's loose-box. This time he let her come up to him, and she pried high and low, but under his hoofs she couldn't come, for he stood firm as a rock on his feet, and so she couldn't find the lad.

"Well; you must just show yourself, for I'm sure I can't find you," said the Princess, and as she spoke the lad stood by her side on the stable floor.

"Now you are mine indeed," said the lad; "for now you can see I'm fated to have you." This he said both to the father and daughter.

"Yes; it is so fated," said the king; "so it must be."

Then they got ready the wedding in right down earnest, and lost no time about it; and the lad got on Dapplegrim, and the Princess on Dapplegrim's match, and then you may fancy they were not long on their way to the church.

THE SEVEN FOALS.

THE SEVEN FOALS.

ONCE on a time there was a poor couple who lived in a wretched hut, far, far away in the wood. How they lived I can't tell, but I'm sure it was from hand to mouth, and hard work even then; but they had three sons, and the youngest of them was Boots, of course, for he did little else than lie there and poke about in the ashes.

So one day the eldest lad said he would go out to earn his bread, and he soon got leave, and wandered out into the world. There he walked and walked the whole day, and when evening drew in, he came to a king's palace, and there stood the king out on the steps, and asked whither he was bound.

"Oh, I'm going about, looking after a place," said the lad.

"Will you serve me?" asked the king, " and watch my seven foals. If you can watch them one whole day, and tell me at night what they eat

and what they drink, you shall have the Princess
to wife, and half my kingdom; but if you can't,
I'll cut three red stripes out of your back. Do
you hear?"

Yes! that was an easy task, the lad thought,
he'd do that fast enough, never fear.

So next morning, as soon as the first peep of
dawn came, the king's coachman let out the seven
foals. Away they went and the lad after them.
You may fancy how they tore over hill and dale,
through bush and bog. When the lad had run so
a long time, he began to get weary, and when he
had held on a while longer, he had more than
enough of his watching, and just there, he came
to a cleft in a rock, where an old hag sat and
spun with a distaff. As soon as she saw the lad
who was running after the foals till the sweat ran
down his brow, this old hag bawled out,—

"Come hither, come hither, my pretty son,
and let me comb your hair."

Yes! the lad was willing enough; so he sat
down in the cleft of the rock with the old hag,
and laid his head on her lap, and she combed his
hair all day whilst he lay there, and stretched his
lazy bones.

So, when evening drew on, the lad wanted to go away.

"I may just as well toddle straight home now," said he, "for it's no use my going back to the palace."

"Stop a bit till it's dark," said the old hag, "and then the king's foals will pass by here again, and then you can run home with them, and then no one will know that you have lain here all day long, instead of watching the foals."

So, when they came, she gave the lad a flask of water and a clod of turf. Those he was to show to the king, and say that was what his seven foals ate and drank.

"Have you watched true and well the whole day, now?" asked the King, when the lad came before him in the evening.

"Yes, I should think so," said the lad.

"Then you can tell me what my seven foals eat and drink," said the King.

"Yes!" and so the lad pulled out the flask of water and the clod of turf, which the old hag had given him.

"Here you see their meat, and here you see their drink," said the lad.

But then the king saw plain enough how he had watched, and he got so wroth, he ordered his men to chase him away home on the spot; but first they were to cut three red stripes out of his back, and rub salt into them. So when the lad got home again, you may fancy what a temper he was in. He'd gone out once to get a place, he said, but he'd never do so again.

Next day the second son said he would go out into the world to try his luck. His father and mother said "No," and bade him look at his brother's back; but the lad wouldn't give in; he held to his own, and at last he got leave to go, and set off. So when he had walked the whole day, he, too, came to the king's palace. There stood the King out on the steps, and asked whither he was bound? and when the lad said he was looking about for a place, the King said he might have a place there, and watch his seven foals. But the king laid down the same punishment, and the same reward, as he had settled for his brother. Well, the lad was willing enough; he took the place at once with the King, for he thought he'd soon watch the foals, and tell the king what they ate and drank.

So, in the gray of the morning, the coachman let out the seven foals, and off they went again over hill and dale, and the lad after them. But the same thing happened to him as had befallen his brother. When he had run after the foals a long long time, till he was both warm and weary, he passed by the cleft in a rock, where an old hag sat and spun with a distaff, and she bawled out to the lad,—

"Come hither, come hither, my pretty son, and let me comb your hair."

That the lad thought a good offer, so he let the foals run on their way, and sat down in the cleft with the old hag. There he sat, and there he lay, taking his ease, and stretching his lazy bones the whole day.

When the foals came back at nightfall, he too got a flask of water and clod of turf from the old hag to show to the king. But when the king asked the lad,—

"Can you tell me now, what my seven foals eat and drink?" and the lad pulled out the flask and the clod, and said,—

"Here you see their meat, and here you see their drink."

Then the king got wroth again, and ordered them to cut three red stripes out of the lad's back, and rub salt in, and chase him home that very minute. And so when the lad got home, he also told how he had fared, and said, he had gone out once to get a place, but he'd never do so any more.

The third day Boots wanted to set out; he had a great mind to try and watch the seven foals, he said. The others laughed at him, and made game of him, saying,—

"When we fared so ill, you'll do it better —a fine joke; you look like it—you who have never done anything but lie there and poke about in the ashes."

"Yes!" said Boots, "I don't see why I shouldn't go, for I've got it into my head, and can't get it out again."

And so, in spite of all the jeers of the others and the prayers of the old people, there was no help for it, and Boots set out.

So after he had walked the whole day, he too came at dusk to the king's palace. There stood the king out on the steps, and asked whither he was bound.

"Oh," said Boots, "I'm going about seeing if I can hear of a place."

"Whence do you come, then?" said the King, for he wanted to know a little more about them before he took any one into his service.

So Boots said whence he came, and how he was brother to those two who had watched the king's seven foals, and ended by asking if he might try to watch them next day.

"Oh, stuff!" said the King, for he got quite cross if he even thought of them; "if you're brother to those two, you're not worth much, I'll be bound. I've had enough of such scamps."

"Well," said Boots; "but since I've come so far, I may just as well get leave to try, I too."

"Oh, very well; with all my heart," said the King, "if you *will* have your back flayed, you're quite welcome."

"I'd much rather have the Princess," said Boots.

So next morning, at gray of dawn, the coachman let out the seven foals again, and away they went over hill and dale, through bush and bog, and Boots behind them. And so, when he too had run a long while, he came to the cleft in the rock,

Y

where the old hag sat, spinning at her distaff.
So she bawled out to Boots,—

"Come hither, come hither, my pretty son, and
let me comb your hair."

"Don't you wish you may catch me," said
Boots. "Don't you wish you may catch me," as
he ran along, leaping and jumping, and holding
on by one of the foals' tails. And when he had
got well past the cleft in the rock, the youngest
foal said,—

"Jump up on my back, my lad, for we've a
long way before us still."

So Boots jumped up on his back.

So they went on, and on, a long long way.

"Do you see anything now?" said the Foal.

"No," said Boots.

So they went on a good bit farther.

"Do you see anything now?" asked the Foal.

"Oh no," said the lad.

So when they had gone a great, great way
farther—I'm sure I can't tell how far—the Foal
asked again,—

"Do you see anything now?"

"Yes," said Boots; "now I see something that
looks white—just like a tall, big birch trunk."

"Yes," said the Foal; "we're going into that trunk."

So when they got to the trunk, the eldest foal took and pushed it on one side, and then they saw a door where it had stood, and inside the door was a little room, and in the room there was scarce anything but a little fire-place and one or two benches; but behind the door hung a great rusty sword and a little pitcher.

"Can you brandish the sword?" said the Foals: "try."

So Boots tried, but he couldn't; then they made him take a pull at the pitcher; first once, then twice, and then thrice, and then he could wield it like anything.

"Yes," said the Foals, "now you may take the sword with you, and with it you must cut off all our seven heads on your wedding-day, and then we'll be princes again as we were before. For we are brothers of that Princess whom you are to have when you can tell the king what we eat and drink; but an ugly Troll has thrown this shape over us. Now mind, when you have hewn off our heads, to take care to lay each head at the tail of the trunk which it belonged to before, and then the spell will have no more power over us."

Yes! Boots promised all that, and then on they went.

And when they had travelled a long long way, the Foal asked,—

" Do you see anything ?"

" No," said Boots.

So they travelled a good bit still.

" And now ?" asked the Foal.

" No, I see nothing," said Boots.

So they travelled many many miles again, over hill and dale.

" Now then," said the Foal, " do you see any-thing now ?"

" Yes," said Boots, " now I see something like a blue stripe, far, far away."

" Yes," said the Foal, " that's a river we've got to cross."

Over the river was a long grand bridge ; and when they had got over to the other side, they travelled on a long, long way. At last the Foal asked again,—

" If Boots didn't see anything ?"

" Yes, this time he saw something that looked

black far, far away, just as though it were a church steeple."

"Yes," said the Foal, "that's where we're going to turn in."

So when the foals got into the churchyard, they became men again, and looked like Princes, with such fine clothes that it glistened from them; and so they went into the church, and took the bread and wine from the priest who stood at the altar. And Boots he went in too; but when the priest had laid his hands on the Princes, and given them the blessing, they went out of the church again, and Boots went out too; but he took with him a flask of wine and a wafer. And as soon as ever the seven Princes came out into the churchyard, they were turned into foals again, and so Boots got up on the back of the youngest, and so they all went back the same way that they had come, only they went much, much faster. First they crossed the bridge, next they passed the trunk, and then they passed the old hag, who sat at the cleft and span, and they went by her so fast, that Boots couldn't hear what the old hag screeched after him; but he heard so much as to know she was in an awful rage.

It was almost dark when they got back to the palace, and the King himself stood out on the steps and waited for them.

" Have you watched well and true the whole day?" said he to Boots.

" I've done my best," answered Boots.

" Then you can tell me what my seven foals eat and drink," said the King.

Then Boots pulled out the flask of wine and the wafer, and showed them to the King.

" Here you see their meat, and here you see their drink," said he.

" Yes," said the King, " you have watched true and well, and you shall have the Princess and half the kingdom."

So they made ready the wedding-feast, and the King said it should be such a grand one, it should be the talk far and near.

But when they sat down to the bridal feast, the bridegroom got up and went down to the stable, for he said he had forgotten something, and must go to fetch it. And when he got down there, he did as the foals had said, and hewed their heads off all seven, the eldest first, and the others after him; and at the same time he took care to lay each head at the tail of the foal to which it belonged ; and as he did this, lo ! they all became Princes again.

So when he went into the bridal hall with the seven princes, the King was so glad he both kissed Boots and patted him on the back, and his bride was still more glad of him than she had been before.

" Half the kingdom you have got already,'' said the King, "and the other half you shall have after my death ; for my sons can easily get themselves lands and wealth, now they are princes again."

And so, like enough, there was mirth and fun at that wedding. I was there too ; but there was no one to care for poor me ; and so I got nothing but a bit of bread and butter, and I laid it down on the stove, and the bread was burnt and the butter ran, and so I didn't get even the smallest crumb. Wasn't that a great shame ?

THE WIDOW'S SON.

ONCE on a time there was a poor, poor widow who had an only son. She dragged on with the boy till he had been confirmed, and then she said she couldn't feed him any longer, he must just go out and earn his own bread. So the lad wandered out into the world, and when he had walked a day or so, a strange man met him.

"Whither away?" asked the man.

"Oh, I'm going out into the world to try and get a place," said the lad.

"Will you come and serve me?" said the man.

"Oh yes; just as soon you as any one else," said the lad.

"Well, you'll have a good place with me," said the man; "for you'll only have to keep me company, and do nothing at all else beside."

So the lad stopped with him, and lived on the fat of the land, both in meat and drink, and had little or nothing to do; but he never saw a living soul in that man's house.

So one day the man said,—

"Now, I'm going off for eight days, and that time you'll have to spend here all alone; but you must not go into any one of these four rooms here. If you do, I'll take your life when I come back."

"No," said the lad,—he'd be sure not to do that. But when the man had been gone three or four days, the lad couldn't bear it any longer, but went into the first room, and when he got inside he looked round, but he saw nothing but a shelf over the door where a bramble-bush rod lay.

Well, indeed! thought the lad; a pretty thing to forbid my seeing this.

So when the eight days were out, the man came home, and the first thing he said was,—

"You haven't been into any of these rooms, of course."

"No, no; that I haven't," said the lad.

"I'll soon see that," said the man, and went at once into the room where the lad had been.

"Nay, but you have been in here," said he; "and now you shall lose your life."

Then the lad begged and prayed so hard that

he got off with his life, but the man gave him a good thrashing. And when it was over, they were as good friends as ever.

Some time after the man set off again, and said he should be away fourteen days; but before he went he forbade the lad to go into any of the rooms he had not been in before; as for that he had been in, he might go into that and welcome. Well, it was the same story over again, except that the lad stood out eight days before he went in. In this room, too, he saw nothing but a shelf over the door, and a big stone, and a pitcher of water on it. Well, after all, there's not much to be afraid of my seeing here, thought the lad.

But when the man came back, he asked if he had been into any of the rooms. No, the lad hadn't done anything of the kind.

"Well, well; I'll soon see that," said the man; and when he saw that the lad had been in them after all, he said,—

"Ah! now I'll spare you no longer; now you must lose your life."

But the lad begged and prayed for himself again, and so this time too he got off with stripes; though he got as many as his skin could carry.

But when he got sound and well again, he led just as easy a life as ever, and he and the man were just as good friends.

So a while after the man was to take another journey, and now he said he should be away three weeks, and he forbade the lad anew to go into the third room, for if he went in there he might just make up his mind at once to lose his life. Then after fourteen days the lad couldn't bear it, but crept into the room, but he saw nothing at all in there but a trap door on the floor; and when he lifted it up and looked down, there stood a great copper cauldron which bubbled and boiled away down there; but he saw no fire under it.

"Well, I should just like to know if it's hot," thought the lad, and stuck his finger down into the broth, and when he pulled it out again, lo! it was gilded all over. So the lad scraped and scrubbed it, but the gilding wouldn't go off, so he bound a piece of rag round it; and when the man came back and asked what was the matter with his finger, the lad said he'd given it such a bad cut. But the man tore off the rag, and then he soon saw what was the matter with the finger. First he wanted to kill the lad outright, but when he wept and begged, he only gave him such a thrashing that he had to keep his bed three days. After that the man took down a pot from the wall, and rubbed him over with some stuff out of it, and so the lad was sound and fresh as ever.

So after a while the man started off again, and this time he was to be away a month. But before he went, he said to the lad, if he went into the fourth room he might give up all hope of saving his life.

Well, the lad stood out for two or three weeks, but then he couldn't hold out any longer; he must and would go into that room, and so in he stole. There stood a great black horse tied up in a stall by himself, with a manger of red hot coals at his head, and a truss of hay at his tail. Then the lad thought this all wrong, so he changed them about, and put the hay at his head. Then said the horse,—

"Since you are so good at heart as to let me have some food, I'll set you free, that I will. For if the Troll comes back and finds you here, he'll kill you outright. But now you must go up to the room which lies just over this, and take a coat of mail out of those that hang there ; and mind, whatever you do, don't take any of the bright ones, but the most rusty of all you see, that's the one to take; and sword and saddle you must choose for yourself just in the same way."

So the lad did all that; but it was a heavy load for him to carry them all down at once.

When he came back, the Horse told him to pull off his clothes and get into the cauldron which stood and boiled in the other room, and bathe himself there. "If I do," thought the lad, "I shall look an awful fright;" but for all that, he did as he was told. So when he had taken his bath, he became so handsome and sleek, and as red and white as milk and blood, and much stronger than he had been before.

"Do you feel any change?" asked the Horse.

" Yes," said the lad.

"Try to lift me then," said the Horse.

Oh yes! he could do that, and as for the sword, he brandished it like a feather.

"Now saddle me," said the Horse, "and put on the coat of mail, and then take the bramble-bush rod, and the stone, and the pitcher of water, and the pot of ointment, and then we'll be off as fast as we can."

So when the lad had got on the horse, off they went at such a rate, he couldn't at all tell how they went. But when he had ridden awhile, the Horse said,

"I think I hear a noise; look round! can you see anything?"

"Yes; there are ever so many coming after us, at least a score," said the lad.

"Aye, aye, that's the Troll coming," said the Horse; "now he's after us with his pack."

So they rode on a while, until those who followed were close behind them.

"Now throw your bramble-bush rod behind you, over your shoulder," said the Horse; "but mind you throw it a good way off my back."

So the lad did that, and all at once a close, thick bramble-wood grew up behind them. So the lad rode on a long, long time, while the Troll and his crew had to go home to fetch something to hew their way through the wood. But at last, the horse said again.

"Look behind you! can you see anything now?"

"Yes, ever so many," said the lad, "as many as would fill a large church."

"Aye, aye, that's the Troll and his crew," said the Horse; "now he's got more to back him; but now throw down the stone, and mind you throw it far behind me."

And as soon as the lad did what the horse said, up rose a great black hill of rock behind him. So the Troll had to be off home to fetch something to mine his way through the rock; and while the Troll did that, the lad rode a good bit further on. But still the Horse begged him to look behind him, and then he saw a troop like a whole army behind him, and they glistened in the sunbeams.

"Aye, aye," said the Horse, "that's the Troll, and now he's got his whole band with him, so throw the pitcher of water behind you, but mind you don't spill any of it upon me."

So the lad did that; but in spite of all the pains he took, he still spilt one drop on the horse's flank. So it became a great deep lake; and because of that one drop, the horse found himself far out in it, but still he swam safe to land. But when the Trolls came to the lake, they lay down to drink it dry; and so they swilled and swilled till they burst.

"Now we're rid of them," said the Horse.

So when they had gone a long long while, they came to a green patch in a wood.

"Now strip off all your arms," said the Horse, "and only put on your ragged clothes, and take the saddle off me, and let me loose, and hang all my clothing and your arms up inside that great hollow lime-tree yonder. Then make yourself a wig of fir-moss, and go up to the king's palace which lies close here, and ask for a place. Whenever you need me, only come here and shake the bridle, and I'll come to you."

Yes! the lad did all his Horse told him, and as soon as ever he put on the wig of moss he became so ugly, and pale, and miserable to look at, no one would have known him again. Then he went up to the king's palace, and begged first for leave to be in the kitchen, and bring in wood and water for the cook, but then the kitchen-maid asked him——

"Why do you wear that ugly wig? Off with it. I won't have such a fright in here."

"No, I can't do that," said the lad; "for I'm not quite right in my head."

"Do you think, then, I'll have you in here about the food," cried the cook. "Away with you to the coachman; you're best fit to go and clean the stable."

But when the coachman begged him to take his wig off, he got the same answer, and he wouldn't have him either.

"You'd best go down to the gardener," said he; "you're best fit to go about and dig in the garden."

So he got leave to be with the gardener, but none of the other servants would sleep with him, and so he had to sleep by himself under the steps of the summer-house. It stood upon beams, and had a high staircase. Under that he got some turf for his bed, and there he lay as well as he could.

So, when he had been some time at the palace, it happened one morning, just as the sun rose, that the lad had taken off his wig, and stood and washed himself, and then he was so handsome, it was a joy to look at him.

So the Princess saw from her window the lovely gardener's boy, and thought she had never seen any one so handsome. Then she asked the gardener why he lay out there under the steps.

"Oh," said the gardener, "none of his fellow-servants will sleep with him; that's why."

" Let him come up to-night, and lie at the door inside my bed-room, and then they'll not refuse to sleep with him any more," said the Princess.

So the gardener told that to the lad.

" Do you think I'll do any such thing?" said the lad. "Why they'd say next there was something between me and the Princess."

" Yes," said the gardener, "you've good reason to fear any such thing, you who are so handsome."

" Well, well," said the lad, "since it's her will, I suppose I must go."

So, when he was to go up the steps in the evening, he tramped and stamped so on the way, that they had to beg him to tread softly lest the King should come to know it. So he came into the Princess' bed-room, lay down, and began to snore at once. Then the Princess said to her maid,—

" Go gently, and just pull his wig off;" and she went up to him.

But just as she was going to whisk it off, he caught hold of it with both hands, and said she should never have it. After that he lay down again, and began to snore. Then the Princess

gave her maid a wink, and this time she whisked
off the wig ; and there lay the lad so lovely, and
white and red, just as the Princess had seen him
in the morning sun.

After that the lad slept every night in the
Princess' bed-room.

But it wasn't long before the King came to
hear how the gardener's lad slept every night in
the Princess' bedroom ; and he got so wroth he
almost took the lad's life. He didn't do that,
however, but threw him into the prison tower ;
and as for his daughter, he shut her up in
her own room, whence she never got leave to stir
day or night. All that she begged, and all that
she prayed, for the lad and herself, was no good.
The King was only more wroth than ever.

Some time after came a war and uproar in
the land, and the king had to take up arms against
another king who wished to take the kingdom
from him. So when the lad heard that, he begged
the goaler to go to the king and ask for a coat of
mail and a sword, and for leave to go to the war.
All the rest laughed when the goaler told his
errand, and begged the king to let him have an
old worn-out suit, that they might have the fun of

seeing such a wretch in battle. So he got that, and an old broken-down hack besides, which went upon three legs, and dragged the fourth after it.

Then they went out to meet the foe; but they hadn't got far from the palace before the lad got stuck fast in a bog with his hack. There he sat and dug his spurs in, and cried, "Gee up, gee up!" to his hack. And all the rest had their fun out of this, and laughed, and made game of the lad as they rode past him. But they were scarcely gone, before he ran to the lime-tree, threw on his coat of mail, and shook the bridle, and there came the horse in a trice, and said,—

"Do now your best, and I'll do mine."

But when the lad came up the battle had begun, and the king was in a sad pinch; but no sooner had the lad rushed into the thick of it than the foe was beaten back, and put to flight. The king and his men wondered and wondered who it could be who had come to help them, but none of them got so near him as to be able to talk to him, and as soon as the fight was over he was gone. When they went back, there sat the lad still in the bog, and dug his spurs into his three-legged hack, and they all laughed again.

"No! only just look," they said; "there the fool sits still."

The next day when they went out to battle, they saw the lad sitting there still, so they laughed again, and made game of him; but as soon as ever they had ridden by, the lad ran again to the lime-tree, and all happened as on the first day. Every one wondered what strange champion it could be that had helped them, but no one got so near him as to say a word to him; and no one guessed it could be the lad; that's easy to understand.

So when they went home at night, and saw the lad still sitting there on his hack, they burst out laughing at him again, and one of them shot an arrow at him and hit him in the leg. So he began to shriek and to bewail; 'twas enough to break one's heart; and so the king threw his pocket-handkerchief to him to bind his wound.

When they went out to battle the third day, the lad still sat there.

"Gee up! gee up!" he said to his hack.

"Nay, nay," said the king's men; "if he won't stick there till he's starved to death."

And then they rode on, and laughed at him till they were fit to fall from their horses. When they were gone, he ran again to the lime, and came up to the battle just in the very nick of time. This day he slew the enemy's king, and then the war was over at once.

When the battle was over, the king caught sight of his handkerchief, which the strange warrior had bound round his leg, and so it wasn't hard to find him out. So they took him with great joy between them to the palace, and the Princess, who saw him from her window, got so glad, no one can believe it.

" Here comes my own true love," she said.

Then he took the pot of ointment and rubbed himself on the leg, and after that he rubbed all the wounded, and so they all got well again in a moment.

So he got the Princess to wife ; but when he went down into the stable where his horse was on the day the wedding was to be, there it stood so dull and heavy, and hung its ears down, and wouldn't eat its corn. So when the young king —for he was now a king, and had got half the kingdom—spoke to him, and asked what ailed him, the Horse said,—

" Now I have helped you on, and now I won't

live any longer. So just take the sword, and cut my head off."

"No, I'll do nothing of the kind," said the young king; "but you shall have all you want, and rest all your life."

"Well," said the Horse, "if you don't do as I tell you, see if I don't take your life somehow."

So the king had to do what he asked; but when he swung the sword and was to cut his head off, he was so sorry he turned away his face, for he would not see the stroke fall. But as soon as ever he had cut off the head, there stood the loveliest Prince on the spot where the horse had stood.

"Why, where in all the world did you come from?" asked the king.

"It was I who was a horse," said the Prince; "for I was king of that land whose king you slew yesterday. He it was who threw this Troll's shape over me, and sold me to the Troll. But now he is slain I get my own again, and you and I will be neighbour kings, but war we will never make on one another."

And they didn't either; for they were friends as long as they lived, and each paid the other very many visits.

ONCE on a time there was a widower, who had a son and a daughter by his first marriage. Both were good children, and loved each other dearly. Some time after the man married a widow, who had a daughter by her first husband, and she was both ugly and bad, like her mother. So from the day the new wife came into the house there was no peace for her step-children in any corner; and at last the lad thought he'd best go out into the world, and try to earn his own bread. And when he had wandered a while he came to a king's palace, and got a place under the coachman, and quick and willing he was, and the horses he looked after were so sleek and clean that their coats shone again.

But the sister who staid at home was treated worse than bad; both her stepmother and step-sister were always at her, and wherever she went, and whatever she did, they scolded and snarled so, the poor lassie hadn't an hour's peace. All the hard work she was forced to do, and early and late she got nothing but bad words, and little food besides.

So one day they had sent her to the burn to fetch water; and what do you think? up popped an ugly, ugly head out of the pool, and said,—

"Wash me, you lassie."

"Yes, with all my heart I'll wash you," said the lassie.

So she began to wash and scrub the ugly head; but truth to say, she thought it nasty work.

"Well, as soon as she had done washing it, up popped another head out of the pool, and this was uglier still.

"Brush me, you lassie," said the head.

"Yes, with all my heart I'll brush you."

And with that she took in hand the matted locks, and you may fancy she hadn't very pleasant work with them.

But when she had got over that, if a third head didn't pop out of the pool, and this was far more ugly and loathsome than both the others put together.

"Kiss me, you lassie."

"Yes, I'll kiss you," said the lassie, and she

did it too, though she thought it the worst work she had ever had to do in her life.

Then the heads began to chatter together, and each asked what they should do for the lassie who was so kind and gentle.

" That she be the prettiest lassie in the world, and as fair as the bright day," said the first head.

" That gold shall drop from her hair, every time she brushes it," said the second head.

" That gold shall fall from her mouth every time she speaks," said the third head.

So when the lassie came home looking so lovely, and beaming as the bright day itself; her stepmother and her stepsister got more and more cross, and they got worse still when she began to talk, and they saw how golden guineas fell from her mouth· As for the stepmother, she got so mad with rage, she chased the lassie into the pigsty. That was the right place for all her gold stuff, but as for coming into the house, she wouldn't hear of it.

Well, it wasn't long before the stepmother wished her own daughter to go to the burn to fetch water. So when she came to the water's edge with her buckets, up popped the first head.

" Wash me, you lassie," it said.

" The Deil wash you," said the stepdaughter.

So the second head popped up.

" Brush me, you lassie," it said.

" The Deil brush you," said the stepdaughter.

So down it went to the bottom, and the third head popped up.

"Kiss me, you lassie," said the head.

" The Deil kiss you, you pig's-snout," said the girl.

Then the heads chattered together again, and asked what they should do to the girl who was so spiteful and cross-grained ; and they all agreed she should have a nose four ells long, and a snout three ells long, and a pine bush right in the midst of her forehead, and every time she spoke, ashes were to fall out of her mouth.

So when she got home with her buckets, she bawled out to her mother——

" Open the door."

" Open it yourself, my darling child," said the mother.

"I can't reach it because of my nose," said the daughter.

So, when the mother came out and saw her, you may fancy what a way she was in, and how she screamed and groaned; but, for all that, there were the nose and the snout and the pine bush, and they got no smaller for all her grief.

Now the brother, who had got the place in the King's stable, had taken a little sketch of his sister, which he carried away with him, and every morning and every evening he knelt down before the picture and prayed to Our Lord for his sister, whom he loved so dearly. The other grooms had heard him praying, so they peeped through the key-hole of his room, and there they saw him on his knees before the picture. So they went about saying how the lad every morning and every evening knelt down and prayed to an idol which he had, and at last they went to the king himself and begged him only to peep through the key-hole, and then His Majesty would see the lad, and what things he did. At first the king wouldn't believe it, but at last they talked him over, and he crept on tiptoe to the door and peeped in. Yes, there was the lad on his knees before the picture, which hung on the wall, praying with clasped hands.

"Open the door!" called out the King; but the lad didn't hear him.

So the King called out in a louder voice, but

the lad was so deep in his prayers he couldn't hear him this time either.

"OPEN THE DOOR, I SAY!" roared out the King; "It's I the King who want to come in."

Well, up jumped the lad and ran to the door and unlocked it, but in his hurry he forgot to hide the picture.

But when the King came in and saw the picture, he stood there as if he were fettered, and couldn't stir from the spot, so lovely he thought the picture.

"So lovely a woman there isn't in all the wide world," said the King.

But the lad told him she was his sister whom he had drawn, and if she wasn't prettier than that, at least she wasn't uglier.

"Well, if she's so lovely," said the King, "I'll have her for my queen;" and then he ordered the lad to set off home that minute, and not be long on the road either. So the lad promised to make as much haste as he could, and started off from the King's palace.

When the brother came home to fetch his sister, the stepmother and stepsister said they must go too. So they all set out, and the good lassie had a casket in which she kept her gold, and a little dog, whose name was " Little Flo;" those two things were all her mother left her. And when they had gone a while, they came to a lake which they had to cross; so the brother sat down at the helm, and the stepmother and the two girls sat in the bow forward, and so they sailed a long, long way.

At last they caught sight of land.

" There," said the brother, " where you see the white strand yonder, there's where we're to land;" and as he said this he pointed across the water.

" What is it my brother says?" asked the good lassie.

" He says you must throw your casket overboard," said the stepmother.

" Well, when my brother says it, I must do it," said the lassie, and overboard went the casket,

When they had sailed a bit further, the brother pointed again across the lake.

" There you see the castle we're going to."

" What is it my brother says?" asked the lassie.

" He says now you must throw your little dog overboard," said the step-mother.

Then the lassie wept and was sore grieved, for little Flo was the dearest thing she had in the world, but at last she threw him overboard.

"When my brother says it, I must do it, but heaven knows how it hurts me to throw you over Little Flo," she said.

So they sailed on a good bit still.

"There you see the King coming down to meet us," said the brother, and pointed towards the strand.

"What is it my brother says?" asked the lassie.

"Now he says you must make haste and throw yourself overboard," said the stepmother.

Well, the lassie wept and moaned; but when her brother told her to do that, she thought she ought to do it, and so she leapt down into the lake.

But when they came to the palace, and the King saw the loathly bride, with a nose four ells long, and a snout three ells long, and a pine bush in the midst of her forehead, he was quite scared out of his wits; but the wedding was all ready, both in brewing and baking, and there sat all the wedding guests, waiting for the bride; and so the

King couldn't help himself, but was forced to take her for better for worse. But angry he was, that any one can forgive him, and so he had the brother thrown into a pit full of snakes.

Well, the first Thursday evening after the wedding, about midnight, in came a lovely lady into the palace-kitchen, and begged the kitchen-maid, who slept there, so prettily to lend her a brush. That she got, and then she brushed her hair, and as she brushed, down dropped gold. A little dog was at her heel, and to him she said,—

"Run out, little Flo, and see if it will soon be day."

This she said three times, and the third time she sent the dog it was just about the time the dawn begins to peep. Then she had to go, but as she went she sung,—

"Out on you, ugly Bushy Bride,
    Lying so warm by the King's left side;
    While I on sand and gravel sleep,
    And over my brother adders creep,
        And all without a tear."

"Now I come twice more, and then never again."

So next morning the kitchen-maid told what she had seen and heard, and the King said he'd

watch himself next Thursday night in the kitchen,
and see if it were true, and as soon as it got dark,
out he went into the kitchen to the kitchen-maid.
But all he could do, and however much he rubbed
his eyes and tried to keep himself awake, it was no
good ; for the Bushy Bride chaunted and sung till
his eyes closed, and so when the lovely lady came,
there he slept and snored. This time, too, as
before, she borrowed a brush, and brushed her
hair till the gold dropped, and sent her dog out
three times, and as soon as it was gray dawn,
away she went singing the same words, and
adding,—

"Now I come once more, and then never
again."

The third Thursday evening the King said he
would watch again ; and he set two men to hold
him, one under each arm, who were to shake and
jog him every time he wanted to fall asleep ; and
two men he set to watch his Bushy Bride. But
when the night wore on, the Bushy Bride began
to chaunt and sing, so that his eyes began to wink,
and his head hung down on his shoulders. Then
in came the lovely lady, and got the brush and
brushed her hair, till the gold dropped from it ;

2 A

after that she sent Little Flo out again to see if it
would soon be day, and this she did three times.
The third time it began to get gray in the east;
then she sang—

"Out on you, ugly Bushy Bride,
  Lying so warm by the King's left side:
  While I on sand and gravel sleep,
  And over my brother adders creep,
    And all without a tear."

"Now I come back never more," she said, and
went towards the door. But the two men who
held the King under the arms, clenched his hands
together, and put a knife into his grasp, and so,
somehow or other, they got him to cut her in her
little finger, and drew blood. Then the true bride
was freed, and the King woke up, and she told
him now the whole story, and how her stepmother
and sister had deceived her. So the King sent at
once and took her brother out of the pit of snakes,
and the adders hadn't done him the least harm,
but the stepmother and her daughter were thrown
into it in his stead.

And now no one can tell how glad the King
was to be rid of that ugly Bushy Bride, and to get
a Queen who was so lovely and bright as the day
itself. So the true wedding was held, and every

one talked of it over seven kingdoms; and then the King drove to church in their coach, and Little Flo went inside with them too, and when the blessing was given they drove back again, and after that I saw nothing more of them.

BOOTS AND HIS BROTHERS.

ONCE on a time there was a man who had three sons, Peter, Paul, and John. John was Boots, of course, because he was the youngest· I can't say the man had anything more than these three sons, for he hadn't one penny to rub against another; and so he told his sons over and over again they must go out into the world and try to earn their bread, for there at home there was nothing to be looked for but starving to death.

Now, a bit off the man's cottage was the king's palace, and you must know, just against the king's windows a great oak had sprung up, which was so stout and big that it took away all the light from the king's palace. The king had said he would give many, many dollars to the man who could fell the oak, but no one was man enough for that, for as soon as ever one chip of the oak's trunk flew off, two grew in its stead. A well, too, the King had dug, which was to hold water for the whole year; for all his neighbours had wells,

but he hadn't any, and that he thought a shame.
So the King said he would give any one who
could dig him such a well as would hold water for
a whole year round, both money and goods; but
no one could do it, for the king's palace lay high,
high up on a hill, and they hadn't dug a few inches,
before they came upon the living rock.

But as the King had set his heart on having
these two things done, he had it given out far and
wide, in all the churches of his kingdom, that he
who could fell the big oak in the king's court-yard,
and get him a well that would hold water the
whole year round, should have the Princess and
half the kingdom. Well! you may easily know
there was many a man who came to try his luck;
but for all their hacking and hewing, and all their
digging and delving, it was no good. The oak
got bigger and stouter at every stroke, and the
rock didn't get softer either. So one day those
three brothers thought they'd set off and try too,
and their father hadn't a word against it; for even
if they didn't get the Princess and half the kingdom, it might happen they might get a place
somewhere with a good master; and that was all
he wanted. So when the brothers said they

thought of going to the palace, their father said "yes" at once. So Peter, Paul, and Jack went off from their home.

Well! they hadn't gone far before they came to a fir-wood, and up along one side of it rose a steep hill-side, and as they went, they heard something hewing and hacking away up on the hill among the trees.

"I wonder now what it is that is hewing away up yonder?" said Jack.

"You're always so clever with your wonderings," said Peter and Paul both at once. "What wonder is it, pray, that a woodcutter should stand and hack up on a hillside?"

"Still, I'd like to see what it is, after all," said Jack; and up he went.

"Oh, if you're such a child, 'twill do you good to go and take a lesson," bawled ou this brothers after him.

But Jack didn't care for what they said; he climbed the steep hill-side towards where the noise came, and when he reached the place, what do you think he saw? why, an axe that stood there hacking and hewing, all of itself, at the trunk of a fir.

"Good day!" said Jack. "So you stand here all alone and hew, do you?"

"Yes; here I've stood and hewed and hacked a long long time, waiting for you," said the Axe.

"Well, here I am at last," said Jack, as he took the axe, pulled it off its haft, and stuffed both head and haft into his wallet.

So when he got down again to his brothers they began to jeer and laugh at him.

"And now, what funny thing was it you saw up yonder on the hill-side?" they said.

"Oh, it was only an axe we heard," said Jack.

So when they had gone a bit farther, they came under a steep spur of rock, and up there they heard something digging and shovelling.

"I wonder now," said Jack, "what it is digging and shovelling up yonder at the top of the rock."

"Ah, you're always so clever with your wonderings," said Peter and Paul again, "as if you'd never heard a woodpecker hacking and pecking at a hollow tree."

"Well, well," said Jack, "I think it would be a piece of fun just to see what it really is."

And so off he set to climb the rock, while the others laughed and made game of him. But he didn't care a bit for that; up he clomb, and when he got near the top, what do you think he saw? Why, a spade that stood there digging and delving.

"Good day!" said Jack. "So you stand here all alone, and dig and delve?"

"Yes, that's what I do," said the Spade, "and that's what I've done this many a long day, waiting for you."

"Well, here I am," said Jack again, as he took the spade and knocked it off its handle, and put it into his wallet, and then down again to his brothers.

"Well, what was it, so rare and strange," said Peter and Paul, "that you saw up there at the top of the rock?"

"Oh," said Jack, "nothing more than a spade; that was what we heard."

So they went on again a good bit, till they came to a brook. They were thirsty, all three, after their long walk, and so they lay down beside the brook to have a drink.

"I wonder now," said Jack, "where all this water comes from."

"I wonder if you're right in your head," said Peter and Paul, in one breath. "If you're not mad already, you'll go mad very soon, with your wonderings. Where the brook comes from, indeed! Have you never heard how water rises from a spring in the earth?"

"Yes! but still I've a great fancy to see where this brook comes from," said Jack.

So up alongside the brook he went, in spite of all that his brothers bawled after him. Nothing could stop him. On he went. So, as he went up and up, the brook got smaller and smaller, and at last, a little way farther on, what do you think he saw? Why, a great walnut, and out of that the water trickled.

"Good-day!" said Jack again. "So you lie here, and trickle and run down all alone?"

"Yes, I do," said the Walnut; "and here have I trickled and run this many a long day, waiting for you."

"Well, here I am," said Jack, as he took up a lump of moss, and plugged up the hole, that the water mightn't run out. Then he put the walnut into his wallet, and ran down to his brothers.

"Well now," said Peter and Paul, "have you found out where the water comes from? A rare sight it must have been!"

"Oh, after all, it was only a hole it ran out of," said Jack; and so the others laughed and made game of him again, but Jack didn't mind that a bit.

"After all I had the fun of seeing it," said he.

So when they had gone a bit further, they came to the king's palace; but as every one in the kingdom had heard how they might win the Princess and half the realm, if they could only fell the big oak and dig the king's well, so many had come to try their luck that the oak was now twice as stout and big as it had been at first, for two chips grew for every one they hewed out with their axes, as I dare say you all bear in mind. So the King had now laid it down as a punishment, that if any one tried and couldn't fell the oak, he should be put on a barren island, and both his ears were to be clipped off. But the two brothers didn't let themselves be scared by that; they were quite sure they could fell the oak, and Peter as he was eldest, was to try his hand first; but it went with him as with all the rest who had hewn at the oak; for every chip he cut out, two grew in its place. So the king's men seized him, and clipped off both his ears, and put him out on the island.

Now Paul, he was to try his luck, but he fared just the same; when he had hewn two or three strokes, they began to see the oak grow, and so the king's men seized him too, and clipped his ears, and put him out on the island ; and his ears they clipped closer, because they said he ought to have taken a lesson from his brother.

So now Jack was to try.

" If you *will* look like a marked sheep, we're quite ready to clip your ears at once, and then you'll save yourself some bother," said the King, for he was angry with him for his brothers' sake.

"Well, I'd like just to try first," said Jack, and so he got leave. Then he took his axe out of his wallet and fitted it to its haft.

" Hew away !" said he to his axe ; and away it hewed, making the chips fly again, so that it wasn't long before down came the oak.

When that was done, Jack pulled out his spade, and fitted it to its handle.

" Dig away !" said he to the spade ; and so the spade began to dig and delve till the earth and rock flew out in splinters, and so he had the well soon dug out, you may think.

And when he had got it as big and deep as he chose, Jack took out his walnut and laid it in one corner of the well, and pulled the plug of moss out.

" Trickle and run," said Jack ; and so the nut trickled and ran, till the water gushed out of the hole in a stream, and in a short time the well was brimfull.

Then Jack had felled the oak which shaded the king's palace, and dug a well in the palace-yard, and so he got the Princess and half the kingdom, as the King had said ; but it was lucky for Peter and Paul that they had lost their ears, else they had heard each hour and day, how every one said, " Well, after all, Jack wasn't so much out of his mind when he took to wondering."

FINIS.

Works by the Same Author.

The Story of Burnt Njal; or, Life in
Iceland at the end of the Tenth Century. From the
Icelandic of the Njals Saga. By G. W. DASENT, D.C.L.
In 2 vols. 8vo, with Maps and Plans, price 28s.

"Considered as a picture of manners, customs, and characters, the
Njala has a merit equal in our eyes to that of the Homeric poems themselves."—*Edinburgh Review, October* 1861.

"The majority of English readers would have been surprised to be
told that in the literature of Iceland there was preserved a story of life and
manners in the heroic age, which for simple force and truthfulness is, as
far as we know, unequalled in European history and poetry, and is not
unworthy of being compared, not indeed for its poetic richness and power,
but for the insight which it gives into ancient society, with the Homeric
poems."—*Guardian, May* 1.

"A work, of which we gladly repeat the judgment of a distinguished
American writer, that it is unsurpassed by any existing monument in the
narrative department of any literature, ancient or modern."—*Saturday
Review.*

"An historical romance of the tenth century, first narrated almost
at the very time and by the very people to whom it refers, nearly true as
to essential facts, and quite true in its pictures of the customs and the
temper of the old Norsemen, about whom it tells, is in these volumes edited
with the soundest scholarship by Dr. Dasent. There was need of a
thorough study of the life and language of the early colonists of Iceland
for the effective setting forth of this Njala, or saga of Njal."—*Examiner,
March* 30.

"This 'Story of Burnt Njal' is worthy of the translator of the Norse
Tales: a work of interest to the antiquary and the lover of legendary
lore—that is, to every one capable of appreciating those sources of
history which are at once the most poetic and the most illustrative of the
character and growth of nations. The events of the story happened while
the conflict of the two creeds of Christ and Odin was yet going on in
the minds of the Northmen. We must pass the book over to the reader's
attentive consideration, for there are few portions of it that are not pregnant with interest and instruction for a reflective mind."—*Athenæum.*

Popular Tales from the Norse. Second
Edition, greatly Enlarged, Price 10s. 6d., containing
Thirteen New Tales, and an Appendix consisting of
Ananzi Stories, as told by the Negroes in the West
Indies.

Contents of Introduction.

I. The ORIGIN OF POPULAR TALES—Comparative
Philology—the Aryan Race.

II. DIFFUSION OF POPULAR TALES—Tell's Master-
shot and Gellert's Grave—Sanscrit Literature—the Pantcha Tantra,
and Calila and Dimna, Somadeva's Stories—Modern African and
Ananzi Stories—Origin of Human Race.

III. NORSE MYTHOLOGY—The Æsir and Frost Giants
—The Wondrous Volsung Tale (The Elder Version of the Nibe-
lungen Lied)—The Norseman's Gods and Faith—Christianity in
the North—The Heathen Gods—The Wild Huntsman—The
Church of Rome.

IV. NORSE POPULAR TALES—The Gods on Earth
—Heathen Gods in Christian Garb—The Norseman's God—The
God of Wish and Wishing Things—Frodi's Quern—The Devil and
Hel—The Norseman's Hell—Dame Habonde and Herodias—
Witchcraft and the Mediæval Witch—Transformation into Beasts-
Were Wolves—Were Bears—The Beast Epic in the North—The
Wolf, Horse, Bull, Dog—The Goat and Little Birds—Giants and
Trolls—The Trolls are Finns and Lapps—The Naked Sword.

V. CONCLUSION—Literature of Popular Tales
Characters in Norse Tales—Norse Nature.

"The loves and feuds of the Powers of Nature, after they had been told,
first of gods, then of heroes, appear in the tales of the people as the flirting
and teasing of fairies and imps. Christianity had destroyed the old gods of the
Teutonic tribes, and supplied new heroes in the saints and martyrs of the
Church. The gods were dead, and the heroes, the sons of the gods, forgotten.
But the stories told of them would not die, and in spite of the excommunications

of the priests, they were welcomed wherever they appeared in their strange disguises. Kind-hearted grannies would tell the pretty stories of old, if it was only to keep their little folk quiet. They did not tell them of the gods ; for those gods were dead ; or, worse than that, had been changed into devils. They told them of nobody ; ay, sometimes they would tell them of the very saints and martyrs, and the apostles themselves have had to wear some of the old rags that belonged by right to Odin and other heathen gods. The oddest figure is that of the Devil in his half-Christian and half-heathen garb. The Aryan nations had no Devil. Pluto, though of a sombre character, was a very respectable personage ; and Loki, though a mischievous person, was not a fiend. The German goddess, Hell, too—like Proserpina—had once seen better days. Thus, when the Germans were indoctrinated with the idea of a real Devil, the Semitic Satan or Diabolus, they treated him in the most good-humoured manner. They ascribed to him all the mischievous tricks of their most mischievous gods. But while the old Northern story-tellers delighted in the success of cunning, the new generation felt in duty bound to represent the Devil in the end as always defeated. He was outwitted in all the tricks which had formerly proved successful, and thus quite a new character was produced—the poor or stupid Devil, who appears not unfrequently in the German and in Norwegian tales.

All this Mr. Dasent has described very tersely and graphically in his Introduction, and we recommend the readers of his tales not to treat that Introduction as most introductions are treated."—*Saturday Review, January* 15, 1859.

APPENDIX—Ananzi Stories.

Why the Jack Spaniard's Waist is Small—Ananzi and the Lion—Ananzi and Quanqua—The Ear of Corn and the Twelve Men—The King and the Ant's Tree—The Little Child and the Pumpkin Tree—The Brother and his Sisters—The Girl and the Fish—The Lion, the Goat, and the Baboon—Ananzi and Baboon—The Man and the Doukana Tree—Nancy Fairy—The Dancing Gang.

In preparation.

The Prose, or Younger Edda. Commonly ascribed to Snorri Sturluson. Translated from the Old Norse, by GEORGE WEBBE DASENT, D.C.L. A New Edition, with an Introduction, in one volume crown 8vo.

Books Suitable for Children.

In One Vol., fcap. 8vo, Price 5s.

Aunt Ailie, by the late Catherine D.
Bell, Author of "Cousin Kate's Story," etc. etc. etc.

Second Edition 16mo., Cloth, Price 3s. 6d. Cloth, Extra Gilt, 4s.

Little Ella and the Fire-King, and
other Fairy Tales, by M. W., with Illustrations by Henry Warren.

In fcap. 8vo, with Coloured Illustrations, Price 5s.

The Diary of Three Children; or,
Fifty-Two Saturdays.

In One Vol., Small 4to, with Illustrations by J. B.

History of Sir Thomas Thumb, by
the Author of "The Heir of Redcliffe," "Hearts-ease," "Little Duke," etc. etc.

Royal 16mo, Price 3s. 6d.

Charlie and Ernest; or, Play and
Work. A story of Hazlehurst School, with four Illustrations by J. D.

4to, Boards, Price 2s. 6d.

The Giants, the Knights, and the
Princess Verbena. A fairy story, with Illustrations by Hunkil Phranc.

LIST OF WORKS

PUBLISHED BY

EDMONSTON AND DOUGLAS,

88 Princes Street, Edinburgh.

———•———

Lord Dunfermline.

Memoir of Lieutenant-General Sir Ralph
Abercromby, K. B., 1793-1801. By his Son James Lord Dunfermline. In 1 vol. demy 8vo.

> "It is peculiarly refreshing to meet with a biography of an individual so illustrious as Sir Ralph Abercromby, from the pen of one so eminent in many respects as the late Lord Dunfermline."—*Caledonian Mercury,* October 3.

> "His grandson, the present Lord Dunfermline, by causing this memoir to be printed and published, has conferred a benefit upon all—and they are fortunately many—who treasure the memory of distinguished men."—*Literary Gazette, October 5.*

John Abercrombie, M.D., Late First Physician to the Queen for Scotland.

Essays and Tracts :—

I. Culture and Discipline of the Mind.
II. Harmony of Christian Faith and Christian Character.
III. Think on these things.
IV. The Contest and the Armour.
V. The Messiah as an Example.
VI. Elements of Sacred Truth for the Young.

Fcap. 8vo, cloth, 3s. 6d.

JOHN ANDERSON, D.D., F.G.S., E.P.S., &c., Author of
'The Course of Creation,' 'Geology of Scotland,' &c.

Dura Den, a Monograph of the Yellow Sandstone and its remarkable Fossil remains. Royal 8vo, cloth, 10s. 6d.

Archæological Catalogue :—

A Catalogue of Antiquities, Works of Arts, and Historical
Scottish Relics, exhibited in Museum of the Archæological
Institute of Great Britain and Ireland during their annual
meeting, held in Edinburgh, July 1856, under the
patronage of H. R. H. The Prince Consort, K.G., comprising notices of the portraits of Mary Queen of Scots, collected on that occasion. Illustrated, royal 8vo, cloth, 21s.

Angelo Sanmartino, a Tale of Lombardy in 1859. Crown 8vo, cloth, 10s. 6d.

" A pretty story enough, and vraisemblable enough for the effect desired
to be produced by the author, which is to awaken in the minds of ordinary English novel readers a lively feeling for the cause of Italian independence."—*Spectator, December* 29.

" We admire the character of Angelo, and heartily commend it to
public favour; it is admirably written; the subject is one dear to every
lover of freedom and honour.—*Commonwealth, December* 15, 1860.

Odal Rights and Feudal Wrongs: a Memorial for Orkney. By DAVID BALFOUR of Balfour and Trenaby. 1 vol. 8vo, price 6s.

" We gather from the book that Mr. Balfour is an Orcadian Laird,
Odaller, or whatever the proper title may be now-a-days. Certainly he
is a sound and careful antiquary, well versed in the local history of the
old Jarldom, and fully entitled to a hearing for anything which he may
say about it."—*Saturday Review, March* 1861.

" To antiquarians, and especially those connected with Orkney, this
book will be a rich acquisition.— *Orkney Herald, October* 23, 1860.

" This book is an interesting contribution to Scottish history."—
Athenæum, January 27.

JAMES BALLANTINE.

Poems. Fcap. 8vo, cloth extra, 3s. 6d.

R. M. BALLANTYNE.

How Not to Do It. A Manual for the
Awkward Squad; or, A Handbook of Directions, written for the instruction of Raw Recruits in our Rifle Volunteer Regiments. With Illustrations. Fcap., sewed, 6d.

The Volunteer Levee; or, the Remarkable
Experience of Ensign Sopht. Written and Illustrated by Himself. Edited by the Author of 'How Not to do It.' Fcap. 8vo, sewed, 1s.

CATHARINE D. BELL, Author of 'Cousin Kate's Story,' 'Margaret Cecil,' &c.

Aunt Ailie. Fcap. 8vo, cloth, 5s.

The Diary of Three Children; or, Fifty-two
Saturdays. Fcap. 8vo, 5s.

M. BETHAM EDWARDS, Author of ' The White House by the Sea.'

Now or Never, a Novel. Crown 8vo, 10s. 6d.

Charlie and Ernest; or, Play and Work. A
Story of Hazlehurst School, with Four Illustrations by J. D. Royal 16mo, 3s. 6d.

J. B.

British Birds drawn from Nature. By Mrs.
BLACKBURN. In 1 vol. folio.

JOHN STUART BLACKIE.

On Beauty. Three discourses delivered in
the University of Edinburgh, with an Exposition of the Doctrine of the Beautiful according to Plato. By J. S. BLACKIE, Professor of Greek in the University, and of Ancient Literature to the Royal Scottish Academy, Edinburgh. Crown 8vo, cloth, 8s. 6d.

Lyrical Poems. By J. S. Blackie. Crown
8vo, cloth, 7s. 6d.

On Greek Pronunciation. By J. S. Blackie.
Demy 8vo, 3s. 6d.

Sir DAVID BREWSTER, K. H., A. M., LL. D., D. C. L , F. R. S., &c., &c.

Memoirs of the Life, Writings, and Dis-
coveries of Sir Isaac Newton. With Portraits. New and Cheaper Edition, 2 vols., fcap. 8vo, cloth, 12s.

"Sir David Brewster's 'Life of Sir Isaac Newton' is a valuable contribution to English literature. It is an account of the life, writings, and discoveries of one of the greatest men that ever lived, by a gentleman distinguished for his profound scholarship and scientific knowledge. The book is worthy of the subject to which it is devoted."—*London Review, December* 15.

"Such works as Sir David Brewster's careful, though rather partial, biography, are of the utmost value in presenting a faithful summary of all that materially illustrates the character of the mind of our great philosopher."—*Quarterly Review, October* 1861.

MARGARET MARIA GORDON (BREWSTER).

Lady Elinor Mordaunt ; or, Sunbeams in the
Castle. Crown 8vo, cloth, 9s.

" To say of this book, that it is written in a style which is worthy of its theme is no greater praise than it merits."—*Morning Post, January* 10.

" The kindly and generous spirit of the book, its quiet and impressive religiousness, the earnestness which characterizes every page, and the sunny cheerfulness which make it the pleasantest of reading, cannot fail to endear it to many of those for whom it has been written. We thank Mrs. Gordon for this last and best of her books most sincerely and cordially."— *The Scottish Press, January* 9.

Letters from Cannes and Nice. Illustrated
by a Lady. 8vo, cloth, 12s.

Work ; or, Plenty to do and How to do it.
Thirty-second thousand. Fcap. 8vo, cloth, 2s. 6d.

Little Millie and her Four Places. Fcap.
8vo, cloth, 3s. 6d.
——————— Cheap Edition. Forty-second thousand. Limp, 1s.

Sunbeams in the Cottage ; or, What Women
may do. A narrative chiefly addressed to the Working Classes. Cheap Edition. Thirty-sixth thousand. Cloth limp, 1s.

The Word and the World. Tenth Edition,
18mo, sewed, 2d.

Leaves of Healing for the Sick and Sorrowful.
Fcap. 4to, cloth, 3s. 6d.

The Motherless Boy ; with an Illustration by
J. Noel Paton, R.S.A. Cheap Edition, limp cloth, 1s.

Rev. James D. Burns, M.A.

The Vision of Prophecy, and other Poems.
Second Edition, fcap. 8vo, cloth, 6s.

John Brown, M.D., F.R.S.E.

Horæ Subsecivæ; Locke and Sydenham,
with other occasional Papers.   2 vols., fcap. 8vo, 7s. 6d. each.

"Of all the John Browns commend us to Dr. John Brown—the physician, the man of genius, the humourist, the student of men, women, and dogs. By means of two beautiful volumes he has given the public a share of his bye-hours, and more pleasant hours than these it would be difficult to find in any life.

"Dr. Brown's masterpiece is the story of a dog called 'Rab.' The tale moves from the most tragic pathos to the most reckless humour, and could not have been written but by a man of genius. Whether it moves tears or laughter, it is perfect in its way, and immortalizes its author."—*Times, October* 21, 1861.

"With his pen Dr. Brown has depicted dogs as powerfully and humanly as Landseer has done with his pencil."—*Oriental Budget, April* 1, 1861.

"The work now before us will be so generally read in Scotland that it is superfluous to describe its contents to the public."—*Courant, June* 6, 1861.

Supplementary Chapter to the Life of the
Rev. John Brown, D.D.   A Letter to the Rev. John Cairns, D.D.   Second Edition, crown 8vo, sewed, 2s.

"It forms an indispensable appendix to the admirable memoir of Dr. Cairns, and it will, if possible, increase the love with which Dr. Brown's memory is cherished."—*Scottish Guardian, January* 5.

"There is a fresh luxuriance in the style, that charms and fascinates the reader."—*Glasgow Saturday Post, January* 5.

Rab and his Friends; Extracted from 'Horæ
Subsecivæ.'   Eighteenth thousand.   Fcap. sewed, 6d.

Rab and his Friends. By John Brown, M.D.
With Illustrations by George Harvey, R.S.A., J. Noel Paton, R.S.A., and J. B.   In 1 vol. small 4to, price 6s.

"With Brains, Sir;" Extracted from 'Horæ

Subsecivæ.' Fourth thousand. Fcap. sewed, 6d.

JOHN CAIRNS, D.D.

Memoirs of John Brown, D.D., senior Minister

of the United Presbyterian Congregation, Broughton Place,
Edinburgh, and Professor of Exegetical Theology to the
United Presbyterian Church, with Supplementary Chapter
by his Son, John Brown, M.D.   Fcap. 8vo, cloth, 9s. 6d.

"The Memoir is exceedingly well written." "Every one should
read the last chapter of Dr. Cairns' Memoir, giving an account of the
closing scene of Dr. Brown's life."—*Scotsman, September* 11.

"In preparing and publishing these memoirs, Dr. Cairns has conferred
upon us a most valuable gift, and has fulfilled his own part with great
discrimination and ability "—*Evan. Christendom.*

SAMUEL BROWN.

Lectures on the Atomic Theory, and Essays,

Scientific and Literary, 2 vols., crown 8vo, cloth, 15s.

Rev. JOHN BRUCE, D.D., Minister of Free St. Andrew's Church, Edinburgh.

The Biography of Samson.   Illustrated and

Applied.   Second Edition.   18mo, cloth, 2s.

J. F. CAMPBELL.

Popular Tales of the West Highlands, orally

collected, with a Translation by J. F. Campbell.   2 vols.,
extra fcap., cloth, 16s.

"Mr. Campbell has published a collection of tales, which will be
regarded as one of the greatest literary surprises of the present century.
It is the first instalment of what was to be expected from any fair state-
ment of the scientific value of popular tales. . . . It required some
striking demonstration of the real worth of popular tales to arouse Gaelic
scholars from their apathy. They have been aroused, and here is the first
fruit, in a work that is most admirably edited by the head of a family
beloved and honoured in those breezy western isles, who has produced a

book which will be equally prized in the nursery, in the drawing-room, and in the library."—*Times, November 5th.*

"They are the 'Arabian Nights of Celtic Scotland,' and as such we recommend them as a present for the young."—*Critic, November 24th.*

"We feel assured that Mr. Campbell's labours will be rewarded with such signal success as shall encourage him to extend them in every direction over the rich field which he has been the first to explore and cultivate."—*Spectator, November 24th.*

"The book is one that no modern student can afford to miss, and that few persons of any age or degree of culture would not come to again and again.—*Daily News, December 28th.*

A New Volume of West Highland Tales. By
J. F. CAMPBELL.   Crown 8vo.   [*In the press.*

F. H. CARTER.

Book-keeping, adapted to Commercial and
Judicial Accounting, with Styles.   By F. H. CARTER, Member of the Society of Chartered Accountants, Edinburgh.   8vo, cloth, price 10s.

Rev. THOMAS CHALMERS, D.D., LL.D.

Life and Works of Rev. Thomas Chalmers;
Memoirs by Rev. W. Hanna, LL.D.   4 vols., 8vo, cloth, £2 : 2s.

————Cheap Edition, 2 vols., crown 8vo, cloth, 12s.

A Selection from the Correspondence of Dr.
Chalmers, uniform with the Memoirs.   Crown 8vo, cloth, 10s. 6d.

Posthumous Works, 9 vols., 8vo.—

Daily Scripture Readings. 3 vols., £1:11:6.
Sabbath Scripture Readings. 2 vols., £1:1s.
Sermons. 1 vol., 10s. 6d.
Institutes of Theology. 2 vols., £1:1s.
Prelections on Butler's Analogy, etc. 1 vol., 10s. 6d.

Sabbath Scripture Readings. *Cheap Edition,* 2 vols., crown 8vo, 10s.

Daily Scripture Readings. *Cheap Edition,* 2 vols., crown 8vo, 10s.

Astronomical Discourses. *New Edition,* cloth, 2s. 6d.

Lectures on the Romans. 2 vols., crown 8vo, 12s.
Institutes of Theology. 2 vols., crown 8vo, 12s.
Political Economy. Crown 8vo, 6s.
Select Works, in 12 vols., crown 8vo, cloth, per vol. 6s.

Vols. I. and II.—Lectures on the Romans, 2 vols.
Vols. III. and IV.—Sermons, 2 vols.
Vol. V.—Natural Theology, Lectures on Butler's Analogy, &c.
Vol. VI.—Christian Evidences, Lectures on Paley's Evidences, &c.
Vols. VII. and VIII.—Institutes of Theology, 2 vols.
Vol. IX.—Political Economy ; with Cognate Essays.
Vol. X.—Polity of a Nation.
Vol. XI.—Church and College Establishments.
Vol. XII.—Moral Philosophy, Introductory Essays, Index, &c.

Characteristics of Old Church Architecture,

etc., in the Mainland and Western Islands of Scotland.
In one vol. 4to, with Illustrations, price 25s.

" Alighting on a book that has discoveries in it is pretty nearly as
good as making the discoveries for one's self. In either case, there is an
impulse to come forward and let the fact be known, lest some other should
be the first to make the revelation. It is thus that we are tempted, with
more than usual promptitude, to notice this book, which contains valuable
and striking novelties from an untrodden archæological ground. . . .
That something might be found in the west had been hinted, in accounts
of some curious relics, by Professor Innes and his friend, Dr. Reeves, but
it has fallen to the author of the present volume to go thoroughly to work
and excavate the neglected treasure."—*Scotsman, April* 24.

" This volume certainly fulfils its title, and gives us an excellent idea
of the Characteristics of the Ancient Religious Architecture of the Mainland and Western Isles of Scotland."—*Saturday Review, July* 27, 1861.

NATHANIEL CULVERWELL, M.A.

Of the Light of Nature, a Discourse by

Nathaniel Culverwell, M.A. Edited by John Brown, D.D.,
with a critical Essay on the Discourse by John Cairns, D.D.
8vo, cloth, 12s.

PROFESSOR DALZEL.

The Annals of the University of Edinburgh.

By ANDREW DALZEL, formerly Professor of Greek in the
University of Edinburgh ; with a Memoir of the Compiler,
and Portrait after Raeburn. In one vol. demy 8vo.

[*In preparation.*

GEORGE WEBBE DASENT, D.C.L.

The Story of Burnt Njal; or, Life in Iceland

at the end of the Tenth Century. From the Icelandic of
the Njals Saga. By G. W. DASENT, D.C.L. In 2 vols.
8vo, with Maps and Plans, price 28s.

" Considered as a picture of manners, customs, and characters, the
Njala has a merit equal in our eyes to that of the Homeric poems themselves."—*Edinburgh Review, October* 1861.

" The majority of English readers would have been surprised to be
told that in the literature of Iceland there was preserved a story of life and
manners in the heroic age, which for simple force and truthfulness is, as
far as we know, unequalled in European history and poetry, and is not
unworthy of being compared, not indeed for its poetic richness and power,
but for the insight which it gives into ancient society, with the Homeric
poems."—*Guardian, May* 1.

" A work, of which we gladly repeat the judgment of a distinguished
American writer, that it is unsurpassed by any existing monument in the
narrative department of any literature, ancient or modern."—*Saturday
Review.*

" An historical romance of the tenth century, first narrated almost at
the very time and by the very people to whom it refers, nearly true as to
essential facts, and quite true in its pictures of the customs and the temper
of the old Norsemen, about whom it tells, is in these volumes edited with
the soundest scholarship by Dr. Dasent. There was need of a thorough
study of the life and language of the early colonists of Iceland for the
effective setting forth of this Njala, or saga of Njal."—*Examiner, March* 30.

" This ' Story of Burnt Njal' is worthy of the translator of the Norse
Tales: a work of interest to the antiquary and the lover of legendary lore—
that is, to every one capable of appreciating those sources of history which
are at once the most poetic and the most illustrative of the character and
growth of nations. The events of the story happened while the conflict
of the two creeds of Christ and Odin was yet going on in the minds of
the Northmen. We must pass the book over to the reader's attentive
consideration, for there are few portions of it that are not pregnant with
interest and instruction for a reflective mind."—*Athenæum.*

" Hurriedly and imperfectly as we have traced the course of this tale
divine, it must be evident to all who have accompanied us in our progress
that there is real Homeric stuff in it. The Saga has a double value, an
æsthetic and an historic value. Through it we may learn how men
and women in Iceland, near a thousand years ago, lived, loved, and
died."—*Spectator, April* 20.

" Mr. Dasent has given us a thoroughly faithful and accurate translation of the ' Njala; or, the Story of Njal,' the longest and certainly the
best of all the Icelandic Sagas. The style is that pure Saxon idiom with
which the readers of his ' Norse Popular Tales' are familiar. To the
translation are prefixed disquisitions on Iceland; its religion, constitution,
and public and private life; and the appendix contains a very amusing
essay on piracy and the Vikings, the biography of Gunnhillda, the wicked
queen of Eric of the Bloody-axe, king of Norway, and afterwards warder
of Northumberland, and a disquisition on the old Icelandic currency."—
Times, April 8.

GEORGE WEBBE DASENT, D.C.L.

Popular Tales from the Norse, with an Introductory Essay on the origin and diffusion of Popular Tales. Second Edition, enlarged. Crown 8vo, 10s. 6d.

A Selection from Dasent's Popular Tales from the Norse. With Illustrations. 1 vol. crown 8vo.

The Prose, or Younger Edda. Commonly ascribed to Snorri Sturluson. Translated from the Old Norse, by GEORGE WEBBE DASENT, D.C.L. A New Edition, with an Introduction, in one volume, crown 8vo.

[*In preparation.*

JAMES DODDS.

The Fifty Years' Struggle of the Scottish Covenanters, 1638-88. Third Edition, fcap., cloth, 5s.

"The volume before us is by a Mr. Dodds, with whose name we were not previously acquainted. His Lectures on the Covenanters were addressed to popular audiences, and they are calculated to be exceedingly popular. . . . They have merits of their own; they are in passages very eloquent; they are full of graphic touches; they appeal with no small success to our sympathies; and, though we cannot endorse the leading idea of the book, we must do it all honour as an advance upon previous ideas on the same subject."—*Times.*

"This is an excellent little book, written in a large-hearted, earnest, pious, and thoroughly manly spirit. . . . . The style is forcible, graphic, and robust; now and then perhaps a little stiff, sometimes pseudo-rhetorical, but, in general, well suited to the subject. . . . . These men, whatever be the reader's prepossessions, are really worth reading about. There was manhood in them."—*Spectator.*

DUNBAR.

From London to Nice. A Journey through France, and Winter in the Sunny South. By Rev. W. B. DUNBAR, of Glencairn. 12mo, cloth, price 3s.

Edinburgh University Calendar, 1861-1862,

Corrected to October 15, 1861, and containing all the new Lists for Examination in Medicine and Arts. Authorized by the Senatus Academicus. 12mo, price 1s. 6d.

M. LAMÉ FLEURY, Auteur de plusieurs ouvrages d'education.

L'Histoire d'Angleterre racontée à la Jeu-

nesse, augmentée d'une table analitique. 18mo, cloth, 2s. 6d.

L'Histoire de France, racontée à la Jeunesse.

18mo, cloth, 2s. 6d.

Rev. A. L. R. FOOTE, author of "Incidents in the Life of our Saviour."

Christianity viewed in some of its Leading

Aspects. Fcap., cloth, 3s.

" It may seem high praise, when we state that sometimes, in the freshness, breadth, and definiteness of the author's thinking, we have been reminded of the posthumous lecture of Foster."—*News of the Churches.*

Fragments of Truth, being the exposition of

several passages of Scripture. Third Edition. Fcap. 8vo., cloth, price 5s.

DR. W. T. GAIRDNER.

Public Health in relation to Air and Water.

By W. T. GAIRDNER, M.D., Fellow of the Royal College of Physicians, Edinburgh, and Lecturer on the Practice of Medicine. In one vol. fcap. 8vo.

By same Author.

Medicine and Medical Education. Three

Lectures, with Notes and Appendix. 12mo, cloth, price 2s. 6d.

Clinical and Pathological Notes on Pericarditis.
8vo, sewed, price 1s.

ARCHIBALD GEIKIE of the Geological Survey of Great
Britain.

The Story of a Boulder, or Gleanings from the
Note Book of a Field Geologist. Illustrated with wood-
cuts. Fcap., cloth, 5s.

"We do not know a more readable book on a scientific subject, and it
will be invaluable to young people, as well as interesting to those who
are already acquainted with the subject it treats of."— *Clerical Journal.*

The Giants, the Knights, and the Princess
Verbena. A Fairy Story, with illustrations by Hunkil
Phranc. 4to, boards, 2s. 6d.

GEORGE GRUB, A.M.

An Ecclesiastical History of Scotland, from
the Introduction of Christianity to the Present Time. By
GEORGE GRUB, A.M. In 4 vols., demy 8vo, 42s. Fine
Paper Copies, 52s. 6d.

Rev. WILLIAM HANNA, LL.D., author of 'Memoirs of
Thomas Chalmers, D.D., LL.D.'

Wycliffe and the Huguenots; or, Sketches of
the rise of the Reformation in England, and of the Early
History of Protestantism in France. Fcap., cloth, 5s.

The Healing Art, the Right Hand of the
Church : or, Practical Medicine an Essential Element in
the Christian System. Crown 8vo, cloth, price 5s.

Homely Hints from the Fireside, by the
author of 'Little Things.' Fcap., cloth, 2s.

> "A collection of excellent counsel on everyday subjects."—*Courant.*
>
> "Many readers will be grateful for its advice, and delighted with its homeliness and pleasant gossip."—*Scottish Press.*
>
> "This little volume contains many 'homely hints' of the most truly valuable kind."—*Falkirk Herald.*
>
> "Some of the 'hints' will be found most acceptable to those who have to regulate the domestic economy of a household, whether large or small; and other parts of the book contain advice which cannot fail to be of service to most people."—*Court Journal.*

Miss SUSAN HORNER, translator of 'Colletas Naples.'

A Century of Despotism in Naples and Sicily,
1759-1859. Fcap., cloth, 2s. 6d.

COSMO INNES, Professor of History in the University of Edinburgh.

Sketches of Early Scottish Social Life. By
Professor C. INNES. Contents : 1. On the Old Scotch Law of Marriage and Divorce.   2. A Sketch of the State of Society before and immediately after the Reformation in Scotland.   3. A Chapter on Old Scotch Topography and Statistics.

Scotland in the Middle Ages. Sketches of
Early Scotch History and Social Progress.   By Professor C. INNES.   With Maps Illustrative of the Civil and Ecclesiastical Divisions in the Tenth and Thirteenth Centuries. 8vo, cloth, 10s. 6d.

> "All who wish to learn what early Scotland really was, will prize it highly."—*Scotsman, January 7.*
>
> "The students of the Edinburgh University have reason to be congratulated on the qualities of their Professor of History, and the general public ought to be thankful for this volume." . . . "More of real history may here be learned in a few hours than from some more pretentious works in as many weeks; and, what is still better, ingenuous youth, if ingenuous indeed, will here take a noble enthusiasm, which will stimulate to long, laborious, and delightful research."—*Dial, November 9.*

Sketches of Early Scotch History. By COSMO INNES, F.S.A., Professor of History in the University of Edinburgh. 1. The Church; its Old Organisation, Parochial and Monastic. 2. Universities. 3. Family History. In one vol., 8vo, price 16s.

" It is since Scottish writers have abandoned the search of a lost political history, have dropped their enthusiasm for a timid and turbulent ecclesiastical history, and have been content to depict the domestic annals of the people, to enter their shops and their houses, to follow them in the streets and the fields, and to record their every-day life—their eating and their drinking, their dress, their pleasures, their marriages, their wealth and their science—that Scottish history has become an enticing study. . . . In this new path none has been more active than Mr. Cosmo Innes." —*Times, April* 3.

" This is a valuable collection of materials, from which future historians of Scotland may extract a solid basis for many portions of their work. . . . . This recapitulation of the contents of the volume before us shews that it is a treasury of valuable documents, from which may be framed a better domestic history of Scotland during the middle ages than we yet possess. It reveals many inner characteristics of a shrewd, enterprising, yet cautious people, as they were floating down the stream of time to blend with their co-civic races in an amicable fusion of political interests."—*Morning Post, April* 8.

" Mr. INNES, who is favourably known to us as the author of a work entitled ' Scotland in the Middle Ages,' has attempted, in his ' *Sketches of Early Scotch History*,' to open up the still tangled wild of his country's annals, down to a later period, joining modern thought and customs to mediæval beliefs and usages. . . . Of the home life in Scotland, Mr. Innes gives us some very attractive notices, passing in review no less than four collections of family documents—the Morton, the Breadalbane, the Cawdor, and the Kilravock papers. Abounding, as these papers do, in social illustrations, and sketching, as they do, the character and spirit of the age, the condition and customs of the people, they cannot fail to instruct and entertain. Touches of reality, pleasant bits of gossip, records of wind and weather, household doings and sayings, are all to be found scattered over these family papers."—*Spectator, April* 6.

. . . . " The length of our quotations prevents us from dwelling on the encomiums this work so really deserves. The charms of literary composition are hardly expected in antiquarian researches. Knowledge and judgment are more looked for, but how well Mr. Innes has combined acumen with the power of investing his subject with interest, the most casual inspection will prove. He has added an important volume to the literature of his country, and doubtless will have many followers in a branch of authorship which is at once instructive and amusing."—*Glasgow Courier, March* 28.

Concerning Some Scotch Surnames. 1 vol.,
small 4to, cloth antique, 5s.

> "We can safely recommend this volume to those who are interested in the subject."—*Caledonian Mercury, October* 26.
>
> "Those fond of etymological pursuits will find in it matter to interest them; and the general reader cannot open it without finding in it something that will suit even his capricious taste."—*Atlas, October* 27.

Instructive Picture Books. 3 vols., folio,
boards, 10s. 6d. each.

I.

The Instructive Picture Book. A few Attractive Lessons from the Natural History of Animals. By ADAM WHITE, Assistant, Zoological Department, British Museum. With 58 folio coloured Plates. Fourth Edition, containing many new Illustrations by J. B., J. Stewart, and others.

II.

The Instructive Picture Book. Lessons from the Vegetable World. By the Author of "The Heir of Redcliffe," "The Herb of the Field," &c. 62 folio coloured Plates, arranged by Robert M. Stark, Edinburgh.

III

The Instructive Picture Book. Lessons from the Geographical Distribution of Animals; or, The Natural History of the Quadrupeds which Characterize the Principal Divisions of the Globe. By M. H. H. J. 60 folio coloured Illustrations.

The New Picture Book. Pictorial Lessons
on Form, Comparison, and Number, for Children under Seven Years of Age. With Explanations by NICHOLAS BOHNY. 36 oblong folio coloured Illustrations. Price 10s. 6d.

DR. IRVING.

The History of Scottish Poetry, from the
Middle Ages to the Close of the Seventeenth Century. By the late DAVID IRVING, LL.D. Edited by JOHN AITKEN

CARLYLE, M.D. With a Memoir and Glossary. In one vol. demy 8vo, 16s.

> " Such a book was demanded to supply a gap in Scottish literature, and being executed with adequate knowledge of the subject, must be recognised as a standard work.—*Spectator, October* 19.
> " The book seems to us to exhaust the subject, and is therefore of permanent value."—*Dumfries Herald, October* 25.

LORD KINLOCH.

A Hand-book of Faith, framed out of a Layman's experience. By the Honourable LORD KINLOCH. Second Edition. In one volume, fcap. 8vo, price 4s. 6d.

Dr. J. G. KURR, Professor of Natural History in the Polytechnic Institution of Stuttgart.

The Mineral Kingdom, with Coloured Illustrations of the most important Minerals, Rocks, and Petrefactions, folio, half-bound, 31s. 6d.

THE DEAN OF LISMORE'S BOOK.

Specimens of Ancient Gaelic Poetry. Collected between the years 1512 and 1529 by the Rev. JAMES M'GREGOR, Dean of Lismore—illustrative of the Language and Literature of the Scottish Highlands prior to the Sixteenth Century. Edited, with a Translation and Notes, by the Rev. THOMAS MACLAUCHLAN. The Introduction and additional Notes by WILLIAM F. SKENE. In one vol. demy 8vo.

Little Ella and the Fire-King, and other Fairy Tales, by M. W., with Illustrations by Henry Warren. Second Edition. 16mo, cloth, 3s. 6d. Cloth extra, gilt edges, 4s.

Rev. Norman M‘Leod, D.D.

The Earnest Student; being Memorials of

John Mackintosh. By the Rev. Norman M‘Leod, D.D.
10th Edition, fcap., cloth, 6s.

"Full of the most instructive materials, and admirably compiled. We
are sure that a career of unusual popularity awaits it. Nor can any
student peruse it without being quickened by its example of candour,
assiduity, and happy self-consecration."—*Excelcior*.

Deborah; or Christian Principles for Domes-

tic Servants; with Extract Readings for the Fireside.
Fcap., cloth, 3s. 6d. Cheap Edition, limp cloth, 1s.

" Altogether this work is well worthy of its author."—*Glasgow Herald*.

Rev. Dr. M‘Cosh and Dr. Dickie.

Typical Forms and Special Ends in Creation.

Crown 8vo, 7s. 6d.

" We are glad to find this work in its second edition. It is an able
and satisfactory examination of one of the most interesting yet difficult
problems of modern science."—*Bradford Review*.

Memoirs of Francis L. Mackenzie; late of

Trinity College, Cambridge; with Notices of Henry Mac-
kenzie, B.A., Scholar of Trinity College, Cambridge. By
Rev. Charles Popham Miles, M.A., M.D., F.L.S. Fcap.,
cloth, 6s.

John G. Macvicar, D.D. Author of ' An Inquiry into
Human Nature,' &c.

The Philosophy of the Beautiful. With

Illustrations. Crown 8vo, cloth, 6s. 6d.

First Lines of Science Simplified, and the

Structure of Molecules Attempted, by the Rev. J. G. Macvicar, D.D. 8vo, cloth, price 7s.

HERMANN MEYER, M.D., Professor of Anatomy in the University of Zurich.

The correct form of Shoes. Why the Shoe
Pinches. A contribution to Applied Anatomy. Translated from the German by JOHN STIRLING CRAIG, L.R.C.P.E., L.R.C.S.E. Third Edition. Fcap., sewed, 6d.

"A sixpenny pamphlet which should be profoundly studied by all who suffer on their toes."—*Examiner, August* 8.

"The English translation of Dr. Meyer's essay (published by Edmonston and Douglas), exact in detail and clearly illustrated by drawings, is enough to enable any man to lay down the law clearly to his bootmaker. It is sixpennyworth of knowledge, that will, we hope, be the ruin of the fashion that has put thousands of people into actual torment of pain, and denies to most of us the full and free use of our legs."—*All the Year Round, August.*

"We cannot too earnestly recommend to all readers the attentive perusal of the little work before us."—*London Review, October* 15.

Nuggets from the Oldest Diggings; or Researches in the Mosaic Creation. Crown 8vo, cloth, 3s. 6d.

ORWELL.

The Bishop's Walk and The Bishop's Times.
By ORWELL. In one vol., fcap. 8vo, price 5s.

J. PAYN.

Richard Arbour; or, the Scapegrace of the
Family. By JAMES PAYN. 1 vol., crown 8vo, price 9s.

"As might be expected, Mr. Payn displays in his more familiar passages the habit of much observation as regards both men and things, which contributes so much to give reality and life to novelists' conception."—*Manchester Weekly Express.*

"The above is a work which we can recommend to those readers who have a *penchant* for a *good* work of fiction."—*Lincoln Herald, August* 20.

E. B. RAMSAY, M.A., LL.D., F.R.S.E., Dean of Edinburgh.

Reminiscences of Scottish Life and Character.
Two vols., fcap. 8vo., 6s. each.

C. T. PERTHES, Professor of Law at Bonn.

Memoirs of Frederick Perthes; or Literary,
Religious, and Political Life in Germany from 1789 to
1843.   Crown 8vo, cloth, 6s.

"We regard this volume as among the most interesting that has been
published of late years."—*Dundee Advertiser.*

A. HENRY RHIND, F.S.A., &c.

Egypt; its Climate, Character, and Resources
as a Winter Resort.   With an Appendix of Meteorological
Notes.   Fcap., cloth, 3s.

JOHN RUFFINI.

Doctor Antonio; a Tale.   Crown 8vo, cloth,
4s.

———— Cheap Edition.   Crown 8vo, boards, 2s. 6d.

"This is a very charming story."—*Leeds Mercury.*

Lorenzo Benoni; or, Passages in the Life of
an Italian, with Illustrations.   Crown 8vo, cloth gilt, 5s.

———— Cheap Edition, crown 8vo, boards, 2s. 6d.

The Paragreens; or, a Visit to the Paris
Universal Exhibition.   With Illustrations by John Leech.
Fcap. cloth, 4s.

JOHN SCARTH.

Twelve Years in China; the People, the
Rebels, and the Mandarins, by a British Resident.   With
coloured Illustrations. Second Edition.   With an Appendix.   Crown 8vo, cloth, price 10s. 6d.

"One of the most interesting books that has been published on that
most mysterious country."—*Morning Post, April 9.*
"Whether Mr. Scarth be right or not in his political conclusions—and
he certainly leaves a strong impression upon our minds that he *is* right—

we have to thank him for a very interesting volume."—*Chambers's Journal, April* 14.

"One of the most amusing and original volumes ever published on China.... He has been at great pains to form correct opinions, and in many cases appears to have succeeded. But the external relations of so vast an empire are too important to be discussed and dismissed in a paragraph. We therefore advise all those who desire to understand the question to study Mr. Scarth's volume."—*Daily Telegraph, March* 21.

"This volume is very readable, sketching the Chinese and their ways in a correct yet lively manner, and containing many judicious extracts and observations on such general subjects as the character and religion of the Chinese."—*Hong-Kong China Mail, April* 25.

"Mr. Scarth's little work will modify the opinions of many among its readers concerning the Chinese Empire. Even for those who have as yet committed themselves to no definite opinions and felt no special interest in regard to the Flowery Land, it is a volume which will repay perusal. It is written from a new point of view, and in a new spirit; and the Chinese question is one with at least two sides. The point of view may be fixed in a few words by saying that a 'British Resident' of twelve years in China is not a British official."—*Saturday Review, May* 5.

GEORGE SETON, Advocate, M.A., Oxon.

Practical Analysis of the Acts relating to the

Registration of Births, Deaths, and Marriages in Scotland. (17 and 18 Vict., c. 80; 18 Vict., c. 29; and 23 and 24 Vict., c. 85). With an Appendix, containing the Statute, Sheriff's Forms, Tables of Burghs, Sheriffdoms, Fees, Penalties, &c., and a copious Index. Fifth Edition. 8vo, cloth, 7s. 6d.

Causes of Illegitimacy, particularly in Scot-

land. With relative Appendices. Being a paper read in Glasgow at the Fourth Annual Meeting of the 'National Association for the Promotion of Social Science,' on the 28th of September 1860. 8vo, sewed, 1s.

The Law and Practice of Heraldry in Scot-

land, by G. Seton. [*In preparation.*

SHIRLEY.

"At the Seaside." Essays by Shirley, Re-

printed from Fraser's Magazine. 1 vol., crown 8vo.

Aemona and the Islands of the Forth.

Notes on an Ancient Oratory or Stone-roofed Cell discovered in the Island of Inchcolme, &c. &c. By J. Y. SIMPSON, Vice-President of the Society of Antiquaries. In one vol. [*In preparation.*

By the same Author.

Archæology: its Past and its Future Work.

An Address given to the Society of Antiquaries of Scotland. In 8vo, price 1s. [*Ready.*

The Skip Jack, or Wireworm, and the Slug.

With notices of the Microscope, Barometer, and Thermometer for the use of Schools. Fcap., cloth limp, 9d.

DR. SOMERVILLE. 1741-1813.

My Life and Times; being the Autobiography

of the Rev. THOS. SOMERVILLE, Minister of Jedburgh, and one of His Majesty's Chaplains. 1 vol. crown 8vo, price 9s.

"His book is eminently graphic and readable, and it is no mean proof of its singular excellence that, following so close in the wake of his more imposing friend, Dr. Somerville should be able to hold his own with perfect ease.... Such, then, are a few of the points of interest afforded by this curious work, which we accept as a most valuable addition to a most interesting species of literature. The style of the book is flowing and graceful; the spirit of it refined and genial. It is excellently edited by a man who knows when to speak and when to be silent—when a foot-note is required and when it is not. We may expect that such a book will become a favourite among those who read for amusement, and, endowed as it is with a careful index, a standard work of reference to those who are in search of facts.—*Times, May* 24.

"The concluding chapters of this volume teem with interest"—*Critic, April* 20.

Dugald Stewart's Collected Works—Vols.

I. to X. 8vo, cloth, each 12s.

Vol. I.—Dissertation.

Vols. II., III., and IV.—Elements of the Philosophy of the Human Mind. 3 vols.

Vol. V.—Philosophical Essays.

Vols. VI. and VII.—Philosophy of the Active and Moral Powers of Man. 2 vols.

Vols. VIII. and IX.—Lectures on Political Economy. 2 vols.

Vol. X.— Biographical Memoirs of Adam Smith, LL.D., William Robertson, D.D., and Thomas Reid, D.D. To which is prefixed a Memoir of Dugald Stewart, with Selections from his Correspondence, by John Veitch, M.A.

Supplementary Vol.—Translations of the Passages in Foreign Languages contained in the Collected Works ; with General Index, *gratis.*

PROFESSOR SYME.

Observations in Clinical Surgery. By JAMES
SYME, Professor of Clinical Surgery in the University of Edinburgh. In one vol. 8vo. Price 8s. 6d.

By the same Author.

Stricture of the Urethra, and Fistula in Per-
ineo. 8vo, 4s. 6d.

Treatise on the Excision of Diseased Joints.
8vo, 5s.

On Diseases of the Rectum. 8vo, 4s. 6d.

Illustration of Medical Evidence and Trial
by Jury in Scotland. 8vo, sewed, 1s.

The Right Reverend The Lord Bishop of London.

Lessons for School Life ; being Selections
from Sermons preached in the Chapel of Rugby School during his Head Mastership. Fcap., cloth, 5s.

History of Sir Thomas Thumb, by the author
of 'The Heir of Redcliffe,' 'Heartsease,' 'Little Duke, &c. &c. Illustrated by J. B. 4to, boards, 2s.

The Two Cosmos. A Tale of Fifty Years Ago.

1 vol., crown 8vo, 10s. 6d.

> "It excels in what we most of all desire in a novel—freshness. . . . . . There is in some passages a good deal of pathos in it; and a writer who is capable of pathos—not mere maudlin, but genuine, manly feeling—belongs to the higher ranks of authorship. Many men have true tenderness of feeling, but, perhaps, the rarest thing in literature is the art of expressing this tenderness without being ridiculous, and of drawing tears of which the reader is not ashamed. Our author has not much indulged his faculty in this way but in one little scene—the deathbed of the elder Cosmo's mother. He has been so successful that one cannot help feeling his superiority."—*Times, January 10th.*

> "To call it merely a good novel is to do an injustice to the narrator, to say that it is the best of the season would not be absolutely correct, but would not be far from the truth. Every one should read it—all who read it will heartily recommend it to their friends."—*Morning Herald, February 2d.*

Memoir of George Wilson, M.D., F.R.S.E.,

Regius Professor of Technology in the University of Edinburgh, and Director of the Industrial Museum of Scotland. By his Sister, Jessie Aitken Wilson. 8vo, cloth, 14s.

> "We lay down the book gratefully and lovingly. To read of such a life is refreshing, and strengthening, and inspiring. It is long since we read any biography with equal pleasure; and assured of its general acceptance, we pass it on to our readers with our heartiest commendation."—*The Scottish Press.*

A Memoir of John Wilson (Christopher North),

late Professor of Moral Philosophy in the University of Edinburgh; compiled from Family Papers, with a Selection from his Correspondence. By his Daughter, Mrs. GORDON.   [*In preparation.*

THE BISHOP OF ST. ANDREWS.

A United Church of Scotland, England, and

Ireland, Advocated. A Discourse on the Scottish Reformation, to which are added Proofs and Illustrations, designed to form a manual of Reformation Facts and Principles. By the Right Reverend CHARLES WORDSWORTH, Bishop of St. Andrews.